take the leap

ANDREA NOURSE

ANDREA NOURSE

————

EDITOR: Bryn Donovan/The Lucky Author

COVER DESIGN: Jeff Jacobs

AndreaNourse.com

To the girl who once quit a lucrative internship with one of her political idols because of a (very very) creepy elevator that was destined to inspire the opening scene in this book.

author's note

Welcome to the book I originally titled *Adventures in Catastrophizing*. This book is special to me for a number of reasons but mostly because Sadie is the most me character I have written. Her fears, her anxieties, and her quirks are all things that come directly from my first-hand experience. Because of this, I wanted to start this book with a few content warnings. I've listed these below.

———

CONTENT WARNINGS

This book contains mentions of childhood cancer, parental abandonment, death of a parent, and on-page panic and anxiety attacks.

one

"WHAT'S the worst that could happen?" asked Ava, my business partner, who also happened to be my best friend.

I pulled my lips in between my teeth and bit down. She knew better than to ask me that question. Did she not know just how loaded that question was? I mean, where do I even start?

"Sadie?" Ava prompted. "We're going to be late."

"Right." I nodded. I knew this. Being punctual was kind of my thing. It was not Ava's. She was the friend I usually lied to and told her an event started an hour later than it actually did. She'd probably still end up late, but I certainly tried. But today, she'd been the one to constantly remind me of the importance of being on time. Being late today was not an option. This meeting was a make-or-break moment for Savie Media, the marketing agency Ava and I owned.

She waved her arms in front of her, urging me forward. "Can we get on the elevator, please?"

I hedged. The simple answer was, yes, of course we can get on the elevator. But with me, nothing was ever simple. I ran a hand through my shoulder-length brown hair, and prayed

Nashville's early spring humidity hadn't already done its frizzy sorcery. "What if we get stuck?"

"Then we call for help. That's what these are for." She held up her phone and shook it.

Ava knew me better than anyone. She knew about my dislike for elevators—and planes, snakes, crowded spaces, rollercoasters, cruise ships, and a dozen other random fears—but I'd never shared *this* specific fear with her. Or any of my wildly imagined fears, and believe me, there were plenty of them.

Ava stared expectantly at me. I let out a sigh. I might as well just tell her. She was stuck with me. Besides, after twenty years of friendship, she wasn't exactly a stranger to my quirks, as she called them.

"Let's say we're in this elevator, and it stalls at the exact moment the world ends. Cell phone towers are down. Phone lines are down. We have no way to communicate. Everything is in chaos out there, but we're stuck in here without a clue. No one is coming because everyone is busy dying or saving other people. We're just trapped until we die in that tiny, cramped box."

Ava locked her gaze on my face. "Sadie, sweetie. Is that plausible?"

"No. But try telling my brain that. It's already worked out every imaginable terrible scenario in which the apocalypse happens while we're stuck in the elevator. So, according to my brain, it is completely possible."

Ava narrowed her green eyes as she studied my face. "So, this has nothing to do with the fact that we're about to ride up to the forty-fifth floor to present the biggest client pitch of our lives? This hesitation is solely because you're convinced the world is on the verge of ending, and we're going to get stuck together and die in an elevator?"

I didn't bother answering her question. Yes, this pitch was a big deal, but so was the impending apocalypse. It was hard to decide which had me more nervous.

"Well, then let's go get trapped in an elevator and die in there rather than getting eaten by zombies or whatever the apocalypse is bringing."

I hesitated for a moment, then leaned forward and pressed the up button on the elevator. "At least we'll die together, I guess."

"Thank heavens for small mercies." I didn't have to look at her face to know she was rolling her eyes.

I followed her into the elevator. As the doors closed, I took a deep breath and held it. Panic started to creep into my veins. It started with a tingle up my spine and was followed by a quickening of my pulse. I tried to shift my thoughts to the pitch we were about to give. But the panic only spread. I clenched my fingers into a fist and squeezed. To further distract myself, I said a silent prayer that the elevator did, in fact, get stuck, and we missed the pitch and had to reschedule for a much later date—a date after I've had more than a few hours of sleep and had plenty of time to practice. I added in a caveat that the apocalypse could wait. We only needed to get delayed for an hour or so. My cell phone was charged, and I always carried emotional support snacks and water with me. So, at a minimum, we'd be fine for an hour or two. But the elevator completed its required task in record time. A strange sensation of both relief and disappointment washed over me.

The doors opened to the lobby of Take the Leap, an adventure planning company that specialized in planning thrilling (terrifying) group excursions. The floors were so shiny that the sun bouncing off the reflection nearly blinded me. A slate grey couch and complementing chairs created a barrier around the front desk, which was built to resemble the edge of a cliff. Just looking at it gave me intense vertigo. I paused at the elevator doors long enough for Ava to turn and give me a very pointed look. *Move*, she mouthed. I nodded and stepped into the lobby.

"Hi, we're here to meet with Tripp James," Ava said. "Ava Reed and Sadie Barnes with Savie Media."

The blonde receptionist barely glanced up at us and nodded before her eyes scanned the space behind us as if she were looking for someone more impressive to gift her attention to. "Have a seat. I'll let him know you're here. Can I get you a water or coffee?"

I started to ask for water, but Ava answered for us. "No, thank you." She grabbed my arm and pulled me back to the sofa. "You have your water bottle, remember?"

"Oh, yeah," I said with a sheepish grin.

"Sadie," Ava whispered as she leaned in close, "what is going on with you today? You're starting to scare me."

I shrugged in an attempt to appear nonchalant. "Nothing."

"Bull. I know you, Sadie, and I can tell when you're lying."

"I'm just nervous, okay? This pitch is a big deal." It was more than that. Savie was at a crisis point, and if we didn't land this client today, we'd both be looking for a job within the next few months. We'd known leaving our comfortable corporate jobs to start our own marketing agency was a risk, but Ava had convinced me it was a chance worth taking. I'm about as risk averse as any one person has any right to be, but I trusted Ava. I knew we worked well together and that we had what it took to run our own company. For the past two years, we'd done a pretty good job at it, too. Then we had two major clients get sold off to bigger companies who had their preferred marketing agencies. Never mind that the only reason they'd even been on the radar of their investors was because of the work we'd done for them.

"Can you try to get it together in the next two minutes?"

"Yes." I nodded. I closed my eyes and allowed my brain to run through every worst-case scenario ... we bomb the pitch, don't sign a new client, go bankrupt, close our business, lose our life savings, foreclose on our house and office space, end up living in an old refrigerator box, and resort to selling feet pictures on the internet to be able to afford a fast-food value meal. Then, I did what I'd learned in therapy, and tucked every last one of those fears into an imaginary metal box, closed the lid, and shoved it into the back of my mental closet. I wasn't going to let fear win today. No, today, I was going to channel my inner badass and we were going to land this client. Tripp James and the Take the Leap team would have no choice but to sign us as their agency of record. "Okay. I'm ready."

Ava clapped her hand on my shoulder and said, "Did you shove all your fears in the metal box?"

"Sure did."

"Good. Now, hand me the key." I pretended to hand her a key and she dropped it into her purse.

"Ms. Barnes and Ms. Reed." A deep voice interrupted us. I leaped to my feet and found myself staring straight into the coral polo-clad solid chest of Tripp James. We'd researched him ahead of the pitch, so we knew all about his blue-grey eyes and rock-hard pecs, but no Google image search could've prepared me for the mountain of a man that stood in front of us. I also knew that he happened to be single. Not that that was necessary information to have for this pitch.

"Mr. James," Ava said and extended her hand. "I'm Ava and this is Sadie." She elbowed my side. I took a step back and held my hand out as well. He shook Ava's hand first and then took mine in a firm and confident grip. His hand was rough, as if he spent as little time in the office as possible. I hoped he couldn't feel all of the nervous energy that had sweated straight into my palm.

"Call me Tripp," he said with a broad smile. The warmth of his smile surprised me. Every picture of him online showcased his chiseled jaw and intense gaze. He rubbed his hand over his scruffy beard. "The team is ready for you. Though, I will warn you, we've been listening to agency pitches for going on six hours now, so I hope you've brought some circus tricks or something to keep us awake."

I laughed nervously and said, "Ava did you remember to bring the trapeze?"

"Darn! I knew I forgot something." She snapped her fingers to convey the missed opportunity.

"Oh, well. I guess we'll settle for a killer presentation."

No pressure. I'd never had a potential client be so blunt. Normally, they never mentioned the competition or just how many pitches they'd suffered through before ours. At least Ava and I weren't big on the normal slideshow presentations, so we wouldn't bore them to tears with an hour-long pitch filled with graphs and charts.

Tripp led us down the bright orange hallway and directed us into a conference room with a giant mural of the entire team skydiving. Looking around, I matched the faces of the people at the table with the smiles on the wall. No one appeared to be over the age of twenty-one, except Tripp. I knew from my research that he'd just celebrated his twenty-eighth birthday, making him a little over a year older than me.

While Ava connected her iPad to their screen, I introduced us to the room. "Thank you for hosting us today. I'm Sadie and this is Ava, we're the women behind Savie." I pulled the box of homemade chocolate chip cookies from my bag and placed them in the center of the table. "We know our work speaks for itself, but we're also not above appealing to your stomachs and your sweet tooth."

A handful of people chuckled politely, but as soon as I

opened the container and the scent of fresh-baked cookies hit the air, every hand around the table reached for a cookie.

"We know you've just sat through a lot of presentations, so we'll do our best to not bore you to tears or put you to sleep. We know it's been a long day for everyone," I said and nodded toward Ava.

She started the video we played before every pitch. It was a thirty-second highlight of the work we'd done over the past two years: the social media launch of a new haircare brand, a rebrand for a local restaurant chain, and a few other campaigns we were proud of. When it finished, she leaned forward and launched into the first part of our pitch.

I stood beside her and kept a neutral smile on my face. During Ava's part, it was my job to read the audience because my specialty was thinking on my feet. If I got the sense that we were losing them, I'd pivot from our original plan. I took in the faces of our audience and tried to gauge their level of interest. Every single one of them looked bored out of their mind. The only person who kept their gaze locked on us in rapt attention was Tripp. We were most definitely losing the room.

Our original idea was to highlight our analysis of everything Take the Leap was doing right and where they could improve and respond to threats from competitors. We had a full plan developed to tackle this in a way that aligned with the company's brand and mission. But as soon as the red-haired boy seated to Tripp's right yawned and caused a chain-reaction yawn around the room that, thankfully, died before it affected Tripp, I knew that plan was the wrong approach.

I clicked my tongue against the roof of my mouth to signal the shift to Ava. She nodded quickly and stepped back to allow me to take over.

"Now is the part of the presentation where, I'm guessing, everyone walked you through the strengths, weaknesses, opportunities, and threats facing Take the Leap. But I won't bore you with the details you already know. We've done the research, and I'm assuming you have, too," I said. "Let's face it, Take the Leap is losing its hold on the market. With the rise of adventure-based businesses like escape rooms and zip-line parks, what used to make Take the Leap unique is what makes it run-of-the-mill now."

Ava shifted nervously behind me. I was supposed to launch into a spiel that praised Tripp and his company for being groundbreaking. I tossed her a look that I hoped portrayed confidence. I had the room's attention now. I just had to keep it.

"But," I said, raising my voice, "what makes Take the Leap special is the exact thing that you've pushed to the back burner. Your adventure matching app."

Tripp sat up straighter. "How do you know about the app?"

I smiled. "I have my ways."

"We haven't launched the app yet."

"No, but you should." I took Ava's iPad and pulled up the email from my twin brother that included my results from the app's quiz. "I beta-tested the app last week. I hope you won't hold it against Seth, but my brother needed someone who might break the quiz algorithm, and I was the perfect candidate."

I turned to make sure my quiz results were on the screen. The profile photo my brother had uploaded wasn't my most flattering photo, but it wasn't the worst either. My brown hair was pulled into a messy bun, and my hazel eyes looked directly at my brother, who was behind the camera. The smirk on my face was the half smile I reserved for my twin that usually communicated my lack of amusement at whatever lame joke he'd just told. At my feet, his dog, Tommy Pickles, laid on his back with his paws in the air, begging for belly scratches. A blank results screen appeared next to the picture. It didn't even have the decency to say *no matches found*. It was just empty.

"Whoa." A murmur of surprised whispers echoed around the room.

"Right? No matches."

"It shouldn't do that," Tripp said, shaking his head. "There is supposed to be a suggestion for everyone."

"Unless you're scared of your own shadow," Ava said, "like Sadie. Look, you've cornered the market on thrill seekers and risk-takers, but what about everyone else? The people who retreat from the mere thought of adventure?"

"Those people aren't exactly our target audience," joked a blond kid sitting at the end of the table. "We don't pander to scaredy cats." A few other people around the table snickered. Tripp shot them each a quick warning glance before clearing his throat and nodding back to us.

"Why not?" Ava asked. "Isn't your slogan *an adventure for everyone*? The company's mission statement is all about taking the extraordinary and making it available for the ordinary."

"Sure, but I guess I'm not following where this is going," Tripp said, sighing. He leaned back in his chair and crossed his arms over his chest. Now, we were losing him, too.

Ava shot me an apologetic look. My stomach twisted in a knot. She was about to pivot big time, and I wasn't going to like it.

"So, let's take someone like Sadie who would never even dream about jumping out of a plane and make her the focus of the social media campaign. We set up a weekly challenge and film the process, teasing a bit each day, before we launch the episode on Friday on your video platform. We show ordinary people that they can do these things."

"Why someone like Sadie?" Tripp asked. He raised an

eyebrow and shifted his gaze between me and my quiz results on the screen behind me.

"Because someone like her is the perfect candidate. You saw the results. There isn't an ounce of adventurousness in her bones. Her idea of thrill-seeking is driving five miles per hour over the speed limit."

"No, I get that. But why not her?" I wasn't a fan of the tiny hint of excitement in his voice. What was he plotting?

I laughed. "Because that's a terrible idea," I said before I could stop myself.

"No, it's brilliant," Ava said. "Sadie would be perfect. She's approachable and relatable to the average person. And we'd be able to keep the budget in check by using in-house talent."

I scoffed at being referred to as *talent*. The idea was almost as preposterous as my fear of being caught in a malfunctioning elevator during the apocalypse. But judging by the looks on the faces of everyone else in the room, I was the only one who saw the obvious flaws in this plan. I was outnumbered. Tripp clapped his hands together as if to signal he'd come to a decision. A tiny smile quirked at the corners of his mouth.

"I love it," Tripp said. "Send over the contract and let's do this. We can let the lawyers hammer out the details. I'd like to get started as soon as possible."

"Wait, what? Don't you want to review with your team? Take some time to go back over the pitches. I mean, we didn't even go through our pitch."

"I don't need to. You two are the first ones to truly understand our purpose. We're more than just a company catering to bachelor parties and finance bros trying to one-up each other. I think I can speak for the entire team when I say, welcome aboard Savie."

A round of applause and cheers erupted from the room. "Let's do it!" Ava said, feeding off their excitement.

I gritted my teeth and glared at Ava as she shook Tripp's hand. This was not at all how I'd seen this day going. I'd never been the face of a campaign before. What if I ruined everything? What if I caused the demise of two businesses—Savie and Take the Leap? My stomach twisted in knots the more I thought through just how terrible of an idea this was.

But, as Ava had asked earlier, *what's the worst that could happen?*

two

"YOU'RE MAD," Ava said as she started the car.

I didn't answer immediately. Instead, I pulled my phone out of my bag and sent Seth a quick text to let him know that I'd accidentally, maybe a little on purpose, shared the app during the presentation. "Yes," I said as I shoved my phone under my leg.

"Yes, you're mad, or YES! that pitch was epic, Ava, thanks for landing us a new client?"

"Neither," I said, shaking my head, "both—all of the above. I don't know. What the heck are you thinking Ava?"

"I was thinking we'd lost them until you launched into the bit on the app, which I thought we'd decided not to mention. That whole thing about being worried your brother would get in trouble for breaking his NDA with Take the Leap?"

"I took a leap," I said with a sheepish grin. "I just sent him a text to give him a heads up." Seth was going to be pissed, but he'd understand. He'd shown me the app because he knew we were desperate to sign a new client. I also signed a non-disclosure agreement when I agreed to beta-test the app for him.

Thankfully, showing my results to the company the app was for didn't violate anything.

"So, did I. And to be fair, I didn't expect Tripp to suggest you be the guinea pig in the campaign."

"You kind of did, though."

Ava sighed. "I mean, maybe? I just said someone *like* you."

"While laying out the perfect case for me to be the someone."

"I kind of felt like you'd already done that by sharing your results. You abandoned the backup plan. I just jumped in to finish the pitch. You know how much we need this business."

She was right, of course. We needed Take The Leap. She'd done exactly what she'd needed to do to keep us in the mix, and it had paid off.

When we arrived at our home-office space in Berry Hill, a small neighborhood in South Nashville, I sulked out of the car and straight into the house. We'd bought the house with the intention of using it fully for our business. Her dad, a real estate developer, had originally purchased the home in foreclosure, so we'd gotten it for a great price. But neither of us had expected the cost of running our own company to make it nearly impossible for us to pay rent on our apartment and a mortgage on the business. Luckily, the layout of the four-bedroom house worked perfectly for two single women running a small business. Downstairs, the main living area also hosted our two offices. The dining room served as our one meeting space, and the kitchen offered a break room and a space to prepare snacks and refreshments for any clients we hosted. In the living room, we'd created a welcoming area for clients complete with a massive television that looped our highlight reel, and plush furniture. Our bedrooms and personal space were upstairs. Ava's dad helped us add a door to the stairs to keep curious clients from entering our personal lives.

I threw the tote bag holding my laptop and purse on the couch and headed straight into the kitchen. Before we left this morning, I'd set the timer on the coffee pot to brew us a fresh pot to have ready when we returned from the meeting. Without thinking, I pulled out two mugs and made a cup for both of us—a splash of cream and no sugar for Ava, and a lot of cream and sugar for me. I handed her the mug and sulked back into my office.

Booting up my laptop, I ignored the sound of Ava pacing the floral rug behind me. While everything loaded, I straightened the papers on my desk. Not that they were messy, but a few corners were slightly askew. I kept a tidy office and house. I'd developed an impressive filing system for Savie that Ava both respected and avoided. Despite her love for statistics, she preferred chaos. The only reason our office was presentable for client meetings was because of me. I'd never met a vacuum or mop I didn't befriend.

I wanted to be mad at her. I wanted to yell at her and question her sanity, but I knew she was right. The idea she proposed was the best one we'd had—better than any of the ones we'd brainstormed ahead of the pitch. Compared to the original proposal we'd come up with, it was downright genius. It was the kind of campaign that would put us back on the map. I hated to admit it, but the entire ride home I'd mapped out the entire plan. I just needed to stew for a few more minutes before I shared this with Ava.

"Are you going to ignore me for the rest of the day?" Ava pouted.

"I want to, but no. Sit down before you wear a hole in my rug." Ava sat in the chair I kept next to my desk. "We need to set some parameters if we're going to do this."

"Oh, we're doing this." She held up her phone and showed me the email that had just come through from our lawyer. "I had Amanda bump the retainer to cover the cost of putting you front and center on the campaign." Amanda was Ava's cousin and our lawyer. She gave us a fantastic family discount, and in turn, referred her new business when we could.

"Tripp's lawyers are reviewing the contract and adding in the unique language to capture the full scope of this project. Hopefully, we can get the contract executed this month and have the first month's retainer in the bank before …" Ava trailed off. She didn't have to finish the sentence. We needed that money to come in before we bounced checks for the bills we couldn't afford to pay.

It took less than a week for the contract to come back. The next Tuesday morning, I opened my email to find the contract in an email from Amanda. I skimmed through the contract. When I got to the addendums Take the Leap had added, I gasped. "Did you see addendum C?"

Ava shook her head and peered over my shoulder the read the section. "Oh."

I propped my elbow on the desk and rested my chin in my hand. None of this should've been a surprise. I'd been on the back-and-forth emails going through the requirements, but seeing things this plainly written in a contract suddenly made it all feel too real.

"Amanda agreed to this change?" *In the event Sadie Barnes does not complete the Take the Leap Challenge as outlined in section five, Savie agrees to void the contract and refund TTL 75% of the retainer paid to the date of incompletion.* "So, if I don't jump out of a plane, we're going to end up paying them for months of work? No."

"Sadie, we both already agreed to this," Ava said. "They originally wanted a full refund, remember. We negotiated them back to 75%."

I turned my attention back to the contract and section five. The Take the Leap Challenge, as Tripp had named it, consisted of a minimum of six adventures. The first five would be determined with the help of Tripp, the app, and the partners of Savie (Ava and me), but the final challenge was outlined in bold letters. **Tandem Skydiving**. They'd even written in Tripp James and Sadie Barnes as the two parties required. I was going to be contractually obligated to jump out of a perfectly good airplane. Was that even legal?

I didn't even want to be a passenger on an airplane, let alone leap out of one. I drove everywhere. I hated flying. The few times I'd done it, I'd required a heavy dose of Benadryl or alcohol to keep my anxiety in check. In other words, I knocked myself out.

The blond brat in the meeting had been correct in calling me a scaredy cat. I was quite literally scared of almost everything. I don't pass cars on two-lane roads. I don't drive excessively fast. I don't try new foods or drinks. I know what I like, and I don't want to test the waters. I don't do dating apps or dating in general—falling in love is far too risky. Anything other than eating, sleeping, breathing, and flowing through my normal routine wasn't worth the risk of something bad or catastrophic happening. I found joy in things like getting lost in the fictional worlds of fantasy and romance novels or television shows and movies. Fiction was far better than reality.

"I know," I said, "and keeping 25% is better than nothing, but it still feels drastic."

"They're taking a chance on us. Or so Tripp James claims. We're unproven when it comes to campaigns like this for companies of their size."

"Isn't their whole business model about taking risks?"

"Apparently, that doesn't apply to their finances."

"So, either I agree to skydive with him, or we lose the contract?"

"Essentially, yes."

"And if we don't sign Take the Leap or another client this month, we're screwed."

Ava didn't answer. She didn't have to. She leaned against the door frame and studied me for a moment before speaking. "I know this is asking a lot of you, but Sadie, what if this turns out to be a good thing? You're always saying you need to get out of your comfort zone and try something new."

I leaned back in my chair and crossed my arms over my chest. She was right. My therapist had recommended some exposure response therapy to help me conquer some of my smaller fears—especially the ones that impacted my day-to-day life. "Sure, when it comes to ordering a new meal at a restaurant or changing my drink order. Not *this*."

"But maybe you try some cool new stuff with Tripp James, who, by the way, isn't a bad guy to be forced to spend time with, and, I don't know, have fun?"

I knew what she was hinting at. But another fun fact about me—I don't date. Or, at least not in the traditional sense. I'd gone to dinner or drinks with members of the opposite sex on occasion. Usually when Ava or Seth decide they've met the one person on the planet who might break through my walls. They were almost always wrong. But I'd humor them and play along for a night or a few weeks, then I'd list all the reasons it wouldn't work and end things before either of us got too attached. I wasn't the type of girl who daydreamed about meeting a prince on a white horse and having the perfect wedding and the perfect house with the perfect kids and the picket fence. This small house that I shared with my best friend and our business was all I needed. I didn't need a man or anyone to come along and disturb the status quo that served me well. Besides, I'd heard enough dating horror stories from Ava and all the blind dates her mom had set her up on over the years.

"Fun?" I asked. "That's highly improbable."

"More improbable than a freak accident happening while you try something new?" she asked.

"Yes. It won't be fun. It will be terrifying. And best-case scenario, I don't die. I can assure you, that even if I survive, I will not have fun. I will hate every second of it and you'll owe me big time."

"Are you saying yes?"

I click on the electronic signature request for the contract and type in my name. I don't know what comes over me as I do it, but a surge of energy explodes inside my body. The thing is, I love our business. Working alongside Ava has been the most rewarding and fulfilling work of my life and the thought of losing that scares me so much more than the thought of jumping out of a plane while strapped to Tripp James.

"No, I'm not saying yes. I'm saying, I'll do this, but I am doing it for us and Savie and because I don't want us to fail. I'm also expensing all the alcohol I'm going to need to consume before I do any of these insane challenges." I was mostly joking. Company-sponsored alcoholism wouldn't be a good look for Savie or me.

Ava squealed and ran to her office. An email confirming all parties had signed the contract pinged into my inbox less than a minute later. She ran back into my office with a bottle of champagne.

"Let's start those drinks now!" She popped the top and a shower of champagne splashed onto my face.

"For the record, I hate this, and I hate you." I threw back the rest of my coffee and held the mug out for her to fill.

three

THE NEXT WEEK, we found ourselves back in the elevator at Take the Leap. I'd lobbied Ava and Tripp to have our client kick-off meeting at our offices, like we typically do, but I was overruled. Tripp preferred hosting meetings at his office, and Ava thought it would be good to start this ridiculous challenge by helping me conquer my fear of elevators. She'd even sent me multiple articles on the benefits of exposure therapy.

"Don't hit me," she said as we walked into the elevator and used her body to block the button panel.

"What are you doing?"

"Nothing." She then proceeded to do, well, nothing. The elevator doors closed, and we just stood there. I glared at her. She averted her eyes and didn't move. My heart raced in my chest as the seconds ticked by. A sharp chill ran up my spine and sent a tingle over my scalp. I hated every bit of this. The four walls around us didn't move, but the space felt tighter. Just as the panic was about to completely take over my body, the doors popped back open, and two older men in suits boarded with us. "What floor," she asked innocently. When they answered, she dutifully pressed the button for their floor along with the forty-five for us.

"I hate you," I whispered into her ear.

"I know, I'm sorry," she said back with a grin. "But now that your adrenaline is pumping, you'll be nice and ready to talk about skydiving and base jumping."

I didn't dignify her with a response. Instead, I leaned back against the wall and tried to regain control of my breathing. I picked at the cuticle on my thumb and channeled my anxious energy into my hands. She'd meant well; I know she did, but she'd thrown me off so much more than she'd ever understand or realize. Once I lost control of my insane imagination, it was hard to reign it back in. In the minute or two that we'd sat in that unmoving box, my brain had run through every imaginable horrific ending. We'd broken the rules of the elevator, and as silly as that might seem, it terrified me. She'd also completely removed any sense of control I'd had over this entire situation. The only thing keeping me in this elevator with her was the knowledge that Take the Leap's first-month retainer was sitting comfortably in our business bank account. I shook off my annoyance and refocused my attention on the meeting we were about to walk into. Ava apologized again, and I forced a smile.

The receptionist, who we knew now was a grad student named Chloe, welcomed us with a smile and ushered us straight to Tripp's office. Today, we'd be meeting with Tripp and his vice president of marketing, Liam Chase, AKA the blond kid who'd called me a scaredy cat. I tried not to let this fact and the knowledge that he'd barely been out of kindergarten when I'd graduated high school bother me. He had an impressive resume, even if he was basically an overgrown toddler.

"No cookies today?" Liam asked, not bothering to hide his disappointment.

"Sorry, I only bake in the dating stage of the process," I replied. I smiled what I'd hoped was a casual, cool smile.

"Bummer."

"I did bring donuts from Bites by Bates," Ava said, setting the bright pink box on the desk. "No offense to my partner here, but I promise these donuts are even better than her cookies."

"I doubt that," Tripp said, "but before we get too comfortable, we wanted to give you a quick tour of the office and introduce you to a few of the key members of our team."

Ava and I nodded our agreement. I fell into step beside Tripp. He was a good foot taller than me, and when he smiled down at me, I expected to be hit with the familiar feeling of inadequacy. Almost everyone looked down at me at five-foot-one, and I'd grown used to their looks of *aww, so cute* when they did. Thanks to my petite stature, I didn't look a day over twenty-one, much less my actual age of twenty-seven. I was used to being underestimated. So, when I caught Tripp's eye, his look of respect and admiration completely took me by surprise. There wasn't even a trace of *how adorable* in the way his intense gaze met mine. I smiled back and knew that this was a man I wanted to get to know. Weird. It was an unfamiliar feeling, and I wasn't quite sure what to do with it.

Tripp and Liam guided us through the maze of the office and introduced us to their creative teams and customer relations support staff. They showed us the brainstorming rooms where they came up with their monthly adventures for Quest subscribers: the members paid $99 a month for unique excursions only available to them. I couldn't imagine anyone paying nearly $100 to risk their lives on surprise adventures, but they had close to 200 members. I had no idea there were so many options for thrill seekers. I'd wrongly assumed that jumping out of planes and off cliffs was it, but according to the Tripp, there was so much more.

We made our way through their accounting department, which wasn't like any other accounting team I'd ever seen. It seemed like everyone had at least an arm full of tattoos and two extra holes on their faces, well, except Tripp. He had a few tattoos, but no visible piercings. Each of their cubicles was plastered with photos of them doing one extreme thing or another. It seemed like everyone in this company was completely sold on their mission.

"You have a very impressive team," I said. "From our research, we knew this, but seeing it in action is completely different."

We made our way back to Tripp's office. Ava and I sat beside Liam in the chairs across from Tripp's desk.

"Just wait until you see the actual work we do," Liam said, his voice beaming with pride.

"Ready to get started?" Tripp asked as he shut the door to his office. "We've got a lot to cover today."

We spent the next two hours reviewing every nook and cranny of Take the Leap's business—where they were growing, where they were struggling, what had worked in the past, and what they'd never tried. By lunchtime, my head was swimming with ideas. While I didn't truly get their business, their enthusiasm was contagious. Not that I was ready to dive into my piece of this challenge yet.

"It sounds like you've been doing everything right, but that there has been a natural ebb and flow to the business." Ava was reading their latest annual report. "You mentioned doing some research? Do you have that handy?"

Liam pulled up a presentation on his laptop and cast it on the television across from Tripp's desk. "We did a few focus groups and then a Quest member survey last spring. As you can see, the focus group results were mixed, but gave us some good insight into what we've been doing right. It also confirmed that we know our target audience well."

"We just aren't reaching new customers. Our Quest members have an overall satisfaction rating of 98%, but only 65% of them would recommend us to their friends or family." Tripp handed over a printout with the survey results.

"Did you dig into why there's a discrepancy?" I asked.

"We have some assumptions," Tripp replied.

"Let me guess, the average, non-thrill-seeking consumer doesn't find the website or social media approachable. They take one look at the extreme activities and nope out before they get a chance to dig any deeper. So, if someone's family members or friends are like me, they know there is no chance they'd be interested?"

"Something like that." Tripp rubbed his hand over his bearded chin. "Which is where you all come in. We completely understand our core audience, but to continue to grow, we need to reach more people."

"Right. And we have some thoughts on that," I said. "Aside from the social media campaign we'll discuss later, we'd like to share some insights from the research we conducted in preparing for the pitch."

I let Ava take it from there. She was the analytical brain, and I provided the creative strategy. We worked well together in these settings. She could take the most boring data sets and work them into easy-to-understand and exciting charts and graphs. Tripp and Liam paid close attention as she unraveled the brilliance behind our plan. They were all in.

"Which leads me to the app," Ava said as she finished going over the research. "Sadie?"

"Right, so as you know, we've had some insider access to the app during development."

"Your brother?" Tripp asked. I couldn't tell if he was amused or annoyed by our insider access to the app. His gaze locked on my face. I tried not to squirm under the intensity of his stare.

"Seth," I said in confirmation. "As I mentioned before, he needed to test functionality against someone who might break the system. After we signed our contract, I pulled Seth into the campaign planning. We worked out a few different models to make the quiz and results more friendly to the risk-averse crowd."

Liam interrupted. "I'm sorry, but I am still unclear on how targeting people who are nowhere near our target audience will help us grow?"

"Completely valid question," I said, smiling, "why would someone like me want to take a quiz like this? Why would I even be looking at Take the Leap?"

"Exactly."

"Well, Liam, would it make more sense if I told you that our research shows that while risk-averse people like me are not likely to sign up to go base jumping or to ride in a hot air balloon, they might be interested in something more tame like a calm, lake kayak excursion or even indoor rock climbing? Something less extreme but still adventurous? And if those people come to your website looking for those types of experiences, they don't find them right away."

Tripp nodded. "It looks like we don't offer those experiences." They did, but you had to really dig to find them, and they weren't highlighted on their social media.

"And on the app, the quiz doesn't consider any of those things. If my choices are parasailing or skydiving, I'm choosing none of the above. But, if I were offered indoor rock climbing or an escape room, I'd be more inclined to make that selection. It wouldn't be an automatic yes, but I also wouldn't reject the idea immediately."

"Baby steps," Ava chimed in.

"With the social campaign, we bring those opportunities to the forefront. We shift away from only showcasing the big scary stuff and sprinkle in the smaller but profitable excursions."

"So, we start small and then build up to skydiving," Tripp said. He glanced across the table and locked his gaze on me. His lips curved into a bright, wide smile. "Just how small are we talking?"

I shook my head. "I don't know yet."

"Bungee jumping?" Tripp suggested.

"Indoor?" I asked.

Liam laughed. "No one wants to watch someone bungee jump indoors. We have a great spot over Percy Priest Lake. It's stunning at night."

"So, when I said *start small,* your first thought is jumping off of a bridge in the dark?"

"Well, we only have five challenges to get you ready for the big finale."

"Ugh. Don't remind me. I'll worry about that one when it's time to worry about it."

I lied. I was already worrying about it. Last night, I'd had a nightmare that I was in my birthday suit, strapped to Tripp, and free-falling from a plane without a parachute. I woke up just before we hit the ground. So, I'll most definitely be worrying about that particular challenge for the next several weeks. But they didn't need to know that.

"But speaking of the five challenges," I said, "I think we also need to add in some of the more approachable ones. Those would be part of the campaign but wouldn't count towards the contractually required ones."

Liam frowned. "Why would we do content on an escape room or something that doesn't fit our current model?"

He was really focused on sticking to what they do and not adventuring outside their usual tricks. Almost like the opposite of me. "Because the goal is to attract new customers. The ones who look at the bungee jumping and immediately scroll or click off the site. We add in some lesser challenges to show the variety available."

"I like that approach," Tripp said. "Liam, I know we're used to doing things one way, but we brought Sadie and Ava in to challenge us. And they're right, we need new customers." Tripp stood and walked toward the white board wall beside us. He handed me a dry-erase marker, and I stood to join him.

"Liam, what are some of the challenges you consider less extreme?" I asked, readying myself to write.

Liam shifted in his seat like he was trying to get comfortable. "Hmm. Well, we do a few hikes in the Smoky Mountains. Would you consider that more tame?"

Me? No, I wouldn't, but this wasn't completely about me. So, I wrote hiking on the board. "Tripp?"

He stood beside me and nodded as if deep in thought. The edges of his eyes crinkled. "Canoeing?"

"Good!" I said a bit too enthusiastically. I added it to the list and then added my own: bicycling. Under that, I added camping and ice fishing.

"Ice fishing?" Tripp asked with a small laugh. "That might require some traveling, but that's a fun idea, and something I've never done before."

Tripp and I started bouncing ideas off each other, and after fifteen minutes, we had a solid list pulled together. Liam and Ava, for the most part, sat back and watched us banter. Tripp never talked over me, no matter how many times I unintentionally interrupted him. I liked the way he leaned in to listen when I spoke up.

"Tripp," Chloe said, popping her head in the door, "your next meeting is starting in two minutes."

"Oh, right, I forgot about that, thanks," he said. I handed him the marker and stepped back to admire our work.

"This is a good start," Ava said. "You guys make a great team."

"Now, we just need to figure out the other five challenges and narrow these down a bit. We could look at booking another meeting tomorrow or later this week?"

"Actually, Sadie, I think it would be best if we worked on these solo—just the two of us. We need to build rapport and trust if we're going to push you out of your comfort zone," Tripp said.

"That's a good plan," Ava said. I glanced at her quizzically, but she winked back. "Liam and I can start working through the details of the remainder of the campaign and pull together some storyboards."

"Sure, that works for me." Another lie. While Tripp's smile and warm eyes made me feel all melty and comfortable, I knew that would not bode well for my goal of avoiding anything too scary or risky. I wasn't sure I could say no to those eyes.

four

TRIPP DIDN'T WAIT TOO long to get our brainstorming session scheduled. Two days after our initial meeting at his office, I met him for coffee and to plan the next stage of the campaign.

"I made a list," Tripp said and handed me a sheet of paper. "These are all of the more extreme adventures we offer and a few we've been considering adding."

I didn't want to, but I took the paper. We're sitting at a small table outside a coffee shop near Take the Leap's downtown Nashville office. Reading down the list, a knot the size of the moon formed in my stomach. I was going to have to do some of these.

Hot air balloon ride. Rock climbing. Rollercoaster. The list went on and on. I turned the page over and found even more things I'd never even thought of but knew, without a doubt, that I had zero desire to consider, much less try.

I hated this campaign more all the time. Why couldn't we have pitched a mattress company or a bookstore? Those are the kind of challenges I can handle.

"It's a lot, I know." He almost sounded apologetic. His blue eyes darkened with sympathy. I searched them for something closer to mocking but only found sincerity. At least he came along with all of this ridiculousness.

"Which of these are least likely to kill me?"

"All of them."

I rolled my eyes and laughed. "You mean all are likely to kill, injure, or maim me?"

"None of the above."

I pointed to the first item on the list. "Roller coaster. I once saw an episode of *Grey's Anatomy* where the roller coaster flew off the tracks and hit a funnel cake stand. People on the ground were burned with the hot oil from the stand, and two people got trapped in the roller coaster car. Then, their friend fainted, and it turns out she had a tumor."

Tripp's face shifted from a jovial expression to one of slight concern as he considered this for a moment. "Do you know why that makes for good TV?"

I pulled my lips into a straight line. "Because it's terrifying?"

He laughed and shook his head. "Yes, but also because it would never actually happen."

"Freak accidents happen all the time."

"Okay, so how about a ride-along in a race car? A professional driver, extreme safety gear, and a controlled environment—all of those sound nice and safe to me."

"Until the driver has a random medical emergency and slams into the wall, trapping both of us in a burning car."

"Are all of your scenarios inspired by medical dramas? If so, we might want to start by changing up your streaming queue," he said, smiling.

"No, I just have a very vivid imagination. For example, there is more than one way to die in a race car. Let's say a tire blows—same outcome. A freak rainstorm comes out of nowhere, and the driver loses control." I sat back in my chair and crossed my arms. "I can sit here all day and catastrophize every single item on your list."

"Catastrophize?" His mouth stumbled over the word.

"It's one of my talents. I learned in therapy that it's a common trauma response." The smile dropped from his face as soon as I said the word *trauma*. He opened his mouth to say something, but I didn't want to dive into my childhood with a brand-new client, so I spoke up before he could ask any questions. "And, if it were an Olympic sport, I'd have a gold medal and hold all of the world records. Go on, try me." This was a challenge I was actually up for. I could do this all day.

His lips quirked up into a smile. "Escape room?" He picked one of the less crazy options I'd given them. But, of course, I could still outline its danger.

"The mechanisms to unlock the doors malfunction because there is a building fire."

"Kayaking?"

I laughed. "Are you trying to challenge me, Mr. James? Because this is child's play." He waved his hands, encouraging me to go on. So, I did. "The boat tips over, trapping me underwater, and I drown. A water moccasin pops into the boat and bites me."

"Spelunking."

"The cave collapses, and we're trapped underground until we suffocate or die of dehydration."

"Can you do this for everyday, normal tasks, too?"

I glanced around the coffee shop's patio. "Absolutely, I can. Right now? Active shooter, earthquake, out-of-control city bus," I said and lifted my untouched muffin. "Or I could choke on this."

He shook his head, and his smile faded. "How do you have fun?"

"I curl up in the safety of my home and read or binge-watch my comfort shows."

"Like *Grey's Anatomy*? Even though it seems to inspire some of your more exaggerated fears?"

I might have balked if he'd been the first person to say this to me. But he wasn't, and I didn't. I'd heard it all before. To everyone else, I sounded ridiculous, and I got that. No one, not even my twin brother or my closest friend, understood what it was like inside my head. I'd spent years in counseling and done EMDR therapy to try and sort through the traumas that had led me to this stage in life. Eye Movement Desensitization and Reprocessing is a type of therapy to help lessen the triggers and stress associated with trauma. Basically, you think about the memory and the feelings that come with it and what you want those feelings to be and let your eyes follow a moving light. It was weird and definitely helped improve my relationships with friends and co-workers, but the fears remained. So, I learned to live with it. I learned to find joy and happiness in the safety of simple things like reading or getting lost in a TV show. I'd come to terms with all the things I'd never do. It's not like I wanted to do them, either. So, I wasn't missing out on anything.

"Have you ever been so paralyzed with fear that the thought of just breathing was too much?" I asked. He shook his head. "It's like the world and time just stop. My life doesn't flash before my eyes or anything dramatic like that. I don't think I actually believe any of these things will happen because, logically, I know they won't. But the mere idea of it makes it feel plausible. Is it rational? No, but that's just how my brain works."

"Is that why you always hesitate at the elevators?" he asked, and I nodded. "Can I ask why?"

"Why what? Why am I scared of elevators? Why do I

doomsday every tiny thing? If you ask me, it's just simple self-preservation."

Tripp considered this for a moment. "Do you know why I started Take the Leap?" he asked.

"No, but I've been dying to ask." I knew my story, but I'd been curious what would cause someone to turn out the exact opposite of me.

"My little brother," he said.

"I didn't know you had a brother, just your sisters." Our research into Tripp James showed that he was close to his family. They were all part owners in the business and big supporters of his.

"Noah. He came along when I was fifteen. He was a surprise baby, and I was just excited to finally not be the only boy. I love my sisters, but when they hit those tween and teen years, it got rough being the only boy in the house."

I swallowed back the dozens of questions that sprang to my mind. There was only one way this story would end, and it wasn't mine to interrupt.

"Noah was a lively baby. He was always laughing and playing. He brought a whole new energy to the house. But just before he turned four, he started to slow down. He was lethargic and tired all the time. It was leukemia. I donated bone marrow and took a semester off from college to stay home and help Mom and Dad. I stayed with him that entire year."

The lingering pain of grief tugged his lips into a deep frown. Seeing it so plainly on his face brought up memories of my own grief. My throat tightened as tears welled in my eyes. His fingers twitched on his mug, and I was overcome with the need to comfort him. But I couldn't find words adequate enough to convey my sympathy. Instead, I offered a soft smile and nodded for him to continue.

"He really got into watching the X-Games and every extreme sport we could find video of. His favorite thing to watch, though, was skydiving videos. For his fifth birthday, my sisters and I all went skydiving. We recorded the whole thing and played it for him. He got so excited knowing we'd done that just for him. He died two days later."

Knowing how the story would end didn't make that last sentence any less heartbreaking. "I'm so sorry." It felt like such a useless thing to say, but I didn't know what else to offer.

"It was hard for everyone. I still miss him every day, and I often find myself wondering what kind of person he'd have grown up to be. That first year was difficult for all of us, but for my parents especially. On his birthday the next year, my sisters and I surprised our parents with another skydiving trip. They came with us, and we all jumped together. We've done it every year since."

"That's the story that needs to be in the About Us section on your website. I mean, wow. It's a beautiful tradition. Terrifying but beautiful. I imagine Noah is watching and cheering you all on."

"I like to think so." A soft smile returned to his face. "Sometimes I like to imagine that he's hanging around the office watching me work."

"And that's why you do the annual Leukemia and Lymphoma Society fundraisers." He nodded. "So, why isn't that story on the website? There's no mention of Noah anywhere."

At this, his head dropped. "In the early days, it was. I talked about Noah in every interview when I started the company. Then we brought in a branding agency that decided it wasn't edgy enough and didn't match the image we needed to portray to attract a decent client base. It made me look too *soft*."

Wow. My eyes widened in horror. Now, I was truly speechless. Ava and I would never recommend removing the heart and soul from a company, especially not one founded for such an altruistic reason.

"Tripp, I don't even know what to say to that. Noah and your family are what make you and your company so amazing." I barely knew the man, but his love for his family was so clearly written all over his face. "And being soft isn't a bad thing."

"Well, hopefully we can change that, right? That's why we're here; to reinvent Take the Leap."

We sat together in silence as we finished our coffee. I watched closely at the way he carefully brought his mug to his lips and took a sip. He closed his eyes for a split second as he savored the taste. There was so much more to this man than his Instagram profile let on. I felt a strong urge to keep peeling back the layers of Tripp James, but I suppressed it. He was a client, and I wasn't interested in anything more than that. Even if I was, the last thing I needed in my life was a boyfriend who jumped out of planes for a living. Or a boyfriend in general.

"So, bungee jumping?" I asked after an employee came to clear our mugs and plates.

"Is that where you want to start?"

"Want to is a bit of a stretch, but sure, let's go with that."

"Excellent choice. I know just the place to practice." A hint of mischief danced in his eyes. "How do you feel about trampoline parks?"

"I have no feelings about them."

"Nothing to catastrophize there?"

"I mean, of course there is. Broken legs. Vomit or other bodily fluids in the foam and ball pits. A snapped spine from a poorly executed landing. The possibilities are endless here, Tripp."

He narrowed his eyes and studied me. "You're a very interesting woman."

"So, I've been told. Usually immediately after someone accuses me of being boring and never having fun." I raised an eyebrow at him to remind him of his earlier questions. He raised his hands in defense.

"I'm just trying to get to know you. We're going to be spending a lot of time together over the next few months, and I'm going to have to help you through all of the challenges."

I pointed down to the list. "Only four more to choose."

"Do you want to go ahead and pick them?"

"Easy there, spider monkey, one terrifying thing at a time."

five

AFTER COFFEE WITH TRIPP, I headed back to our office to decompress. I'd peopled far too much over the last twenty-four hours, and all I wanted was silence and a dark room. And maybe a few hours to escape into a fictional world. Unfortunately, Ava was waiting for me at the front door. I didn't even have time to sit in my car and stare into the void.

"So?" she asked. "How did it go?" She'd never admit it, but she'd been worried I was going to mess this whole thing up. She hadn't wanted me to be alone with Tripp long enough to sell him on another idea. Especially after I'd already tried to talk her out of it a number of times.

"I'll be jumping off a bridge in less than two weeks." I collapsed onto the sofa we kept in the sitting room for casual client meetings. "It went well. Tripp is a nice guy. He does all this in honor of his little brother, Noah, who died of cancer two days after his fifth birthday. The whole family is involved."

If human irises could actually transform into hearts, Ava's eyes would've permanently melted into that shape long ago. She swooned an actual swoon and sunk into the couch beside me. She had a flair for drama. "Does he rescue kittens and puppies on the weekend, too?"

"Stop," I said and playfully slapped her arm. "We're not developing any client crushes, okay? This client may actually get me killed, so I don't want you getting too attached to them. We should also have Amanda update my will...just in case."

"And you think I'm the dramatic one? I've got nothing on you."

"Speaking of being dramatic, I need about ten hours where no one speaks to or looks at me. Can you manage without me?"

"I've already stocked your room with snacks and tea, and the next episode of *Grey's* is queued up for you."

"The heated blanket?"

"Plugged in and ready to smother you into introvert heaven." She knew me well.

"Thank you! You're the best," I said as I made my exit. "Oh, and don't let me start doom-scrolling bungee jumping disasters, okay?"

"I've already blocked those search terms on your social media and browser settings."

"Can you do that?"

"Do you think I can do that?" she asked flatly.

"No, but I'll pretend you can."

"Good."

I tossed a grateful smile at my friend and dragged myself up the stairs. True to her word, Ava had loaded my room with everything I needed to hide out for a few hours. Before I dove into my solitude, I pulled out my laptop to do a bit more research into Tripp and the James family. I'd thought our initial deep dive into him and his business had been thorough, but we'd somehow missed the story behind Take the Leap. He'd told me pretty much everything, but I still felt the itch to keep learning more. I chalked this up to plain old curiosity about a new client and my desire to do the best we could for them. There definitely wasn't any other motivation behind my inquisitiveness. Nope. None at all.

It took a little digging, but I was able to uncover the early news articles on Take the Leap's founding and the James family, which included the photo of Tripp and his sisters skydiving for Noah's fifth birthday. While the idea of skydiving still scared the crap out of me, I was drawn to the four smiling faces in the photo. If I focused on their smiles, I could ignore the fact that the photo was taken mid-air, a few thousand feet off the ground. Despite everything they were going through at the time, the four healthy James siblings looked as if they'd left every single one of their worries and fears on the plane they'd just leaped out of. And if I didn't overanalyze the photo, I could, for a second or two, see why this had become their thing.

But not overanalyzing wasn't something I was capable of doing. I overanalyzed everything. My brain never stopped. I was like an internet browser with a thousand tabs open. After enjoying their happy faces in the photo for less than two minutes, my mind jumped to the possibility that the James parents could've lost all of their children in a matter of days. Imagine if their four oldest kids' parachutes had failed. Didn't they think about that before they stupidly jumped out of a plane? How did people do this? How did *enough* people choose to skydive to sustain the hundreds of companies dedicated to the sport? Was it even a sport?

Before I could delve into an internet rabbit hole of skydiving research, I slammed my laptop shut and shoved it aside. Despite my plans to use this time to unwind, I'd spent my first hour of solitude doing what I do best—obsessing. At least it hadn't been on my life dangling at the end of a bungee cord, but now that was all I could think about. I'd started to look up *Tripp James Bungee Jumping* just before I'd closed my computer. That was a path I didn't need to take tonight.

I hit play on the episode Ava had queued up for me and tried to shift my focus away from our new client and let myself get completely sucked into Meredith Grey's ridiculously dramatic life. Ten minutes in, I realized that any attempt to distract myself was futile. My brain refused to let go of Tripp, Take the Leap, and my impending doom. Just as I was about to give into temptation and start researching all the ways the bungee cord could fail, my phone rang with an incoming video call. I groaned. My brother couldn't just text like a normal millennial. He had a strange affinity for FaceTime.

"Hey," I answered with very little enthusiasm. But as soon as I saw my brother's wide grin and dimples, my frustration melted. Ava insisted we had the same smile, but my brother's had a certain charm to it that I lacked. I hated that it usually worked on me.

"So, bungee jumping, huh?" my brother asked. His smile widened as he tried and failed to hold in his laughter. He swiped at a wisp of brown hair. He was overdue for a trim, and it was forever getting in his eyes. Just like mine did every time I let my bangs grow out. Aside from being nearly a foot taller than me, we really did look a lot alike.

Personality wise, we were polar opposites. He's a big fan of Take the Leap and a Quest member. His favorite activity to do with the company was parasailing. He went a few times a year, which is how he'd met Liam and Tripp. Through his work on the app, he was able to give Ava and me the heads-up that they were looking for a new digital marketing agency. When I'd told him we were serious about submitting, he'd laughed. As if the idea of his sister helping market a company that was the very antithesis of everything she was was preposterous. Sure, I'd been skeptical about how I'd be able to connect with the brand, but that wasn't my job. Or at least, it shouldn't have been my job. My job was to imagine campaigns that would appeal to their target consumers, not people like me. Yet here we were doing the exact opposite and I only had myself to blame.

"Who told you?"

"I had a meeting with Tripp and Liam this afternoon." The more he talked, the less impact his charm had on me.

"Great," I groaned, "so are you calling to laugh at me or to remind me just how lame you think I am?"

"Neither actually." I didn't believe him for a second. "I was actually calling for something else."

He frowned. His tone shifted from jovial to serious. Concern flooded over me. I wasn't going to like whatever he was about to say. "Okay."

"Dad called me this morning."

I bit my lip to keep from responding. I let the silence between us linger until he spoke again. But he knew me too well and kept quiet. My throat tightened.

"Can we go back to you laughing at me?" I pulled the phone further away from my face with the hope that he wouldn't see the hint of tears that formed in my eyes.

"He's coming to Nashville soon and wants to meet us for dinner."

"Did you tell him to go—"

"I told him we'd love to," Seth said, cutting me off.

"You answered for me?" Unbelievable.

"He said you weren't answering his calls or returning his texts."

"Perhaps that's because I don't want to talk to him." Or because I had his number blocked. It's hard to say.

"He's coming to town anyway." Seth carried on as if I hadn't said anything. Our conversations were often like this—

both of us having a one-sided conversation without the other person's involvement. "Dinner is the least we can do."

"Well, I think that's the night I'm bungee jumping."

"I haven't told you the date, yet."

"Doesn't matter, I'd rather jump off a bridge than share a meal with Brett." I couldn't even bring myself to call him *Dad*. He hadn't earned the name or the affection that came with it.

"Great, I'll pick you up around six, then?"

"I won't be home."

"You don't know the date."

"That's fine, I'll just avoid being home at six every night for the rest of my life."

"One meal. We haven't seen him in over a year." Which was also the last time Seth had surprised me with a dinner with him. This was becoming a pattern.

"Whose fault is that?"

"And it's almost our birthday, which means it's also—"

"I know what it means, and I don't want to spend that day or any day with the man who spent our entire lives blaming us for it and then left us to be raised by his mother." With that, I ended the call and flopped backward. So much for spending the rest of the day as a recluse. I pushed myself up and got off the bed.

"Do we have any whiskey left over from New Year's?" I asked Ava as I sulked down the stairs. We didn't usually keep liquor in the house, but we'd hosted a New Year's Eve gathering for our clients a few months ago.

"Maybe?" Ava answered. "Why? Did Seth call?"

I raised my eyebrows at her. "What do you know?"

"Nothing." She answered too quickly.

"Lying liar who lies. When did you talk to Seth?"

"While you were meeting with Tripp. I called him to get access to the beta test for the app. He may have mentioned something about he who shall not be named."

"Did he mention when?" Ava shook her head. "I don't know what makes him think he can just spring this on me. It's just rude."

"Do you want to talk about it?" she asked, already knowing the answer.

"No, I want to continue avoiding him and everything he brings up." Ava followed me into the kitchen and watched as I searched the cabinets for any remaining whiskey. When I came up empty-handed, I settled for a Diet Coke and a stack of Oreos. I handed her the rest of the package of cookies and leaned against the counter. "It's like he knows the exact wrong moment to re-insert himself into our lives."

"Is there ever a right moment?" She twisted open an Oreo and scraped off the cream. She handed it to me. I scraped the cream off two of my cookies and stacked them on top of the cream she'd given me. Then I handed her my remaining cookie pieces. She was the cookie to my cream—decent apart but perfect together. This was one of the reasons we were best friends. We'd sat next to each other one random lunch hour in elementary school. She's had a pack of Oreos, and I'd watched in absolute horror as she scraped off the cream and set it aside. When she caught me staring at her wide-eyed, she'd asked if I wanted it. We've been inseparable ever since. I may be hard to love, but give me sugar, and I'll be as loyal to you as I am to myself.

"No, I suppose there isn't."

"What makes this moment the exact wrong one, then?"

I considered her question for a moment before answering. I could lie and tell her that all moments were wrong, and this one wasn't any more special, but we'd both know that it wasn't. "With the new client and this whole challenge thing, it just feels like I'm already opening myself up to more vulnerability than I'm comfortable with."

"That's fair, but let me say something without you freaking out," she said and handed me another round of cookie cream. "Maybe that makes this the best time."

I knew why she'd believe that. Ava was an optimist. She was kind and forgiving and always looking for the one tiny flicker of brightness on the darkest of nights. It was another reason we worked well together. I was the doomsday queen. I'd find the one dark spot on a sunny summer day and burrow myself in the cool darkness.

But that didn't mean I agreed. "No," I answered flatly, "he decided he didn't want to be my dad a long time ago. I've accepted it and everyone else needs to, too. Including him."

I scrapped the cookie crumbs off the counter and into my hand, dumping them in the trash on the way to my office. Along the way, I picked up the pair of shoes Ava had discarded in the hallway and straightened the Nashville skyline painting that refused to hang right.

"You know you're going to have to deal with this one day, right? Seth won't let you give up on him."

"Probably not, but he also can't force me into a relationship with Brett." I tucked my legs beneath me as I sat down at my desk. "Can we please talk about bungee jumping or something else. Anything."

"I printed out a list of all the adventures on Take the Leap's website. I figured we could rank them from best to worst. That way you don't go into each planning session blind. Or maybe we could just go ahead and pick your next four?"

"No," I said, "I can't handle the mental gymnastics. What if we just cut them all up and drop them in a jar? Then after we complete one, we draw the next one. But use this list from

Tripp, instead. He added a few that weren't on their website." I pulled the list from my pocket and passed it to her.

"Can you handle that? You'd have no control."

She knew me too well. "Probably not, and I reserved the right to change my mind, but I also know I can't sit across from Tripp and outline my impending doom four more times. I'm afraid I'll let him talk me into something worse each time."

"Because of his seductive blue-grey eyes or his megawatt smile?" Ava teased.

"Neither. Both. I don't know. Maybe he has another long-dead relative that he camps on cliffs for. You know where they tie a tent to the side of a cliff and sleep in midair."

"Or maybe you think he's cute and want to try something even scarier than skydiving?"

I scoffed. "I cannot think of anything scarier than that."

"Dating."

I gasped, feigning horror. "That's not scary, that's just downright terrifying."

six

THE TRAMPOLINE PARK WAS EMPTY. Even though it was 10 a.m. on a Wednesday, I'd assumed there'd at least be a dozen young kids running around getting their germs everywhere. But it was just Liam, Ava, Tripp, their content creator, Kyle, and me. We had the place to ourselves, and I wasn't quite sure how I felt about that. On the one hand, the witnesses to my embarrassment would be minimal. On the other hand, there wouldn't be a rush of tiny humans distracting everyone from watching me.

I still didn't understand how the trampoline park would help prepare me for a bungee jump, but I'd much rather start here than head into my first challenge without an ounce of preparation.

"Here," Tripp said and handed me a pair of neon yellow and green socks. I turned them over in my hand and stared at him blankly. "They have grippers, so you don't bust your butt out there."

"If they think silicone dots on the bottom of socks will keep me safe, they haven't met me." I smiled and took the socks. "But safety first!"

Liam rolled his eyes and turned his attention back to Ava and Kyle. They were setting up lighting and going over the shots they wanted to be sure to capture. I tried to ignore their conversation, but every few seconds, one of them would say my name, and I'd strain to listen.

"Penny for your thoughts?" Tripp asked.

I glanced up at him, startled. I hadn't seen him approaching. "Pretty sure you can guess without dropping a coin."

He laughed and placed his hand on my shoulder. The unexpected touch startled me, but at the same time, butterflies filled my stomach. He gave it a gentle squeeze and pulled away quickly. The butterflies lingered. "This should be the fun part. But I'm sure you've already imagined a million ways you might die today."

"Or snap my spine. I didn't know a trampoline required so many warning signs. Or a three-page safety waiver."

"Lawyers can ruin the fun in just about anything."

"I did consider that career path for a while."

"A lawyer who kills fun?"

"A lawyer who keeps the world safe," I said, smiling. "Though, you piss off the wrong person and—" I traced a line across my neck with my finger. Tripp shook his head when I lolled my head to the side and stuck out my tongue.

"Well, I for one am glad you chose marketing. You'd have been a wonderful lawyer, I'm sure, but your creativity would've been wasted."

I ignored the simultaneous rush of pride and embarrassment at his compliment and shrugged. "So, what's the plan here? Is someone going to just shove me into a foam or ball pit? Do I just bounce on a trampoline until my fear of jumping off of a bridge magically fades away?"

"Something like that, yeah." Tripp grinned.

"Fantastic. Let's get this over with."

I followed him out into the empty park. Kyle, Liam, and Ava trailed behind us. I was acutely aware of their whispered commentary and the fact that the camera was not only rolling but also fully focused on me.

Up until this moment. I'd been able to pretend my shiny, happy self wasn't the actual face of this entire campaign. Every reaction, every fear, every vulnerability of mine would be on full display for the nearly two million people that follow Take the Lead on social media. I wasn't sure which was more terrifying—doing the challenges or being made to look like a scared fool on social media in video and photographic content that would live much longer than me. At least no one knew who I was outside of our existing client base and my friends and family, and hopefully, we could keep the client exposure to a minimum. I shuddered at the thought of presenting marketing plans to a room full of people who had, for example, watched me pass out while riding a rollercoaster.

Tripp led me out to one of the smaller trampolines. I took a tentative step onto it and immediately pulled back. While, logically, I knew the ground was solid, it felt like anything but. The pliable material looked like any flat surface, but the minute my body weight applied any hint of pressure, it gave way. My heart thudded in my chest. Liam snorted and made a snide remark under his breath. I couldn't quite hear him, but it didn't take a genius to figure out what he'd said.

A hand wrapped around mine. I glanced down and found my fingers intertwined with Tripp's. His palm was warm and rough and reassuring against mine. He gave my hand a sturdy squeeze before he tugged me forward. I lost my balance for a moment, but his other hand landed on my hip and immediately steadied me. A flood of warmth inundated my senses. It was so strong that I barely noticed the trampoline under my feet. What is happening? Is he getting butterflies too? No, I'm sure he's just being supportive and making sure we don't get lame content. With Tripp guiding me, I walked to the center of the trampoline.

"I'm going to stay still. Just jump when you're ready." His voice was so quiet that only I could hear him. There wasn't an ounce of judgment or ridicule in his voice. Liam and Kyle were both snickering behind us. I could hear Ava quietly scolding and trying to shush them. "Ignore them and focus on me, okay?"

It was ridiculous, though. This was a small trampoline in a completely controlled environment. There were absolutely zero reasons to be scared and worried. Kids did this kind of stuff with wild abandon all the time. Well, kids who weren't me. They didn't worry about broken necks or double bounces that broke bones or a trampoline ripping wide open sending them careening onto a concrete floor. This was fun. Or it should be fun.

Honestly, I wasn't even sure I knew how to jump. When was the last time I'd tried? Probably during some plyometric exercise in one of those workout DVDs that Ava talked me into doing back in college. Even then, I always followed the low-impact modifier. Jumping led to jiggling and the wild freedom of all of my bits and pieces. Suddenly, I became hyper-aware of the camera on me catching every inch of me. I'm not usually self-conscious, but I also wasn't used to being the face of a campaign.

"I can't do this," I whispered to Tripp. "This is a bad idea. I don't know how to jump, and everyone is going to make fun of me and laugh when they see this video."

Why had I agreed to this? Tears welled in my eyes. I felt like such an idiot—both for my reaction and for my inability to just freaking jump.

"This is so stupid," I said. "I'm stupid."

"Breathe, Sadie," Tripp said. He leaned in close, and his lips grazed my ear. If I hadn't been in the midst of a mild panic attack, I'd have melted under the contact. He placed his hands on either side of my waist and started bouncing. I shook my head as the ground beneath me gave way to our weight. "I know you don't know me, but try to trust me, okay? I've got you."

Without thinking, I nodded. *I've got you.* His words melted something frozen inside of me. My body warmed. I felt my knees loosen and bend. My feet didn't leave the surface, but slowly, I began to bounce along with him. After a minute or two, he jumped a bit higher. When my feet finally left the ground, he released his hold on my hips. I grasped his hands and held onto them as we began to jump higher. We fell into a rhythm. The more we jumped, the more my mind relaxed. I let go of his hands and was surprised to find I was enjoying myself. Tripp backed away from me and eventually stepped off of the trampoline. I started laughing.

I caught Ava's eye and smiled back at her. "Look at you!" she mouthed at me. Her face beamed with pride.

I jumped for what felt like hours. I bounced from one trampoline to another, zigzagging across the park. It was freeing, how loose it all felt. At some point, I even forgot about the cameras and audience. I was just having fun.

"Okay, that's enough trampoline content," Liam said, yawning. "Let's move over to the climbing area."

Wait, what? I slowed my jumping. I turned back to the group and found Tripp's smiling face. Like Ava, he looked like a proud parent. "Why do I need to climb?"

"So, you can jump off their little platform," Liam said and smirked. "Think you can handle that?"

No, not at all. I wasn't about to tell him that and give him the satisfaction. Liam seemed to be enjoying my discomfort which made me dislike him and want to prove him wrong.

"Sure," I said.

We moved our setup across the park. A small fenced-off area filled with rock climbing walls, pedestals of various heights, and something that looked like a baby bungee jumping platform awaited us, and I wondered why we hadn't started here. Just looking at the area made my heart and mind race. I conjured up dozens of images of snapped ropes and my body lying prone and broken on the hard floor.

But I kept it together as Tripp helped me into a harness and stepped into his own. "How do you want to do this?" he asked.

"I don't."

Tripp laughed and shook his head. "We can either start small and work our way up to the platform jump, or we can start there and just focus on that."

I scanned the climbing area and weighed my options. I could delay the inevitable and give Liam a dozen extra opportunities to laugh at me, or I could just go for the one thing I wanted to do least. Neither option appealed to me. I chose the path of least resistance ... and humiliation.

"Let's just go for it."

Tripp nodded with a grin. "Good choice." Once again, he grabbed my hand. This time, I was prepared for the contact. I noted how well my hand fit in his, and then promptly shoved the thought aside. He led me toward the ladder. It was only about eight feet up, but it looked like Mount Everest from where I stood. A lump rose in my throat as I looked up at the metal I'd soon be climbing.

"Only one of us can go up at a time," Tripp said.

"What? No, I am not going up there alone."

"Technically, only one of us can go up because there is only one rope." He held the offending rope in his hand and showed it to me before he clipped it to the carabiner on my waist. "We're going to break the rules today, though." He started to climb the ladder.

"Wait!" I shouted louder than I'd intended. "You need to be attached to a rope too! It's not safe without it, is it?"

Liam gave a loud snort of laughter. I turned to glare at him. All I wanted was for his boss to be safe. What was so funny about that?

"I'm not jumping," Tripp said, "I'm going to go up with you, and then I'll climb back down to help you land on the ground. We'll repeat that until you can do it on your own."

I wanted to protest more, but he started climbing the ladder. I stared up at him and willed my feet to move. I wrapped my fingers around the step in front of me and placed my foot on the bottom rung of the ladder. I'd climbed things before. At barely five feet tall, I was used to climbing step ladders and standing on things to reach medium-height shelves. So, I pretended that was all I was doing. This was just four small stools stacked on top of each other. Four small step stools. I repeated this over and over with every step. When I reached the last one, my eyes blurred with tears. I blinked them away and met Tripp's gaze.

"I was expecting more of a fight." He took hold of my arm and helped pull me up. I remained crouched for a moment before standing to join him. I kept my gaze locked on his face. I feared if I looked anywhere else, like down, I'd completely lose it.

"I had to turn my brain off," I said once I'd composed myself. "It helps that the ladder is sturdier than the trampoline."

"When you're ready, I'm going to climb back down." He grabbed the rope in front of me and tugged it. The rope gave a little but remained firmly attached to the ceiling. "This is long enough to get you to the ground, okay? It's strong enough to hold 800 pounds. You are safe."

"Safe," I echoed. There wasn't an ounce of trust in my voice.

Tripp leaned in and whispered into my ear. "Between this rope and me at the bottom, you're safe, Sadie. Okay?" The confidence in his voice filtered through my ears and into my brain. I let his words circle a few times in my mind until I'd memorized the sound. "I've got you."

"Safe." This time, I almost believed it. Tripp guided me a few steps forward but stopped shy of the edge. He locked his eyes on mine one last time and waited until I gave him a small nod. Then, he climbed back down. My eyes followed him back down the ladder and then to the ground below me.

"When you're ready."

"Jump?"

"That's the idea," Liam said. I ignored him and focused on Tripp.

Wrapping my hands around the rope, I pulled it just as Tripp had. It felt sturdy. I dared a look over the edge. Instead of seeing the ground, I saw Tripp smiling up at me. *You're safe, Sadie. I've got you.* His words echoed in my mind. And I actually believed him. I trusted this man I barely knew. I didn't let any other thoughts enter my head. I trained every ounce of energy onto those three words and the man who'd uttered them. Then I stepped forward.

My feet found the air...

And then I was falling.

Before I could even react, I was on the ground and Tripp had his arms around me. He hadn't needed to catch me—the rope had done a good enough job—but he was a man of his word. He'd been ready and waiting for me.

"Damn!" Liam hollered.

"Holy crap," Ava said. "She didn't even hesitate."

"Heck yeah, sis!" At that, my head snapped to the right. Seth, my brother, was standing beside Kyle. A look of complete disbelief was plastered on his face. What is he doing here?

Tripp read the puzzled look on my face. "He said you all had dinner plans tonight and wanted to know when we'd be done so he could pick you up."

That little scheming brat.

seven

"THIS IS NOT OKAY, SETH," I said, seething. "You cannot show up at my work and spring this on me." I pressed my shaking hands deeper in between my legs. Anger pulsed through my veins.

"Dinner? It's just a meal. You eat it every day." His tone was far too jovial for my current disposition.

"Dinner with him." I wasn't in the mood to play verbal tennis.

"Well, to be fair, I did tell you we were having dinner with Dad, and that I was picking you up."

"It had to be today?"

"No, it just happened to be today."

My brother didn't bother hiding his amusement at my irritation. I glared at him from the passenger seat of his car and debated my escape options. We were currently on I40 heading into downtown, so now wasn't the ideal time to attempt my first tuck and roll out of a moving vehicle. Though, I did wonder if Tripp offered that kind of adventure. Maybe I could use the training for my brother's future attempts at twinnapping. My next best option was to schedule a rideshare to pick me up as soon as we arrived at the restaurant. When I pulled my phone out of my bag, Seth tsked his tongue against his teeth.

"Don't even think about it," he warned.

"Think about what?" I asked, feigning innocence. But my brother knew me too well.

"Finding a rideshare to meet you at the restaurant. Dinner with Dad and Mel is happening whether you want it to or not."

"Mel?" He'd conveniently left out the part about our step-mother joining us.

"Did I not tell you?"

"You failed to mention that crucial piece of information. Anything else you want to add?" I loved my brother dearly but wasn't above considering murder at the moment. His death and my arrest would solve the impending doom of dinner, but the long-term consequences weren't worth it. I'd probably miss him, too. Maybe.

So, I gritted my teeth and decided to stew in silence for the remainder of the drive. I ignored his every attempt at small talk until he gave up. It was the longest ten-minute car ride I'd suffered through in recent memory.

When we arrived at the restaurant, Seth had the audacity to ask me to "behave." I scoffed and rolled my eyes. Sure, his request was completely reasonable, but it wasn't as if I needed him to remind me. I turned toward him and painted the fakest smile across my face. I bared my teeth and kept the uncomfortable grin locked in place as we walked inside. At least he'd picked one of my favorite restaurants for my torture.

"Welcome to Brine's, how many?" the hostess asked.

"Four if you count the unwanted guests," I said before Seth could answer.

Shaking his head, Seth said, "Reservation for four. Seth Barnes." The hostess nodded and checked her computer before informing us that the rest of our party was already seated and leading us toward the back of the restaurant. Despite my deep desire to be anywhere but here, the overwhelming scent of garlic and marinara sauce reminded me just how hungry I was. Who knew trampolines could work up such a big appetite?

My hunger quickly soured when we arrived at the table.

Brett and Mel were waiting with nervous smiles. As much as I hated to admit it, every time I looked at Brett it was hard not to see that we were related. He had the same hazel eyes and brown hair that we did. Like Seth, Brett was tall and lean. Growing up, Gran used to say Seth got his athleticism from our dad, and I got my creativity from Mom. Not that I could've confirmed that piece of information.

Mel stood to greet me, but I chose to ignore her outstretched hand. Her chocolate brown eyes dropped toward the floor at the rejection, and I immediately felt bad. Reluctantly, I offered her a side hug and caught the subtle scent of lilacs in her blonde hair.

They'd ordered a bottle of the sweet white wine I liked for the table. I knew from past forced family bonding experiences that Brett would try to pretend like he knew me. He'd ask about work and throw in some new tidbit that I was certain Seth had fed him. Then he'd feign interest in whatever hobby he'd seen me obsessing over on social media. The wine, always the same and always my favorite, was always step one in the *Convince Sadie I'm a Good Dad* game we played every few months. He'd yet to win a single round. I had years and years of practice under my belt.

Seth took the seat next to Mel, knowing I wouldn't. I, begrudgingly, plopped myself between him and Brett. My brother passed a knowing glance toward me. Another plea for me to be on my best behavior. *No promises*, I thought and hoped for the millionth time that twin telepathy was a real thing. It wasn't. Judging by the smug grin on his face, he took my lack of response as acquiescence.

"So, Sadie," Brett said as he poured me a glass of wine, "I hear you and Ava just landed a big new client."

"We did."

"And Seth said something about you joining him on some of those extreme sport things he does?" Mel chimed in.

"Yep." I took a long, slow sip of the wine, careful to not down the entire glass. I'd be polite and play along as much as my resentment would allow me, but I wasn't going to drink too much or offer more than one or two-word answers. If my *father* wanted complete sentences, he should try and show up more than once or twice a year.

Seth cleared his throat and kicked me under the table. I shrugged in response. He should really know how this game is played by now. We'd been doing it since we were teenagers.

"Sadie was actually practicing for her bungee jump this weekend when I picked her up. The campaign they came up with is brilliant," Seth said.

I bit back my smile. It was brilliant, and I appreciated that my brother recognized this, but I wasn't taking the bait. Awkward silence engulfed us before Brett decided to speak up again.

"Wow, bungee jumping? That seems a little out of character, Sadie. I know your brother loves chasing adrenaline rushes, but you and Seth couldn't be more opposite when it comes to that stuff."

"It is," I agreed. Every bit of this was out of character.

"What inspired the campaign?" Brett asked, trying to get more out of me.

"The app."

"What app?" Mel asked.

"Seth?" I nodded toward my twin. It was his app; he could

talk about it. Plus, I knew he couldn't resist an opportunity to take a deep dive into the nerdy end of the pool. Just as I'd predicted, Seth launched into a spirited monologue on the app he was developing for Take the Leap. Brett and Mel were so enthralled with his speech that they completely forgot I was there. Just how I preferred it.

When the waitress came to take our order, Seth paused long enough to order appetizers and another bottle of wine before we each ordered our meals. I was hoping to avoid multiple courses and a long-drawn-out meal, but it appeared my brother had other plans. I groaned silently and slumped back in my chair when the waitress left us alone to continue our conversation.

Thankfully, Seth picked up where he left off. I crossed my arms over my chest and watched as Mel and Brett stared at Seth and nodded along as if they understood what Angular and UI/UX meant. I'll give them some credit; they could both play the part of the doting parent well. Although Mel hadn't exactly received the warmest welcome to her stepmom role, she seemed to at least somewhat care about the lives of the spawns of her husband. Even if he didn't.

Mel was wife number three for dear old Dad. First had been my mother, but she'd died and left him with newborn twins. When we were two, he met and married Claire, who hadn't much cared for kids, especially not toddlers. So Brett shipped us off to Nashville to live with his mother while he started a new life that didn't involve the daily reminder of his dead first love. When Claire left him for her divorce lawyer, Brett didn't come back to claim us. Instead, he left us with Gran and carried on as if he were living his best childless, bachelor life.

Then Gran died and my heart broke beyond repair, and we spent an awkward two years living in her old house with Brett and his new bride, Mel. By then it was too late. I'd spent fourteen years of my life without him and wasn't about to welcome him back with open arms.

"Wait? What do you mean Sadie broke the app?" Mel asked, laughing. Hearing my name pulled me out of my thoughts and back into the conversation.

"She matched with literally nothing. I'd built it to offer everyone an answer, but I didn't factor in the completely risk-averse people." My brother and Brett both laughed along with Mel. "From what Ava and Tripp tell me, the app and Sadie's completely boring life is what saved their pitch."

I rolled my eyes. "No, what saved the pitch was *my* idea to pull the app into our plan and shift our presentation."

"She speaks!" Seth said and threw his fists in the air in victory. *Damn.*

"Whatever."

"Tell me more about the pitch and what you'll be doing," Brett said.

I sighed. I couldn't answer that with just two words. As much as I hated the idea of doing all of these challenges, I was proud of the campaign we'd put together. It was innovative and had the potential to make a huge impact for our client.

"Basically, it's an experiential campaign. I'll do challenges alongside Tripp James, the founder of the company, and we'll document and share the entire process. The goal is to show people the wide variety of experiences that Take the Leap offers and to make them more appealing to normal people."

"Did you mention skydiving?" Brett asked Seth. He sounded a little nervous. Or scared? Maybe concerned? I wasn't sure which, but none of the options were on brand for him. He'd never so much as offered me a bandage for a paper cut, much less expressed interest in my well-being.

"That's the last challenge. Bungee jumping is up first. Then there will be a few others before that."

"Like what?" Brett asked. There was definitely something off with the way his voice shifted.

"Sadie?" Seth asked. He kicked me under the table again. I rolled my eyes at him.

"We don't have them all planned out, yet. But the list of ideas includes things like hot air balloon rides, skateboarding, rock climbing, kayaking, and some other stuff like that."

Brett's eyes went wide as he studied my face. "Isn't that, I don't know, dangerous?"

"Yes, that's kind of the point."

He shifted in his seat. "I don't know how I feel about you doing all of that, Sadie Bug." I bristled at the use of Gran's nickname for me. "What if something goes wrong?"

"It won't," Seth said before I could agree with Brett.

"I'll be fine." I didn't believe the words even as I said them, but the change in Brett's demeanor was freaking me out.

"I'm just worried about you. It seems like a lot to take on for one client."

"Brett, I'm in good hands. Tripp and his team know what they're doing."

"They do," Seth agreed, "and they'll make sure she's taken care of. You have nothing to worry about."

"I'm her dad. I have everything to worry about. I just don't want anything to happen to you."

I didn't bother hiding my amusement. "Really? Are you serious right now?"

"Sadie," Seth said, warning me.

"You're worried about me? Now? I'm an adult. The time to worry about me was when I was two and essentially orphaned. You don't get to worry about me now. You lost that privilege a long time ago."

"I've never stopped worrying about you or loving you, Sadie, you know that."

"I don't know that. Nor do I believe it." I slid my chair back and stood quickly. Brett stood to stop me, but Mel placed her hand on his arm. "Don't. It's okay. Thank you for coming tonight, Sadie. I know this isn't easy for you," she said, turning her attention back to me.

I bit back the sarcastic response that burned on my tongue. Instead, I looked down at Mel and offered an apologetic smile. I truly meant no harm or ill will toward her. She wasn't to blame for his past choices. Before I could say another word, I grabbed my purse and headed to the door.

As soon as my back was to them, tears welled in my eyes. I blinked them away and told myself the crying could wait. I refused to risk letting them see me show a single ounce of emotion.

A gentle hand grabbed my shoulder. "At least let me drive you home," Seth said.

I shook my head. "I'll get a rideshare or call Ava. Go back. Enjoy your dinner."

Seth had always been more tolerant of Brett. He'd forgiven him for abandoning us. He'd even managed to build a relationship with him. He could call him *Dad* without so much as a hint of bitterness or sarcasm. Unlike me. I wasn't sure I'd ever be able to forgive him, much less want him to be a part of my life.

How dare he show up and act as if he had a say in anything I did?

eight

AFTER THE ATTEMPTED dinner with Brett, jumping off of a bridge didn't sound so bad. That didn't mean I was excited to be standing on a bridge over a lake at eight o'clock on a Friday night. I wrapped my arms around my waist and tried to ignore Ava and Liam standing near the edge of the bridge. They were discussing camera angles. With every other word, Ava glanced at me and forced a smile. She'd had to shove me into the car to get me here, so she wasn't about to let me out of her sight. I was a flight risk with a fear of falling, to quote the queen herself, Taylor Swift.

"Are you ready?" Tripp asked. He stepped beside me and bumped his shoulder against mine.

"Sure. Totally. Definitely ready for all of this." I swept my arms in front of me as I chewed my lower lip. "But you know, I wouldn't be opposed to breaking into the trampoline park and doing a few more baby jumps." Before Seth dragged me to dinner with Brett and Mel, I'd jumped off the mini platform a grand total of five times. I felt like a pro and ready to take on an actual jump. But that was more than forty-eight hours ago, and I'd had plenty of time to imagine the bungee cord snapping in two and sending me to my death in the frigid waters of Percy Priest Lake.

He chuckled. "You've got this, Sadie." A rush of warmth flowed through me at the way his voice softened when he said my name. I shook it off and glanced down at the harness in his hand. It looked only slightly sturdier than the one I'd worn at the park. He'd already stepped into his, but the collective team decided that getting me into the harness would make for great content. I'd tried to argue, but had been sorely outnumbered. As if the humiliation of being terrified of everything wasn't enough, now everyone would get a front-row seat to watch me get an ultimate wedgie.

"All right, Sadie," Ava said as she and Liam stepped into the bubble of warmth Tripp had created around us. I shivered. She handed Tripp and me our helmets. Both were equipped with cameras to help capture every angle. "Fair warning, these are already recording. We don't want to risk missing anything."

"Unless you want to jump twice," Liam said with a laugh.

"Nope. Once is already one too many times."

"We've also got a camera attached to the base over there." He pointed at the base where we'd be launching to our deaths. "And, Tony, the guy who runs this place, is also wearing a camera. Kyle is down at the base of the lake to capture additional on-the-ground footage, and Ava and I have things covered up here."

It sounded like a lot of cameras, but again, I didn't want to do this more than once. "Should we have one more on the ground? Didn't we discuss someone in a boat or something to get another angle?"

"Right," Liam said and glanced at Ava, who offered a reassuring smile. "Between the helmet cameras, the one under the bridge, and Tony's, we should be good. "

Ava said, "Look, we've got the content portion under control."

I asked, "Lighting? Is that good?"

Liam nodded toward Tony, who flipped on two large lights that flooded the area. "Yup. Anything else to ask to delay the inevitable?"

I ignored the annoyance in his voice and shook my head. I'm sure I could come up with a dozen more questions, but he was right. Stalling was pointless.

Liam and Ava stepped back toward the edge of the bridge. I watched them walk until they were both in position. They had their phones trained on me as I slipped the helmet onto my head and tightened the strap. I turned to Tripp and gave what I hoped was a confident smile.

"Let's get you strapped in," he said with a smirk. He held the harness out and I stepped into it. I was careful to keep my head angled away from him so we didn't bump helmets. He slid the straps over my thighs and tightened them. His fingers brushed over the soft material of my leggings sending a flood of heat from my core all the way to my face. I glanced around, suddenly very aware of all the eyes locked on me. Could they tell how my body was reacting?

"Does that feel snug? Too tight? Too loose?"

I cleared my throat. "Um, I think it's okay." I wasn't sure how it was supposed to feel, but it felt like I was being tied into a thigh noose. "Does making it tighter make it safer?"

He smiled at me. I searched his face for a hint of mocking or even frustration but didn't find any. All I found was a warm and inviting smile that offered reassurance. "You should be able to feel the straps but not feel like they're cutting into your skin."

I frowned. "There might be a little cutting going on." I reached down to loosen one of the belts at the same time he did. Our fingers tangled for a moment. His hands, though rough, felt soothing against my skin. I jerked my hand back and mumbled an apology as he continued adjusting the strap. Once it felt snug, I nodded curtly and took a few steps back.

"It's good. Thank you," I said and avoided making direct eye contact with him.

"We don't have all night here. Some of us have lives to get back to," Liam said, shouting at us.

"Coming," I said right as Tripp replied, "We do, actually have all night, Liam. We're not going to rush Sadie, remember?" His voice carried a stern, warning tone.

Liam shrugged off the warning. "Whatever you say."

"Liam, do we need to find another member of the team to lead this campaign?" Tripp asked.

"No, sorry, boss," Liam muttered. I caught him roll his eyes when he turned back to the rest of the crew.

In front of me, Tripp squared his shoulders. The muscles in his jaw tensed. I met Ava's wide-eyed stare. I'd never heard anyone at Take the Leap speak harshly towards Tripp. They all seemed to love him, but the tension between Liam and Tripp was palpable. Whatever nerves I'd managed to ignore resurfaced as Tripp's demeanor shifted. I hadn't realized just how much his positive energy had calmed me.

I took another tentative step toward the jump platform. After five steps, I was at the railing that surrounded the base. I glanced toward the darkness on the other side of the bridge and gasped. My heart raced. My legs felt like Jell-o, and an odd icy feeling radiated from my core.

I can't do this. I can't do this. I stopped walking; my head shook from side to side as if it were being pulled by an invisible string. Fear wrapped around my entire body and pulled me toward the ground. I braced my hands against the pavement and lowered my forehead to the ground.

My vision blurred with tears I hadn't been expecting. Not now. I could not cry in front of Tripp or Liam, but especially not in front of the cameras. From the corner of my eye, I saw a blur of blue rush toward me. Ava knelt beside me and placed her hand on my back. On the other side of me, another body hovered. Tripp.

"Sadie?" Ava whispered. "Sweetie?" Her tone was filled with concern.

"I can't—" My voice trembled as I tried to finish my sentence. "I thought I could do this, but I can't. I can't, Ava."

"Breathe, okay? Just breathe." Tripp's deep voice soothed into my ear. "In. Out." He emphasized each word and paused to breathe with me.

I closed my eyes, squeezing them shut as tight as I could. Tears moistened my cheeks. I swiped my hands across my face to clear them away. Tripp continued to whisper his urges to breathe. After a minute or two, I let my focus shift to his voice. I took a few tentative breaths along with him and felt my pulse slow to a more manageable rate. My legs steadied beneath me, and I pushed myself back to standing. Tripp and Ava flanked me, both keeping their hands on my back to hold me up.

"Okay?" Tripp asked once I was fully upright again.

"No." I didn't bother lying. It was pretty obvious that I wasn't. "I'm sorry, this was a terrible idea."

A silent conversation seemed to pass between Ava and Tripp as I glanced between them. Tripp gave a quick nod, and Ava gave me a quick squeeze before returning to Liam's side at the edge of the bridge. Liam's glare of annoyance shone nearly as bright as the spotlights. My face flushed as I remembered all the cameras recording me. I would not be watching any of this footage.

"What if we did it together?" Tripp asked.

"Together?" I wasn't sure what he meant. The plan was for him to jump first and for me to follow.

"A tandem jump. We'll both be harnessed and strapped in, but I'll carry you. You'll just be along for the ride."

He pulled out his phone and showed me a video. The fact that he had it cued up and ready to go on his phone told me he'd anticipated this.

In the video, a man and a woman stood together on a ledge a lot like the one in front of me. She had her legs wrapped around his waist as he held her. They were face-to-face and looked rather intimate. He wanted me to wrap my legs around his waist and let him cradle my butt in his arms as we leaped off a bridge together. Yeah, no. Not going to happen. I glanced up at Tripp and immediately regretted the mental images of my arms and legs entwined with his somewhere other than this blasted bridge that popped into my mind.

I didn't know which scared me more—jumping alone or jumping while canoodling with Tripp.

"I ... I don't know." I could feel the heat rising up my neck and face. Tripp took my hand and guided me slowly toward the platform where Tony was waiting patiently.

"I've got you, Sadie. Remember?" He said it the exact way he'd said it at the trampoline park. I forced myself to shove any and all thoughts of our bodies touching to the side and instead focused on the task at hand. I had to jump. This was the first challenge of five. I couldn't chicken out now. I owed it myself and Ava. I glanced over at her. She tossed me a thumbs up, but I could see the questions in her eyes.

I drew in a shallow breath and exhaled through my teeth. "Let's get this over with."

"Together?" He moved closer to me and placed his hands on my hips. Tony clipped a bungee cord to each of our harnesses and tugged. My body pulled forward and I fell against Tripp's chest. He wrapped his arms around me and lifted me. Instinctively, I wrapped my arms around his shoulders and legs around his waist. I buried my head into his shoulder and used every ounce of self-preservation I had remaining to pretend I wasn't feeling anything other than panic. Because panic was the *last* thing I was feeling right now. I felt every single inch of him, and it was causing my mind and heart to race. He shifted, nudging me a bit higher with his knee until I rested comfortably in his arms. I stifled a gasp as my hips settled against his. His hold on me tightened as he walked toward the edge. "On three, okay?"

I nodded, not daring to look at him or over the edge. I closed my eyes and braced myself.

"Open your eyes, Sadie, please?" I shook my head. Not going to happen. I felt him sigh but he didn't push it. I rested my forehead on his shoulder. The cool night air brushed against my skin as we approached the last few inches of the platform.

"On three," he whispered. "One... Two... Three."

I pulled myself closer to him when his body twitched to jump. Clenching my jaw, I held in my scream when I felt him lift off the ground and leap into the open air.

I buried my face deeper into his shoulder and inhaled sharply as the rush of air exploded around us. Tripp's laughter shook his body. Curious, I opened one eye and snuck a look up at him. His head was tilted back, and he had the goofiest grin on his face. I couldn't help but smile. He glanced down and caught me watching him. His smile widened.

I opened both eyes and watched in horror as we fell closer and closer to the lake. The top of my helmet grazed the top of the water before we were yanked back up. My hold on Tripp loosened a bit, and I let my gaze shift around us. We were at the mercy of the bungee now. It jerked us up and then down. Fast at first, but the pace slowed.

When we stopped bouncing, I let out the breath I'd been holding and mentally scanned my body. It appeared everything was still intact. I was whole. And alive. And wrapped in the very strong arms of Tripp James. With the fear of dying removed, I was reminded once again of just how close to Tripp I was. I could feel every breath he took—his rising chest and the puff of air as he exhaled onto my cheek.

Nervous laughter bubbled out of my mouth and came out in a weak giggle. I let go of Tripp and clamped my hand over my mouth. A small boat appeared beneath us, and the driver guided us in. I wobbled when my feet touched the bottom of the boat, but Tripp helped keep me upright. As soon as the bungee clamp was released, I sank onto the seat and tried to catch my breath. Between the adrenaline and the giggling, I was sure I looked like an insane person. Tripp watched me. The stupid grin plastered on his face remained.

"Holy crap. I did it. We jumped off a bridge," I said once I calmed down enough to trust my voice. "I didn't die!"

nine

IT TOOK me three days to recover from the bungee jump. I spent half of Saturday in bed, alternating between more nightmares of the disaster I avoided or illicit dreams of Tripp. On Sunday, I shifted my energy to baking cookies and eating them. By Monday, I still wasn't ready to face reality, but I sucked it up and rode with Ava to Take the Leap's offices to review the footage from the trampoline park and bridge.

This was the first time I'd been back to their office since Ava had pulled the stunt with the elevator. As we drove over, I mentally prepared myself to tackle the elevator without any intervention or stalling. When we walked into the lobby, I stayed one step ahead of Ava and beat her to the elevator. Without saying a word, I pressed the up button and stood to wait for the doors to open. Once inside, I hit the button for our floor and stepped to the back of the space.

"Who are you?" Ava asked. "And what have you done with Sadie?"

"You shouldn't be surprised that I'm taking control. Especially after the crap you pulled last time."

"Fair point. Are you ready for this?"

We hadn't spoken much over the weekend. She'd had a date with the son of a friend of her mom's, and I'd pretty much stayed in bed and spent the entire weekend reading.

"I think so, I'm just hoping it doesn't turn out to be too humiliating," I said as we exited the elevator on the forty-fifth floor. "Hey, Chloe, we're here for Tripp and Liam."

"They're down in the content editing room, do you know how to get there?"

"We can manage, thank you!" Ava said and guided me down the hallway to the right. "The good news is that everyone in the editing room was there, so none of this will be new for us. And I'm sure it all looks great."

"You mean the part where I panic at the trampoline park or the part where I break down on the bridge?"

Before I could answer, Tripp greeted us in the hallway. He directed us into the room where Liam and Kyle sat in front of two large monitors. The video on the screen was frozen on an image of me and Tripp talking at the trampoline park. In the image, he was staring down at me with a look on this face that I don't quite know how to read. Amusement? Curiosity? Admiration? Or, more likely, annoyance at whatever I'm saying.

Kyle tapped the play button and the sound of my voice filled the room. Cringing, I braced myself. It was one thing to see my face on screen, but it was another to have to sit and listen to myself talk.

"I think this banter is good, here," Kyle said. "Liam wants to cut it."

"Why?" Ava asked. "It's pretty amusing, and helps the audience get a sense of who Sadie is."

"Yeah, but it's also kind of weird. Or lame or flirty. Honestly, I don't know," Liam said. His usual cockiness was gone, instead he glanced at Tripp as if he were asking permission to speak freely. "We have a brand image to uphold."

Tripp's face dropped. *Too soft.* I recalled the conversation we'd had at coffee. Liam thinks the banter could hurt their image.

"We're revamping the brand," I said, "remember? The whole point of this is to bring in a new audience, which means we need to show both sides of the brand—the extreme, edgy side and the approachable, friendly aspect."

Tripp cleared his throat, "Sadie's right. We leave the banter."

"And all those sweet nothing whispers of *I've got you?*" Liam choked out a laugh as he gagged. "Like what was that?"

A rush of pink flushed over Tripp's face. I smiled up at him and covered my face with my hands to hide my blush. *Sweet nothings.* Seriously? He was just being supportive. Liam opened his mouth to speak again, but Tripp silenced him with a glare.

"It shows viewers that your team is concerned about their safety and wants everyone to feel safe on whatever excursion they book," Ava said, jumping in to break the awkward silence.

"We're trying something new here, Liam, and we need everyone on board. Now, let's move on."

"Speaking of trying something new," Kyle said, pulling our attention back to him, "I think we need to get some footage of Tripp introducing Sadie and the campaign. If we just drop this on the feed, it's going to feel out of place. We can film that today, if that works for you guys?"

Tripp glanced at me. I shrugged in response. "Sure, we can do that. I'm presentable enough, I think." I glanced down at the pastel striped shirt and jeans I was wearing. I'd done my hair and makeup this morning as well.

"You look perfect," Tripp said, his voice heavy.

Liam coughed and stared at him with his face twisted in a look of disgust. He quickly shook it off and grabbed a camera from the shelf behind the monitors. "Let's get this over with, then. We have a lot of editing to do."

Tripp and I followed him back into the lobby. He directed us to stand side-by-side in front of the Take the Leap logo. We decided to improvise a quick conversation that could be used in the video. Tripp introduced me, and I shared a bit about Savie and myself.

"Stay tuned for the full video later this week," I said and nudged Tripp with my shoulder, "I get a little too wrapped up in this guy, here." The words fell out of my mouth before I could stop them. Ava stared at me with her mouth hanging open. Rather than keep talking myself deeper into a hole I wouldn't be able to climb out of, I snapped my mouth shut.

"Hey, I have no complaints," Tripp joked back. His hip bumped against mine as he slid his arm behind me and rested his hand on the small of my back. I resisted the urge to close my eyes and lean into his touch.

"That's enough," Liam said and turned off the camera. "We should probably stop before you completely implode our brand image."

Tripp shifted beside me and dropped his hand. I stepped away from him. We made our way back to the editing room and returned to our seats. Before we could start the editing again, we were interrupted by a familiar voice at the door. I exhaled a deep sigh.

"Seth?" Ava asked and turned to face my brother. "What are you doing here?"

"I was meeting with the technical team to go over some of the app updates and they mentioned you were working on the footage. Mind if I crash the party?" he asked and took a seat next to me without waiting for a response.

"Sure, make yourself at home," I said, rolling my eyes.

"This is weird," Liam said. His gaze drifted between my

brother and me. "It's like you're the same person but yet not at all."

"We are twins, man," Seth said.

"If you didn't look so much alike, I don't think I'd have believed you. She is nothing like you. Wait until you see her lose it on the bridge." Liam snorted a laugh.

Seth drapped a protective arm around my shoulder. "I'm just proud she did it."

"Suck up," I whispered to him, "I'm still pissed about dinner."

"I know."

"All right let's get this going, I've got a budget meeting at two," Tripp said. His gaze met mine for a moment. Rather than look away, I kept my eyes locked on him. I searched his face for a hint that I hadn't read too much into his continued support of me. But all I saw was the face of a man who knew exactly what he wanted. Could that be me, I wondered? Did I want it to be? If anyone else noticed the look that passed between us, they didn't say anything.

Kyle hit play again, and I covered my eyes when the video cut to footage of me at the trampoline park. When it got to the part where I started jumping while holding Tripp's hands, I dared to take a peek between my fingers. I couldn't quite hear his whispered reassurances, but I could read the words on his lips. The same warmth I'd felt that day spread through me again. Why did those three words cause such a dramatic reaction? Rather than obsesses over the question I didn't know how to answer, I shifted my attention back to the video.

I barely recognized the woman on the screen. She was smiling and laughing and jumping on a trampoline. She climbed up a ladder and jumped down into the arms of a man who looked genuinely happy to have her. Again, I wasn't going to dwell on that random thought. Tripp was doing his job, and so was I.

For the next two or so hours, we worked our way through the rest of the content to narrow it down into one long video and a few shorter options to share on social media. After the trampoline park footage, I stopped hiding behind my hands. Ava patted her hand on my knee as Tripp paced the floor behind us offering directions on what audio to add or what clips to cut and include. He paused beside me every few minutes as if to make sure I was doing okay. I'd smile and to reassure him I was fine. Watching the footage hadn't been as painful as I expected, but I focused all my attention on Tripp. He was natural on camera, and the way he looked at me sent a thousand errant and unproductive thoughts of all the things we could do off of camera through my head. I squashed each and every one of them.

I was already risking my life by doing this nonsense, I wasn't about to risk anything else—like my heart.

ten

WHEN AVA and I arrived at the Take the Leap offices for the campaign kickoff party the next week, Tripp greeted us with a smile. I'd broken my cookies-are-only-for-courting-clients rule and baked up a few batches of chocolate chip cookies for the party, mostly because baking distracted me from dreading this whole ordeal. I would've spent the entire night baking if Ava hadn't hidden the flour and sugar after the third batch.

"The whole team is here and ready to kick this campaign off with a bang!" Tripp said, beaming. "Your brother is here, too. He's back with the tech team, going over everything for the app. He said something about servers and traffic, and then I tuned him out."

Laughing, I said, "Wise choice. He'll talk about that stuff for hours upon hours."

"You guys really went all out." I followed Ava's hands as she waved around the room. The entire space was decorated. Much to my surprise—and horror—they'd created movie posters for the video featuring one of the photos of me clinging to Tripp for dear life as we hovered over Percy Priest Lake,

Thankfully, you couldn't see my face. But Tripp's scruffy, chiseled face was on full display. A vainer person might be sad the marketing materials focused on the supporting character, but I was grateful. No one would be focusing on me when they could stare at the pure joy on Tripp's face ... or at the rest of him.

Ava wandered off to chat with Liam and the content team, leaving me alone with Tripp for the first time since the jump. He'd sent a few texts and emails to check in, but I'd kept the communication professional. Much to my unexplainable disappointment, so had he. This was a new, confusing feeling for me, and I'd never had a client, or anyone, affect me quite like he had. The fact that he was a client made this even more confounding ... and frustrating.

"How have you been? Feel any different now that you're a daredevil?"

I shook my head. "Nope, still the same old chicken I've always been. But now I know what it feels like to fall off a bridge." *In your arms*, I thought, but didn't dare speak out loud.

"Are you ready for the world to see it?" he asked. His voice carried a hint of concern.

"Ready for everyone to see me panic on a bridge? No, but I am excited to see how the campaign is received."

"Were you okay with how it all turned out? I'm sure it wasn't easy to rewatch. I know I hated watching the footage of me." We'd all had to watch the final video several times, so at this point, I was almost numb to it.

"Which was basically all of it."

"Right," he said with a laugh. "But you're still the star."

"Unfortunately."

"Don't say that. You look fantastic and represent us well."

"Which part do you think I looked most fantastic in? The part where I was terrified of a trampoline or when I had an emotional breakdown on the bridge?" I cringed at the memory. Thankfully, those parts were edited artfully and didn't show just how exposed and scared I'd felt.

"All of it," Tripp said without hesitation.

The compliment sent a thrill of heat over me. I tried to ignore it. He was just talking about work. "I appreciate that, I really do."

"So, I was thinking we could look at doing one of the tamer videos next. Give you some time to recover from the adrenaline rush."

"I think I'd be up for something a little less, um, thrilling. Are there any extreme challenges we go do lying down? Uh, I mean, like napping." Flames of embarrassment rushed over my skin. I wanted to crawl under the carpet and hide.

An unreadable expression passed over his face. He opened his mouth to speak but got tongue-tied. He coughed and cleared his throat and said, "I'm not sure that's an activity we could do together."

I decided to quickly change the subject. "The place looks great! I don't usually love parties, but you did a fantastic job."

"My team deserves all the credit. Liam and the marketing group go all out for parties."

Before I could respond, Liam unleashed an air horn to get everyone's attention. I covered my ears and cowered behind Tripp. The shrill, loud sound startled me. Tripp turned back and gave me an apologetic smile. I tried to return the smile but couldn't force the curve into my lips, which were trembling from the sudden rush of fear. Loud, unexpected noises are yet another item on my long list of things that terrified me.

I felt Tripp brush his hand against mine. I glanced up and met his questioning stare. "Okay?" he asked.

I laughed it off and said, "Sure, that just startled me." He gave my hand a quick squeeze and let go too quickly. I shook off the brief thought that I might have been okay if he'd held on a little longer. I wasn't quite sure what to do with the empty ache I felt at the absence of his attention.

"All right! Leapers!" Liam yelled to the crowd once the buzz of conversation slowed. "Who's ready to kick off Take the Leap 2.0?" A roar of cheers, screams, whistles, and clapping filled the air. He gestured to Tripp who gave me one last smile before joining Liam at the front of the room.

A staff of waiters clad in Take the Leap gear, complete with harnesses like the ones we'd worn last Friday, circled the room to hand out flutes of champagne, Tripp launched into a speech.

"Thank you all for your hard work these last few months, especially the past forty-eight hours. You've been working day and night to get the website and app ready for this moment. Months of trial and error and sleepless nights have brought us to this moment. I'm proud of the work each of you have done to bring Take the Leap into the company that it is, and I cannot wait to see where we go next." He raised his glass and locked his gaze on me. "And a special thank you to Savie's Ava Reed and Sadie Barnes for being the masterminds behind this new campaign, but most importantly, thank you to Sadie who is quite literally taking the leap right alongside me. To Take the Leap!" Everyone shouted it back to him and threw back their glasses.

The office went dark as several screens around the space queued up with their social media pages. "Take the Leap 2.0 goes live in 3 ... 2 ... 1 ..." As soon as Tripp said one, confetti and balloons floated down from the ceiling and the video began to play.

I hadn't seen the social media edits of the videos, but knew they started similar to the long one I'd watched earlier. I didn't need to witness them again, so I snuck out of the lobby and ducked into the first open office I could find. Pulling the door closed behind me, I stepped into the dark office and relished in the silence and calm. The door muted chatter from the employees and the music overlay from the video. I breathed a sigh of relief. One challenge done, four more, and a skydive to go.

Looking around the dark office, I realized I'd managed to sneak into Tripp's office. I recognized the plush chairs from the few meetings we'd had in here. Sinking into one, I closed my eyes and thought back through everything that had to be done now that the campaign was live. There was so much work to do, but I could handle that. Ava and I were used to late nights and deadlines. It was the rest that scared the daylights out of me. I needed to get the challenges over with.

No matter how attractive or kind Tripp was, or how safe he made me feel, there could never be anything more than a passing crush between us. Not that he would want that. But on the off chance he did, it just wasn't in the cards for me. I may be willing to try these terrifying adventures one time, but I wasn't about to even consider the one thing that scared me the most.

"Oh, sorry. I wasn't expecting anyone to be in here," Tripp said, startling me out of my reverie. I turned and offered a weak smile.

"I hope it's okay that I'm hiding out in your office. I wasn't up for another viewing of the video."

"Why do you think I'm here?"

I was pretty sure the question was rhetorical, but I said, "To avoid me?"

Tripp dropped into the seat beside me with a sigh. "No, actually, I was looking for you."

He was? The tiny trill of satisfaction that sent through me tickled out a smile. "Making sure I didn't already make a run for it?"

He laughed softly. "No, you don't strike me as the type of woman to bail on people."

"Really?" His observation was surprising but also made me feel seen and understood.

"I mean, you fought through your fear and jumped off a bridge with me, and you sat through a four-hour editing session with Liam and Kyle."

That had been almost as painful as the crippling fear I'd experienced on the bridge. At least Liam had been forced to witness just what an ass he'd been to me during the trampoline park practice session. He hadn't actually apologized, but at least he seemed somewhat apologetic.

"I know what it's like to be on the other end of leaving, and I don't want to ever be the reason someone experiences that," I said, offering more honesty than I'd intended to. "But that's enough Debbie downer talk for a party. How's the team's response to the video been so far?"

"Everyone seems to be proud of the work. The social media team is monitoring views and comments, and Seth and the developers are celebrating a successful launch of the app. Downloads are a little slower than we'd hoped, but at least it's gone smoothly."

"That's great," I said, mulling over his comment on the soft download numbers. We'd set our goals high for the app, but we also knew the rollout would be slow.

Tripp's phone buzzed in his pocket. He slipped it out and glanced down at the screen. A crooked smile danced on his lips. A quick stab of jealousy pricked my heart. A smile like that was reserved for someone special.

"We should probably get back out there," I said, and stood abruptly. "I'll let you have a few minutes alone."

"My mom's a fan of the video," he said and held up his phone, showing me the screen.

Wow, Tripp! Video looks great. You and Sadie did a great job. I raised a true gentleman. Love that you're finally sharing this side of yourself with the world! Noah would be proud.

The crooked smile straightened into a wide, bright smile that reached his eyes. His happiness was contagious.

I knew exactly what she meant, though. Every video or image of Tripp on Take the Leap's social media lacked the charisma he exuded in person. Normally, he embodied the tough, extreme sport persona, but in the new videos, he seemed more relaxed and natural. And, of course, his gentleness and patience with me showed a completely different side of him. In the short time I'd known him, he'd been nothing like the bruh character he played so well online. Based on what his mom's text had said, this version of Tripp was the real version of him.

"She's right, you know, we made the right call in keeping in the banter and the less extreme scenes."

"I hope so. It's definitely a risk, and Liam hasn't been shy about telling me he thinks it's a mistake."

"Do you think it's a mistake?"

His eyebrows furrowed as he considered his answer. "No, I don't. You're bringing out a side of myself that I haven't seen in a while."

It was my turn to get lost in thought as I overanalyzed this. "How?"

Smiling, he answered without hesitation, "I feel like I'm getting to re-experience the adventures with you, and it's giving me a whole new perspective on how I'm seeing our business and mission. I've never met anyone like you, Sadie, and it's refreshing to have someone that challenges me to think outside my own experience."

I hadn't considered this before. I was the one trying new things and being pushed out of my comfort zone. It hadn't occurred to me that Tripp might be going through some of the same feelings. Sure, none of these adventures would be new to him, but allowing himself to be seen as something other than the guy who jumps out of planes for fun was a new experience for him.

eleven

THE NEXT MORNING, we got straight to work on the next video. I'd wanted to try one of the less extreme options, but Ava reminded me that we had to keep the interest of the audience. So, it was time to draw a challenge from the bucket hat Seth had donated for the cause. My brother had insisted it was his lucky hat and tried to convince me that using it would ensure my safety and survival. Though his heart was in the right place, it didn't do much to give me any more confidence.

We'd set up the tripod and camera Liam insisted we use to capture the moment of the challenge reveal and did a quick run-through of how it would go. He'd opted out of spending the morning at Savie's office to partake in such a boring endeavor, and I wasn't mad about it. Tripp was growing on me, but I couldn't say the same about Liam. His snarky comments and obvious annoyance with me hadn't won me over. But he had sent an email congratulating us on a mostly successful launch. Their website traffic had a 55% increase in the first twenty-four hours after the video was posted, but the app downloads weren't anywhere near our target. I tried not to focus on the negative results with the app, it was still early, but

I was disappointed. I didn't want to talk about the millions of people who'd seen the video. I'd wisely avoided the comment section. Ava had strict instructions not to mention anything she read.

"You only put the ones we discussed in here, right?" I asked as she handed me the hat. "No online dating or anything insane like that, right?"

"Sadie Genevieve Barnes, you just might be the only person who thinks dating is more insane than skydiving."

"I didn't say it was more insane or extreme than skydiving. I just want to make sure you didn't slip anything in here that isn't on the Take the Leap menu."

"Like make out with Tripp?"

My heart did a tiny somersault at the mention of Tripp's lips anywhere near mine. I blinked away the mental image that was already forming, but not before it was seared into my brain. "Well, that is oddly specific, but yes, exactly."

Ava smirked. "I think you're secretly wishing I did."

"Nope. I am pretty sure those types of adventures are not offered by Tripp or Take the Leap. They aren't an escort service."

"I'm willing to bet that Tripp would be up for that challenge."

"Shut up, Ava! Seriously, did you slip anything in here that you weren't supposed to?"

Sighing, Ava shook her head. "No, I resisted the temptation to include anything in there that might actually improve your life." She checked the camera one last time and had me move a few inches to the left. "Perfect. Ready?

I rolled my eyes, nodded, and stuck my hand inside the hat. I rifled through the slips of paper and tried to run my fingers over the writing to determine what was on each. While I didn't want to agonize over each of the adventures, drawing one at random should totally count as one of the challenges. I didn't do things at random. I needed lists and planning and charts and spreadsheets. I curled my fingers around one of the papers and pulled it out. I handed it to Ava.

"You don't want to look first?" she asked.

"Nope. I already have no control, why not pass the responsibility of reading my fate to you as well?"

"Dramatic, but okay." She glanced at the camera and grinned. It was clear she was enjoying this way more than I was. I resisted the temptation to chew on my thumbnail as I watched her unfold the paper. "All right, ladies and gentlemen, for our next amazing Take the Leap adventure, our dear Sadie will be …"

She paused and stared at the paper. She bit her lip and shot me a look that said, *are you sure.* When I shrugged, she took that for approval and cleared her throat. "A hot air balloon ride! This is so cool. I've always wanted to do one of those romantic hot air balloon rides at sunset."

I rolled my eyes. "Then you go. I'll wave from the ground." Once the words left my lips, I wanted to take them back. The thought of Tripp in a romantic moment with anyone other than me sent a thrill of jealousy rushing through me.

"Ha! Like you'd be okay with me and Tripp canoodling in a tiny basket while you watched from below." We both looked at the camera. She clamped her hand over her mouth. "I mean, these are your challenges, not mine."

"Well, we're editing that before you send it over." I reached over and hit the stop button. "Dude!"

She cringed. "Oops. Sorry, but can we finally admit that you like him and want to kiss his perfectly scruffy face?"

"No. Never." I denied it, but we both knew that was a lie. Even though I didn't date much, I got crushes more often than I cared to admit. Window shopping was safe. No commitment.

No one to break your heart when they find someone better to drape their dress over.

"Liar. Not that it matters, because you *totally* don't like him, but the buzz around the Take the Leap office is that he's crushing on you. Hard."

"Really?" I asked with far more enthusiasm than I'd meant. "Why?"

She cocked an eyebrow and smirked. "Again, not that it matters. Right?"

"Right." It definitely didn't matter. The butterflies I felt around him would eventually die off. He'd find someone to share his crazy lifestyle with, and I'd go back to pining over fictional characters and Chris Evans.

"Do you want to tell Tripp, or do you want me to send him an email?"

"Tell me about what?" a deep and way too familiar voice asked from the lobby of our office.

Crap. How long had he been standing there? Did he hear the entire exchange between Ava and me? I kind of wished I could crawl under my desk and pretend the last thirty seconds had never happened.

When I turned around, I must have looked like a deer caught in the headlights of an oncoming freight train.

Tripp smiled and said, "Sorry, I wasn't sure if the protocol was to knock or just come in."

"No, no, all good," Ava said quickly. "Liam mentioned you might stop by to talk through the next steps. I forgot to mention it to Sadie."

"Yes, you did," I said through gritted teeth. Could he see the crimson flooding my cheeks? I tried, and failed, to shake off my mortification. In order to save whatever dignity, I had left, I changed the subject. "Ava and I just drew the next challenge."

"So, what's next, Sadie?"

"Um," I said, stuttering, "hot air balloon ride. But we didn't clarify that one. Will we be tethered to the ground and just going up? Or are we traipsing around the world?"

"That's up to you," he said with a wink.

"Tethered." I didn't hesitate. After the last challenge, I'd like to at least keep some particle of myself attached to the earth. I'd expected everything after bungee jumping to feel less scary, but I'd been wrong. Imagining myself in a floppy basket while hanging from a balloon made me lightheaded. A hot air balloon ride sounds relaxing and fun, unless you've already pictured yourself plummeting to the earth without a bungee cord to keep you at least somewhat safe.

"That sounds like a plan. Let me send Liam a quick text so he can work on getting that scheduled."

"While you're here, do you want an office tour?"

He glanced around the open area and nodded. "That would be great."

I led him through the living room and into the conference room while Ava told him all about the process we'd taken to transform the two-level home into an office and residential area. He oohed and aahed at all the right places and asked polite questions about the decor.

I trailed behind them, trying not to watch him walk. How had I missed how well he wore his jeans? That's something I should've noticed sooner, considering how much taller than me he was. I had a direct line of sight to his perfect posterior. As my thoughts wandered into the inappropriate, I chased them back to reality.

"In addition to being the creative force behind Savie, Sadie also designed this entire space. She picked out all the art and the colors," Ava said, beaming.

"It's a fantastic space," Tripp said as he stopped to admire the abstract painting of the Nashville skyline I'd purchased from a local artist. "I can definitely see your personality in these paintings. The vibrant colors and mixed mediums."

"I tried to find a good blend of both Ava and me. She's a fan of the more modern and industrial style, where I prefer what I call the Midwest Granny aesthetic. Florals, pops of color, and a hint of classic. It wasn't easy, but I love how it turned out."

I led us into Ava's office to show him the deep grey walls and photography I'd selected for her. Most people were surprised to learn that Ava, the bright bubble one, leaned into darker colors and preferred a more muted pallet. No one expected me to have the office with the bright pink walls and vibrant Rifle Paper floral rug and curtains I'd had made to match, but I loved the hint of happiness the colors brought to my office. It was a nice contrast to the darkness that usually occupied my brain.

"So, what was it that you wanted to go over?" I asked as we made our way back into the living room. Our office wasn't big enough for a long tour, and I wasn't about to offer him a tour of my bedroom. Client tours never ventured up the stairs.

"Well, I was actually thinking we could knock out one of the smaller adventures today. Give you a bit of a break from being pushed out of your comfort zone."

"And off of bridges?"

"Technically, you jumped," Ava added helpfully.

"Sure, I did. Anyway, what did you have in mind?"

"It's a nice day out. How do you feel about hiking or nature walks?"

"Are there snakes? Or bears? Or cliffs?"

"Probably."

"Then, not great."

He laughed. "I know a few trails that are pretty tame. They're even paved."

"Who's filming?" I asked. The thought of Liam tagging

along and laughing every time I jumped because I heard leaves crunching in the woods made me want to throw up. But I wasn't too keen on the idea of being alone in the woods with Tripp. Especially if he planned to wear those jeans. But at the same time, I could most definitely imagine spending the entire day enjoying the view.

"Just us." He pulled the two head cameras we'd worn for the bungee jump from his bag. "Liam said between these and any footage we get on our phones should be good."

"Let me guess, he's bored by lame hikes?"

Tripp winced. At least I wasn't alone in noticing just how miserable all of this seemed to make his young marketing director. "That and he's stuck at the office working with the social media team to develop a response plan for the comments and feedback."

I winced. I hoped with every fiber of my being that Liam hadn't been right about the shift in branding. "That bad?"

"Yes and no," he said, sighing. "We knew to expect some negative feedback, but the comments seem to be more critical than even Liam expected."

I glanced at Ava and frowned. We'd just gotten word that our one other client was moving on to a bigger agency, meaning Take the Leap was our last client. This wasn't good.

"I read some of the social commentary," Ava said, "and, while I agree, it did lean more negative, there were some positives. Your female audience is pretty significant, and they all seem to relate to Sadie."

"It's the male audience that's been particularly brutal." Tripp scowled as he said this. "But it's just the first video, and I know the point is to draw in a new audience, which will take time to build."

"Agreed," I said, surprised at my optimism. I really did

believe in this campaign and knew Tripp did too, despite Liam's objections.

Ava said. "Sadie and I planned to spend the day gearing up for the next video and phase of the plan, but I've got that under control if you want to go change and get ready. Besides, it will be good to get ahead of the content."

"Are you sure?" My question was genuine. I didn't want to leave her to do all the boring work while I was out galivanting through the woods or whatever with Tripp.

"Yes, go. We both know you'd just spend the day looking up hot air balloon crashes."

Laughing, Tripp asked, "Yes, let's get away from the internet today. Go put on something comfortable. I promise not to take you anywhere too scary. After all, the goal is to try something less intense."

But it wasn't the snakes or bears of cliffs that had me scared. It was being alone with him.

twelve

TRIPP HELD the door to his Jeep open for me. Of course, he had a Jeep. It had two doors, was shiny and black, and screamed *I do cool things*! I drove a sensible four-door hybrid sedan. I'd splurged on a sunroof that I rarely opened, but I did thoroughly enjoy the heated seats. My car rarely saw much action beyond the occasional road trip, while his Jeep still had mud caked to the trim from whatever adventure he'd recently been on.

I climbed into the passenger seat and tried to smile back at him as he shut the door, but I must have failed because he looked at me in confusion and said, "What?"

"Nothing, I was just thinking all you need to complete the Jeep Dude look is a backward ballcap and some Raybans."

His grin widened and he held up his index finger telling me to wait. "Close your eyes."

"Why?"

"Humor me."

I obliged and closed my eyes. I didn't give into the temptation to peek when I heard him open the driver's side door and ease into the seat. Instead, I waited patiently for him to tell me it was okay to look. When he did, I shouldn't have been surprised to find him wearing a backward cap and sunglasses. They weren't the Raybans I'd been expecting, but they were still slick and cool and the sight of him sent my mind racing down a rollercoaster of daydreams that involved him in little more than the hat and sunglasses.

I managed to squeak out a barely audible *perfect* before I quickly diverted my attention somewhere else. He turned the engine and backed out of the drive. Staring out the window, I caught a glimpse of Ava staring wide-eyed out the front door. I knew without looking that she'd already sent me a text or two commenting on the Tripp transformation we'd both just witnessed. He went from the big city CEO to Hallmark romance movie small-town hero guy with a hat and a pair of sunglasses. I mean, he was always eye candy I wanted to devour, but those two little additions transformed him into book boyfriend material. I didn't need to read her messages to confirm what I already knew.

I cleared my throat. "So, what's the plan?"

"I don't really have one," he admitted. "That's part of the fun."

"Is it?"

"For me, yeah. I mean, don't get me wrong, I do love a good schedule and plan when it comes to my workday, but outside of work? I prefer to wing it."

I considered this for a moment. "I don't think I've ever done that. I make lists to prepare for making other lists."

"You like structure, I get that." I waited for him to add in the punchline and make fun of me, but he didn't. Interesting. Liam for sure would've had something to say, but not Tripp. There wasn't even a hint of mocking in his voice. "Did you make any lists of the tamer adventures?"

"You know I did." I tried not to focus on the fact that he

was heading straight for the interstate without a plan or GPS app. He drove with confidence even though he had no clue where we were going. I swiped away the text notifications on my phone and opened my notes app. "You already mentioned hiking. I also had roller skating, train ride, horror movies, karaoke, escape room, though I wouldn't consider being trapped in a room *tame*, but whatever."

"Mind if I throw one out that might not be on your list?" he asked.

I hedged. "I suppose that depends on what it is."

"Fair. It might be too tame, even for you."

I laughed and shook my head. "Now that does sound like a challenge. What did you have in mind, Mr. James?"

"The zoo."

"The zoo? Interesting. There are snakes and bears and wild animals. So, that does check off a few of my random fears." His suggestion surprised me. I was expecting him to suggest a zip line or something the exact opposite of tame. Or, worse, something like going to the mall to make fun of all of my silly phobias.

"But they're in cages."

"Cages that someone could open or fall into," I said, "and we do kind of have to hike. They also have this rope bridge thing near the spider monkeys that I've been scared to try. Not that I am suggesting we do that. Not at all."

"Come on, Sadie, I'll hold your hand." The suggestion of physical contact rendered me speechless. The silence hung between us like the thousand-pound weight of unasked and unanswered questions. Ava's suggestion that he might have similar feelings toward me that I did for him lingered in my mind. I didn't know what to do with that information or with the hint of hopefulness that clung to his voice.

"We'll see. But I am definitely not going into that area that's dark and musty and crawling with snakes."

"You'll have to pick one. Snakes or the rope bridge."

"I'll think about it."

Our office was less than ten minutes from the zoo. Since it was still early and a weekday, Tripp found a parking spot near the entrance. He opted to keep his hat and sunglasses on, and I traded my everyday glasses for the prescription sunglasses I was thankful I'd thrown in my bag before leaving. I caught a glimpse of us in the reflection of his Jeep. We looked like a normal couple out for a fun day at the zoo. Well, until he strapped the camera to his hat. For a second, I'd hoped the camera on his hat would be ridiculous enough to make him look less attractive, but it didn't.

"Do I need to strap mine to my head?" I asked, praying the answer would be no.

"Technically, Liam asked for footage from both of us, but I think we'll be fine with this one. Only one of us needs to look like a moron."

"A sexy moron," I said without thinking. I slapped my hand over my mouth and turned away from him. But not before I caught the hint of red sneaking up his cheeks. "Please forget I said that."

Tripp shook his head and smirked. "Yeah, no. That's not going to happen. In fact, I think you should say it one more time so it can go straight to my ego."

Mortified, I covered my face with my hands and mumbled, "Well, *I* am going to forget I said it."

Thanks to my brief moment of stupidity, the first half hour in the zoo was painfully awkward. We stopped to watch the gibbons swinging through their trees and screaming at each other. Then made our way down to the meerkats and the flamingos. Tripp made polite conversation, but I knew the footage his camera was catching would be painfully boring. I could already hear Liam complaining. Besides, this wasn't good for business or whatever this crush thing I had was. Obviously, I was most concerned about the business. So, when we wrapped up at the flamingos, I mustered up the courage to touch him and grabbed his bicep. It was just as firm and inviting as I remembered.

He halted and turned to look down at me.

"I have an idea." I did not want to have this idea, nor did I want to verbalize it. He waited patiently while I dug deeper into my courage well and grabbed another dose. "You know they have a ride here, right?"

"The Soaring Eagle?" I nodded. "What about it?"

"Um, well, I think we might need some more engaging content if we're going to be able to use any of this footage."

"Are you saying I'm boring?" he asked, smirking.

"No, not at all. But I'm pretty sure Liam and your audience will think all of this is lame and boring." It was time to slip out of my Sadie hat and into my Savie role. "The whole point of these less extreme videos are to show that there is a variety of things that Take the Leap offers. Sure, a trip to the zoo is great for me and fun, but what's the adventure? Where's the fun? How would Take the Leap make an average zoo trip more? The Soaring Eagle makes sense."

Tripp was nodding along. His eyes lit up with excitement. "Are you sure? It would make for some great content."

No, but he didn't need to know that. The last thing I wanted to do was climb onto a small plastic seat and ride up a thin line and then plunge 110 feet down and through the air. Honestly, it was like the bungee jump all over again. I did not want to do this, but I knew I had to.

"Sadie?"

"Yes, I'm sure." The only thing I was sure of was that we

needed to do something to spice this day up, but I wasn't okay with it. So, it wasn't a complete lie.

We hadn't brought the extra camera into the zoo with us, so Tripp suggested we use my phone to capture more footage. When I pulled it out of my pocket, I noticed several missed texts from Mel. I rolled my eyes and swiped them away. I didn't need to add any more stress to the day.

"If you need to answer those, you've got time while I buy tickets for the ride."

"No, it's not important. It's just my stepmom." The word felt like sour candy on my tongue. I don't think I'd ever called Mel my stepmom before. At least not out loud.

"Family is always important. They're the only people you can truly count on."

"Maybe in your family." Changing the subject, I glanced at the zip line and said, "Looks like the line isn't long."

Once again, I'd managed to reignite the awkwardness. I could tell he wanted to ask more about my family and the comment, but he, wisely, didn't push it. He just got our tickets and led the way to the Soaring Eagle line, which had dwindled down to one other couple. Not that we were a couple. There were two of us; we just didn't go together. He was adventurous and fun, and I was boring and, well, just boring. Nothing about us made sense, no matter how much mental gymnastics I did every single time he smiled that sexy half-grin at me or how my entire body warmed anytime I managed to touch him. It was just a crush. It would pass. They always did.

When it was our turn, I surprised myself and climbed right into the seat. It probably helped that I was still distracted by Tripp. They strapped me in beside him, and I took a few deep breaths.

"It's going to pull us up backward, okay? Then we'll float

back down. It won't take more than two minutes." He spoke in a low, comforting tone without being condescending. "Ready?"

I exhaled and nodded. "Let's do this." The quiver in my voice betrayed my confidence. The seat jolted and we started moving back. When I gasped, Tripp reached over and grabbed my hand. I didn't bother pulling away or pretending that his hand wasn't exactly what I needed. He laced his fingers through mine, and I tightened my grip. I was so focused on the feeling of how tiny my hand felt inside of his rough fingers, that I didn't notice that we'd almost made it to the top. Somehow, there was even more intimacy in that single handhold than there'd been during the bungee jump.

I hadn't closed my eyes, and as soon as I took in the sweeping view over the zoo and into downtown, I was grateful. It was beautiful up here. I could see the giraffes grazing. Just beyond that, the tall buildings of downtown. A sea of green trees surrounded us. Then I looked down.

"Nope. Nope. Nope." I jerked my head back up and met Tripp's gaze.

"I've got you," he whispered as the zipline released and sent us rushing back down to earth. I kept my eyes locked on his face the entire ride down. The fear melted away.

With every whisper of *I've got you*, I felt myself falling deeper and deeper into him.

thirteen

AVA EYED ME WITH SUSPICION. We exited her car at the open field where I'd be climbing into a basket attached to a massive balloon and hoisted in the air by gas from a giant flame. Normally, I'd assume it was a look of concern or to make sure I wasn't about to run for it, but she'd been looking at me like this ever since Tripp dropped me off after our zoo trip. It was as if she had a sixth sense that something had happened between us. Not that anything had happened. He'd held my hand and calmed my fears. That was all. Or at least that's what I keep trying to tell myself.

"Liam sent over the footage from the zoo."

"Oh?" I asked, pretending to be as nonchalant as I could.

"The zipline ride looked fun. I still can't believe it was your idea."

"What can I say? I'm a regular daredevil."

"Weird how the footage is all from Tripp's perspective, and it's all you."

"Well, he was the one wearing the head camera. I'm sure the audience will be disappointed."

Ava shook her head. "We'll fix that today. I'm just dying to see video footage of Tripp swooning over you."

I rolled my eyes. "Let's focus on the job at hand. And keeping me alive."

"Oh, I think Tripp is *up* for that job," she said. I ignored her innuendo.

There hadn't been any prep work for the hot air balloon. Liam and Tripp both agreed that if I could handle the bungee jump and the zip line, I'd be fine in a hot air balloon tethered to the ground. I hadn't argued. As much as my heart and body were begging me to spend more time with Tripp, my common sense and self-preservation prevailed. My daydreams of spending hours tangled up in him didn't need to add any fuel to that fire. I just hoped the crush would pass before we finished all these challenges so I could go into one without having a dirty dream about Tripp beforehand. Last night, I'd woken up twisted in my sheets after dreaming that I'd finally tasted his kiss. I really wish I had more control over my dream self. She was getting me into all kinds of trouble—even if it was all in my head, it was still distracting.

The Take the Leap crew, Liam, Tripp, Kyle, and a few others I didn't recognize were all gathered in the field. They stood in a semi-circle around the balloon, which was slowly being inflated by massive fans. In my research, I learned this was called cold inflation. Apparently, the balloon needed a burst of cold air before the burners were turned on. I'd tried to understand the science that made it work, but the more I read, the less it made sense. I'd never been a fan of math or science. I'll stick to words and art, thank you very much.

Two large fans filled the black and red striped balloon while two men held it open. Take the Leap's logo was emblazoned on both sides of the massive nylon ball. It was fascinating to watch it go from a big flat envelope to a round-ish balloon. The burner made a loud whooshing sound as it roared to life. Within a minute, the balloon lifted upright, pulling the basket along with it. More workers stepped in to help right the balloon. This felt like such an elaborate process just to capture content for a video. Especially considering we weren't actually planning to fly anywhere.

"Wow." Stepping back from the crowd, I could see just how massive the balloon was.

"Impressive, right?" Tripp asked. I hadn't noticed him walking toward me.

"I feel like this is all too much for what we're doing. This must cost a fortune."

He waved off my comment. "We have a few rides booked for later this afternoon and into the evening." He already had his hat and camera strapped on. The green light indicating that it was recording was lit.

I asked, "How many balloon adventures do you all do?"

"We typically have a few each month. We decided to invest in our own balloon a few years ago and started taking it to local festivals to help promote the business."

"Have you been up in it?"

He nodded. "A few times. My sister Lydia's fiancée proposed to her on this one last summer. I haven't been on it since."

"Romantic. And terrifying. Probably more terrifying than romantic. At least for me. I'm sure your sister loved it, seeing how y'all jump out of a plane once a year." I was rambling. My nerves were getting the better of me. "Are proposals common on these things?"

"Yes. We actually offer a proposal package. It's a sunset ride complete with champagne and roses."

"Has anyone ever dropped the ring?"

He laughed and shook his head. "Let's hope that doesn't happen."

I wanted to ask if the balloon had ever experienced any mechanical issues or run into trees or power lines, but decided to wait until I was safely back on the ground.

We watched the balloon rise to its full height together. Tripp stood so close to me; I could feel the heat radiating off of his skin. My fingers itched to reach for him. I didn't dare move a single muscle. I wasn't in complete control, and if I let myself slip, I knew there'd be no going back.

"We're ready for you, Tripp," the man inside the basket said.

"That's Elliot, the pilot," Tripp said.

He held out his hand, offering it to me. I hesitated but let my hand fall into his. He gave it a gentle squeeze and held on as we made our way to the basket. I listened closely as Elliot explained the process to me. He showed me how to get in and out of the balloon. He must have sensed my nerves because he spent several minutes going over how the tethers worked and how many there were. Five. One for each corner and one at the bottom. Then, he introduced me to the four men who'd remain on the ground and mind the tethers. We'd be going up about 120 feet, which was just a bit higher than the zipline, but the ropes allowed for 150 - 200 feet.

Tripp introduced me to each of the men on the crew. I gave each of them a firm handshake, saying, "Nice to meet you."

"We're ready when you are," Elliot said after he finished going through the safety procedures. He turned his attention back to the balloon and the burner, which he'd use to take us up and bring us back down.

I looked at Liam, who was staring at me as if he expected me to have another emotional breakdown. I didn't plan to, but with me, you never know. "Do you have all the cameras ready? Do I need one of those?" I pointed to Tripp's head cam.

"No, we've got a few inside of the balloon and Elliot will also have one. They're already filming."

"All right. Let's do this, then." I didn't want to put this off any longer. The more time I let pass, the more I'd give into the rising panic. I gripped the edge of the basket and stuck my foot into the bottom notch, just as Elliot had shown me. I lost my balance a bit when I threw my leg over the edge.

Tripp moved to steady me. His hands gripped my waist and helped me finish climbing in. "Thanks," I said in a husky whisper. He climbed in with ease and stood beside me.

"Ready?" I nodded and then immediately shook my head. Fear bubbled in my stomach. Heat rushed up my neck and into my face. The loud woosh of the burner dulled in my ears as my heart raced.

Not again. I closed my eyes and leaned back against the basket. Bracing myself, I took a few calming breaths. Everyone had assumed the hot air balloon ride would be easier for me than the bungee jump had been. In theory, it should've been, but the idea of being off of the ground and floating toward the clouds sent a shudder of panic through me.

"I've got you, Sadie," Tripp said those words in *that* voice again. I wanted to melt into him. I wanted to let go of every single fear that gripped me and hand them over to him. I wanted to give in to the daydreams and fantasies, but I didn't.

Instead, I plastered on a weak smile and said, "I know."

I had sunk back into the corner, putting more distance between us than I wanted to, and nodded at Elliot. *Let's get this over with.* He pulled the lever and sent a fresh burst of blue flame into the balloon. The basket lifted along with the balloon. I lost my footing for a second but regained my balance before Tripp could react. We rose slowly into the air. I kept my gaze locked on the basket floor. It felt like we were in an elevator, which didn't exactly comfort me.

"I'm okay," I said to Tripp pre-emptively. It wasn't the full truth, but it wasn't a complete lie. I didn't dare look up at him or meet his gaze, but I could feel him watching me.

The ride up was smoother than I expected. When we reached the desired height, above the visible tree line but not the full length of the rope, Elliot backed off the burner. We hovered for a moment. The wind gently rocked the basket. When it felt like we'd stopped moving, I loosened my death grip on the basket and allowed myself to peek over the edge of the basket. The view was breathtaking. Trees and hills for miles. Clear blue sky. It was picture-perfect.

As long as I didn't look down.

I didn't plan to look down.

But Tripp took a step toward me. He placed his hand over mine on the edge of the basket. He moved his fingers to interlace with mine. Once again, the desire to let him offer intimacy and comfort took over. I spread my fingers and let his fall between mine. He curled his knuckles, and I let my guard down just enough to allow myself to really feel the pressure and heat of his skin on mine. I leaned into him and gazed out over the horizon. This wasn't so bad. The view was breathtaking, and being next to him brought a sense of calm to me that settled deep into my core. For the briefest of moments, I forgot we were here for work. I imagined this was a romantic date, and we were more than co-workers or friends.

Then out of nowhere, a gust of wind rocked the basket and caught me off guard. I lost my grip on the basket. My feet stumbled backwards. Panicking, I shifted my gaze to where my hand was supposed to be, and my eyes dipped down. I looked straight at the ground. I saw how tiny Ava, and Liam, and everyone were. Even the cars looked tiny. There was no way we were only 120 feet in the air.

My knees buckled and I collapsed to the bottom of the basket. Scooting back into the corner, I dropped my head to my knees. Blinking back tears, I tried to take slow, deep breaths but they came out in gasps. Tripp knelt beside me and put his hand on my back.

"Sadie?" he asked, his voice filled with tenderness. "Breathe, Sadie. I'm here." The sincerity in his voice sent a surge of calm through me, but it did little to break through the wall of panic I hid behind.

"Can we go back down? Now? Please. We're too high. What if we fall? Or the basket breaks? I need to be on the ground. Please?"

I felt him tense beside me, but he didn't move. He remained knelt next to me with his hand on my back. Then he said those three words again, and I was completely and utterly gone. This *crush* was going to be the death of me.

fourteen

MY HEART HADN'T STOPPED RACING in the two hours since the balloon returned to the ground. I'd been pacing the open field ever since Tripp and Elliot helped me out of the basket. Ava and Tripp both kept their distance, but I could feel their gazes locked on me. Everyone else from Take the Leap and the hot air balloon team had moved on to their paying customers. I was acutely aware of the curious stares of the newcomers, but I was too lost in my own thoughts to worry about them.

"Sadie?" Ava asked and fell into step alongside me. "I have to head out. Are you going to ride back with me? Or do you need some more time? Tripp said he'd stick around."

"Huh?" I asked. I paused and looked at her. "Where are you going? Oh, wait. Is tonight that blind date your mom set up?"

Ava nodded. "I don't want to be late. Senator Reed would die of embarrassment if her daughter showed up ten minutes late to a date with her favorite lawyer's son."

"I can call her and tell her it's my fault if you don't want to go." Ava's mother had found another eligible suitor for her daughter. I knew how much she hated those dates, so I put aside the fear of being on the wrong side of Senator Reed's wrath and volunteered as tribute for the best friend who always had my back.

A soft pink blush colored her cheeks. "I am actually kind of excited about this one. I stalked him on social media. He's cute and shares the funniest memes. So, who knows, maybe Mom finally found a good one."

I crossed my fingers and held them up. "Go. I can call a ride share or hitch a ride with Tripp."

"Option two, for sure," Ava said with a wink. "What happened up there, anyway?"

I shrugged. "It was going great until the wind picked up. I think I'd been enjoying it up until that point."

"That's two challenges that haven't injured or killed you," Ava said and glanced at her watch. "Crap, I have to go. But I want details later, okay?"

"No, I will be the one grilling you after your date. I'll have wine and ice cream ready." She leaned toward me and kissed the top of my head. "Good luck!"

She tossed me one last smile and took off running for her car. I watched her for a moment before glancing toward Tripp. I caught his eye and held his gaze. I both loved and hated the way my stomach flip-flopped every time his blue-grey eyes locked on mine. Even from a few hundred feet away, I could see the way the sunlight made them appear to sparkle. We started walking toward each other. I tried to force my pulse to slow, but the closer he got to me, the quicker it raced.

"My ride left," I said, shrugging.

"I saw that. I was about to head out and grab some dinner. Are you hungry?"

Yes.

No.

"Sure," I said, "if I won't be interrupting your Friday night plans."

He shook his head. "I have no plans. There's a great barbecue place a few miles up the road. How does that sound?"

"Perfect." It was messy and about the least romantic meal I could think of, so it was ideal.

We walked side-by-side to his Jeep. My hand twitched with the desire to reach for his hand. At first I ignored it. Then his hand brushed against mine, and I let the urge to touch him win. Without a hint of hesitation, he wrapped his hand around mine. It was amazing how well our hands fit together like custom tailored gloves meant for only us.

In the Jeep, we made small talk. I sensed he wanted to ask about the balloon and what had sparked my panic, but he didn't ask, and I wasn't about to bring it up. So, we talked about the weather and the app downloads. Tripp jumped out when we got to the restaurant and rushed around to open the door for me. He held out his hand to help me climb out of the Jeep. I almost rejected the offer, but then I looked down and remembered just how far off the ground the sidestep was. I took his hand and jumped down. He wrapped his hand around mine firmly as we walked into the restaurant. It was just after five, so they were pretty busy, but we managed to find a small table near the bar. The music wasn't too loud, but the chorus of conversation filled the restaurant.

I took a deep inhale and closed my eyes. The smell of smoked meat and the sweet scent of sauce made my stomach growl. "I didn't realize how hungry I am," I said.

"I imagine this is what heaven smells like."

"No," I said, shaking my head. "Heaven smells like fresh-baked chocolate chip cookies in my grandma's kitchen."

"You might be right." The server came and took our drink

order. Tripp handed me a menu. "They have some delicious barbecue nachos."

"Only if we can do the pulled pork." I love chicken as much as anyone, but I firmly believe that pork and brisket make for the best barbecue. Anytime I shared an appetizer with Ava, we had to get chicken or something with vegetables.

"Good call."

We ordered our appetizers and meals. He opted for the meat sampler, which included sausage, brisket, ribs, and chicken, while I ordered the brisket. We both chose mac and cheese and baked beans for our sides.

"Are you close to your grandma?" Tripp asked. His question caught me off guard. "I only ask because you mentioned her kitchen and chocolate chip cookies."

"Oh, yeah. Um," I said, hesitating. I wasn't sure how much I wanted to share with him. I hadn't been thinking clearly when I mentioned her earlier. "Gran raised Seth and me. She used to make us chocolate chip cookies every Friday after school."

"She sounds amazing. Does she live here?"

"She did, yeah. She died a long time ago."

"I'm sorry to hear that. Where are your parents?" I winced. Tripp frowned and said, "We don't have to talk about this if you don't want to. I've just been curious to know more about you."

"You want to know why I'm scared of my own shadow?" I laughed. "My therapist spends an hour a week with me, and she is still trying to figure that out."

"No, I want to know what makes you, you. You're a beautiful, intelligent, funny, and kind woman. You're creative, and you've built an amazing business." He paused and met my gaze. "I want to know you. Tell me your story, Sadie."

His intensity warmed me from the inside out and made me want to tell him everything there was to know about Sadie

Barnes. "My mom died from complications in childbirth when Seth and I were born. Undiagnosed eclampsia. Brett, my dad, couldn't handle newborn twins alone, so Gran moved up to Kansas City to help him. Then, he met someone new and decided fatherhood wasn't for him and shipped us off to live here with Gran when we were two."

I kept to the facts and tried not to let the retelling of our story get to me. Aside from Ava, I'd never told anyone the full truth. If anyone asked, which they rarely did because I never let anyone close enough to be curious, I simply said Gran raised us, and she was fantastic. Both were true. But the way Tripp was studying me made me want to tell him everything. He leaned in and listened carefully.

"Then, when we were seventeen, Gran had an accident," I said, swallowing back the lump that always rose in my throat when I thought or talked about that night. "Seth and I had snuck out of the house to go to some stupid party. Gran must have heard the door close or something and got out of bed to investigate. She fell down the stairs. Seth and I didn't find her until we snuck back in the next morning."

"Oh, wow. You found her?" he asked in a soft whisper. He reached across the table and placed his hand on top of mine. "Sadie, that's heartbreaking."

"I often replay that night. If we'd stayed home or come home sooner, she'd still be here. If we'd picked up the laundry basket at the top of the stairs like she'd asked. Or if we'd never lived there in the first place. She'd still be here."

"You can't blame yourself, Sadie."

"I can, and I do. Brett does as well. We killed his beloved wife and his mother. No wonder he wanted so little to do with us." No matter how many times my brother and Ava tried to talk me out of this line of thinking, they couldn't. It didn't take a rocket scientist to figure this one out. The math was clear—

Sadie + anything = disaster and death. I couldn't change the past, but I could plan the future to avoid hurting myself or anyone else.

I pulled my hand out from under his and sat back, putting more distance between us. "And now you know the real Sadie. I bet you wish you hadn't asked." I tried to laugh but couldn't force out the sound.

"Not at all. I'm glad you told me."

"Why? So, you can cancel our contract and run for the hills? We probably should add a Sadie disaster clause to our contracts."

"Don't say that."

"Why? It's true. I'm a mess, Tripp. This whole campaign and challenge came about because I'm a joke."

He shook his head. "You're guarded, which makes sense. You've experienced so much heartbreak, and yet you're still here and pushing forward. You think you have to go it alone, but you don't. You've had Seth and Ava, and now me."

"You barely know me," I argued.

"Then let me in and let me know you." Why was he so insistent? Why did he care?

"After everything I just told you, you still want to know more?"

"Yes, Sadie, I want to know more. You're all I think about, and not just because of the amazing work you and Ava are doing. Because every single time you touch me, it's like I've forgotten how to breath. I want to protect you but also show you that the world isn't a scary place. I want to show you that there are people you can count on."

I shook my head. "You want to know how I've never had a relationship last more than two dates? Or how the thought of dating scares me more than jumping out of an airplane? Or how I know, deep down, that no matter how hard I try, I'm never going to be able to fall in love or let someone fall in love with me? Or, that I like the safety in knowing I'll never hurt if I never love? Maybe I like living in my little bubble. I can't even consider living outside of the safety net I've created because every time I do, I see my Gran's lifeless body lying at the bottom of the stairs. I can still taste the stale alcohol on my tongue from that morning."

I shut my mouth. I'd already said too much. I swiped my hand under my eye to catch the errant tear. "Sorry," I said, "I didn't mean to unload all of that on you."

"It's okay, I can take it."

"You shouldn't have to."

"What if I want to?"

How did he always know the exact right thing to say? "Why?" I asked, my voice barely audible.

"Because I like you." He said it matter-of-factly as if there was no other possible explanation.

I sat with this information and let it sink in. It took every ounce of self control to not continue telling him every reason why he shouldn't like or want me. Instead, I lifted my eyes and met his. He held me there in his gaze and didn't let go. He held on when most people, including me, would've given up and walked away.

"Tripp," I said, my voice shaking. "This isn't a good idea, we work together, and for all intents and purposes, you're my boss. You're the client."

His frown deepened as he considered this. "It's complicated, for sure."

"And let's not forget that the campaign is off to a rocky start. What happens if we fail and all of this backfires? I don't know if I can handle losing you as a client, much less as something more." But the thought of never knowing if this could be something more was killing me. In a barely audible whisper, I admitted, "Because, I like you, too."

"Then let's take this slowly," he suggested. "We get to know each other. We spend time together doing these challenges and then outside of work."

It didn't take me long to agree. "I like that idea, but first, I need you to know that Savie and Take the Leap come first, for both of us. Okay?"

"Agreed."

I reached across the table and rested my hand over his. This time, I did it without hesitation or even a second thought. Touching him felt right.

fifteen

THE HOUSE WAS dark and silent when I finally made it home. As much as I wanted to crawl into bed and hibernate until Monday, I'd made a promise to Ava. Based on her lack of text messages, her date was likely going well. I quickly changed into my comfiest pajamas and grabbed a bottle of wine and two glasses. I set them out on the table in the shared living space between our two bedrooms. Then, I grabbed a book and a blanket and curled up on the couch. It was just after eight, so I had a few hours to collect my thoughts before she got home. Tonight was going to be about her, not me.

I opened the book and settled back into the cushions. I read the first paragraph and then reread it. After my fourth attempt to comprehend the basic words and sentences on the page, I slammed the book closed. I had no idea what I'd just read, but I could now recite my entire conversation with Tripp verbatim. It played on a loop in my brain—over and over. With each replay, my heart felt as if it had doubled in size. Is this how the Grinch had felt? Warm and fuzzy and optimistic for what was to come.

"Sadie? Are you home?" Ava called up the stairs.

"Up here!" I yelled down. I threw the blanket off of my face and picked up my book. I'd blame it on the book if she noticed I'd been on the verge of tears. "I have the wine ready!"

"How'd you know it wasn't a pint of ice cream date?" Ava asked when she reached the top of the stairs.

"You didn't send a single text or beg me to rescue you."

Ava let out a long, exaggerated sigh. "I think my mom might have found a good one. His name is Heath."

The grin that spread across her face when she said his name told me a second date was already planned. I couldn't help by smile along with her. If anyone deserved a happy ending, it was her. Ava had the biggest heart and had so much love to give. I considered myself lucky to be on the receiving end of so much of it.

"He's an architect and fosters senior dogs. He's sarcastic and freaking hilarious. My abs are going to hurt tomorrow from laughing so hard."

"What did you guys do?"

"We got dinner at a taco truck and then had ice cream while we walked the riverfront. He's an only child like me and eventually wants a house full of kids."

"Just like you."

"Yeah," she said, swooning a bit. "He owns a house in Wilson County and spends his weekends helping his dad restore old cars."

"He sounds like he checks off all your boxes."

"He does, Sadie. I mean, I feel like we just clicked. There was instant chemistry."

"Did you get a goodnight kiss?"

Ava blushed and nodded. "More sparks."

Seeing her this happy eased every ounce of tension from my body. I giggled. "Aww, yay! When do you see him again?"

She glanced down at her phone and smiled again. "He just

texted to make sure I made it home." She typed out a response, and the smile stayed plastered in place. She was smitten. "Next week. He suggested tomorrow, but I didn't want to interrupt his time with his parents. His mom is getting her garden ready for planting season."

"I'm so glad you had a good night."

"So, what did you do tonight?" She waggled her eyebrows. "I noticed you didn't text me either. Did you and Tripp do anything?"

"We went to a barbecue place and grabbed dinner," I said. I knew without a doubt that the grin on my face looked exactly like the one Ava had when she told me about Heath. She noticed, too.

"And?"

"And you're right."

"I'm sorry, what? Can you repeat that? Maybe let me get it on video."

I playfully slapped her arm. "No, and I'll deny it if you try to use it against me later."

"Whatever." She rolled her eyes and asked, "Well, what happened?"

I gave her the Cliff's Notes version of the conversation we'd had. Including the part where I told him everything that happened with my parents and Gran. As I spoke, my thoughts began to spiral out of control. I let the doubt creep in and remined me how horrible of an idea this actually was.

"What am I going to do?" I asked and looked at Ava. "Why do I do this? It's a terrible idea, right? I'm going to mess this up and then we'll be done for. I'm like relationship repellant."

"No, you're not. You're guarded. But, hey, you opened up to someone tonight. That's hard and brave. I don't think you need to do anything tonight, and I know you didn't scare him off. He doesn't seem like a man that is easy to scare. Eat, drink some wine, and watch a movie. I'll pick so you don't have to think about it."

"Can we still talk about your date and how amazing Heath is?" I truly wanted to hear all about it. Being happy for her would distract me from the disaster that was my life.

"Deal."

While she got up to get the remote, I pulled out my phone to find a message from Tripp. *I had fun tonight.*

I smiled and replied, *I did too.*

I was tempted to beg him to forget everything that had happened tonight and ask him if we could go back to being friends and stick to a professional relationship, but I wasn't sure that was what I wanted. But I couldn't think about that now. I didn't want to think about anything. Thankfully, Ava picked a comedy that didn't involve romance or a heavy plot. There was one more thing needed to do to clear my mind.

"Before you start the movie," I said, standing up, "can we draw the next challenge? I don't want to have to dread it over the weekend."

"You sure? Won't drawing it make you dread it more?"

"Nope. Not knowing is way worse." I got up and ran downstairs to grab the hat from my office. All the while silently praying, *please let it be something tame and not at all romantic.* When I got back upstairs, I held out the hat for Ava. "You draw this time."

"Should we set up the camera?" I shook my head. There'd be plenty of content without it. There always was. She dipped her hand into the hat and shuffled through the slips of paper. I squeezed my eyes shut and waited for her to read the next challenge. "Ohh. This should be fun! Kayaking!"

Fun? It was like she didn't know me at all. "Cool," I said casually. "Well, let's get this movie going."

I grabbed the wine and sat back on the couch, vowing to

shut my brain off completely. I took all my thoughts of Tripp and the replays of the evening, along with the future dread for the kayak trip, and tucked them into my mental box. Once I closed the lid and shoved it deep, deep in the mental drawer, I left it there and focused on the movie.

sixteen

THE NEXT WEEK flew by in a blur of content editing, number crunching, and second, third, and fourth dates for Ava, leaving me plenty of alone time. I spent most of it trying to avoid the comment section on the hot air balloon video. Liam and Tripp both agreed to edit out the mid-air panic attack, which meant we were short on footage. Even with the edit, it was clear I hadn't taken to the adventure convincingly enough. The comments were brutal. I was stiff and off-putting while Tripp was still the fan favorite. Everyone loved him. Well, everyone except the die hard Take the Leap fans. They hated the new content almost as much as they hated seeing a woman as the face of the campaign.

At least the female audience was happy to see this new side of Tripp. I couldn't blame them. I'd watch him watch paint dry.

The app downloads picked up some, but we were still well below the KPIs we'd set. Seth and his team were pulling all-nighters to update the quiz, and Liam's team were dipping into their ad budget to promote it more.

For the most part, we'd managed to pretend nothing weird or awkward had happened between us. We went on working together as if nothing had changed between us, and, really, it hadn't. He just knew more about me than I ever wanted anyone to know.

Today, I'd planned for a nice and quiet Saturday. Ava was out for the afternoon with Heath, so I had the house to myself. I had a *Grey's Anatomy* and *Big Bang Theory* marathon planned. I was carrying my collection of snacks up the stairs when a knock at the door startled me. I paused on the stairs so I didn't make any noise, assuming it was someone selling lawn care or Jesus. I wasn't up for small talk with strangers today. I waited a solid minute before continuing my trek up the stairs.

Another knock caused me to sigh in frustration. What part about a nice and quiet day did the universe not understand? My annoyance melted away when I heard the voice on the other side of the door say my name.

"Coming!" I set the bowl of snacks on the stairs and smoothed my hands over my hair. I'd thrown it into a ponytail rather than washing it this morning, but I was suddenly regretting that choice—along with the old leggings and radio station T-shirt I was wearing. But there wasn't time to change. I pulled the door open, and even though I knew who was on the other side, seeing him standing there in his stupid backward cap and sunglasses caught my breath.

"Hi, Tripp."

"Hi."

"I wasn't expecting anyone today," I said and gestured toward my attire. "Did you need something for work?" It was the only plausible explanation I could think of.

He smiled his adorable half-grin and shook his head. "Sorry to drop in unannounced. I found myself bored and alone. So, I got in the car and started driving. Somehow, I ended up here."

Oh. The new familiar feeling of warmth spread from my

core through my body. "Do you want to come in? I was planning a lazy day with snacks and TV binging."

He glanced around me and into the house but didn't move to come in. "Actually, I was wondering if maybe you'd be up for taking me on one of your adventures."

"Yeah, I don't really have those."

"Come on now, I've seen the way your face lights up when you talk about going to the bookstore or the library. It's a gorgeous spring day. If you could do anything outside of the house today, what would you do?"

I considered his question. "Staying inside and avoiding allergies sounds like a good plan. But I'm guessing you had something else in mind."

"I didn't, really. I'm still not entirely sure how I ended up here." The other half of lips joined in the smile. He slipped off his sunglasses and took a step forward. "You can send me on my way, if you want to. I won't be offended."

I didn't even hesitate. I stepped aside and let him in. "We don't usually use the bottom floor on the weekend," I said and reached to flip on the light at the same time he did. Our fingers brushed. I couldn't ignore the warmth that spread from that tiny touch.

"Are you sure you don't mind if I crash your Saturday?"

"No," I answered quickly. Sure, I'd planned to spend the day alone and doing all my favorite things, but the instant his face graced my doorway, I knew I didn't want to spend it alone. "I had snacks and a few beverages ready to head up."

He slipped off his shoes, placed them by the door, and removed his hat and sunglasses. He stuffed his hands into the pockets of his jeans and glanced around the room. He looked nervous almost. I hadn't ever seen him look anything other than calm, cool, and collected. I kind of liked this new, shy version of him.

I led the way to the stairs and retrieved the bowl of snacks. Tripp took it from me and climbed the stairs behind me. When we reached the top, I gestured around the open living area. He'd seen the office space last time he was here, but he'd yet to see our living area. "This is our space. Ava's room is over to the right, and mine is on the left."

"Is it weird living where you work?"

"Sometimes, but the commute is great," I said. "So, I'd planned to watch *Grey's* or *Big Bang*; do you have a preference? My backup plan was reading, but that might be boring."

"Let's go with *Big Bang*, I love the opposites attract dynamic. What season are you on?"

"Oh, I've seen the whole show, but this rewatch, I'm on season three."

"How many times have you watched this?" I hesitated before admitting that I'd watched the entire show three times. At least. "That's only one more than me."

"You have time to watch entire seasons of shows?"

"What do you think I do after work every night?"

"Well, as Nashville's most eligible bachelor under 40, I imagine you have a line of screaming girls waiting for a ride in your Jeep. When you're not wooing the town's single women, you're jumping out of planes and traveling the world in a hot air balloon." I sat on the couch and scooted closer to the armrest to make room for him, but he didn't sit down. He leaned against the wall and crossed his arm over his chest. He locked his gaze on me. I tried not to squirm on the couch but failed.

"You have quite the imagination, Sadie."

"Overactive, according to most of my former teachers."

"Just right," he argued. "But in this case, you're wrong. I go home and feed my cats, read, watch TV, or, depending on the day, crash early."

I bit my lip and debated my next question. "So, you don't spend your weekends wining and dining the bachelorettes?"

Tripp shook his head and laughed. "Not as often as my reputation would lead you to believe. I've spent the past ten years dedicated to Take the Leap and haven't had much time or energy for anything else. I'd hoped once things picked up a few years ago, I'd have time, but the demands kept coming."

It made sense. His business had exploded in the beginning, then when it started to dip recently, he'd put all of his efforts and energy into keeping it going. "You're married to the job, I get that. I've often referred to Savie as our child, it takes more time than most people realize."

"It's a good thing we love what we do, though."

"It makes it all worth it," I said. "Wait, did you say cats? As in more than one?"

"Three."

"You have three cats?" I didn't believe him. At all.

"Elliot, Derek, and Taylor." An adorable hint of red crept up his cheeks. Those names sounded oddly familiar.

"Hold up. As in Stabler, Shepherd, and Swift?" He nodded, confirming my guess. "No. Seriously?"

"Would you believe me if I said my sisters were Swifties and named them for me?"

"Based on how red your face is right now, no. Not at all. Mr. James, you continue to surprise me." He pushed off the wall and strode toward the couch. Rather than sitting next to me, he sat on the edge of the coffee table.

"Busted. My sisters are all big fans, but so am I. We went to all three of her shows in Nashville last year. We always listen to *Fearless* before a jump."

"Do you jump head-first, fearless?"

"Every time." He leaned forward. "Are you sure this is okay?"

"What?"

"Me being here. I know we haven't really talked much since the hot air balloon. I don't want to push you. You can tell me to bugger off." He said it in a horrible British accent. Laughing, I shook my head.

I could. But I didn't want to. "As long as you don't bring up my family or tell me you were rooting against Penny and Leonard, you can stay. I'll even let you sit on the couch."

I patted the cushion on the other side. He cocked his head to the side and studied me for a moment. Then, got up and moved to the couch. He sat on the cushion beside me. I could still feel the heat radiating off of him.

"I mean, Priya's cute, but she's no Penny."

I scoffed. "You're lucky I've already watched the breakup seasons and you aren't spoiling anything. But how dare you." I tossed one of the decorative pillows at him. He caught it with ease and tucked it behind his head.

"Well, let's get this binge-watch going. We've got all day."

I settled into my spot on the couch and turned the TV on. I'd queued up *Grey's* but switched over to *Big Bang* and started the episode. When the intro began to play, I raised the remote to skip it, but Tripp started to sing along under his breath. I let it play through and was tempted to restart the episode so I could hear him sing again. But it would play again in twenty-three minutes. I could wait.

I snuck another peek at him while the episode played. I couldn't believe he was sitting on my couch in my house. He seemed like he fit right in. If I let myself daydream, I could see him here every Saturday and Sunday. Except, there wouldn't be a couch cushion between us. I shut that daydream down before my overactive imagination ran completely wild.

"Are you bored yet?" I asked after a few episodes.

He stretched his arms over his head and arched his back. "Not at all."

I shifted closer to him so that his arm fell around my shoulders when he dropped them back down. I nestled into the crook of his arm and inhaled deeply. He smelled like a warm summer day, and I didn't hate it. He wrapped his hand around my arm and inched me closer to him. We both shifted until we found a comfortable position.

If you'd have told me two months ago that I'd spend my Saturday afternoon curled up on the couch with Tripp James, I'd have laughed. I'd never have guessed that there was a soft, kind man beneath the rough and tumble exterior he exuded. He was nothing at all like I'd expected. He had cats named after my favorite musician, he adored his family, he knew all the words to TV show theme songs, and he was patient and gentle. It was as if every day I spent with him uncovered a new side of him. If I'd seen this version of him in our early brand research, I wouldn't have hesitated to pitch them for even a second.

I sat up and jumped off the couch. "I have an idea."

Tripp startled and stared up at me, confused.

"You know how we're getting all these comments from your core audience about how different the content is and that they don't recognize you?"

"Yeah?" He leaned forward and focused his attention on me.

"That's because no one knows your story. They don't know about Noah or your family or how these adventures are healing and cathartic. They only know the story they've been told through branding." He was nodding along now. "I think we need to tell that story. We need to show the heart behind TTL and your mission. That's the piece that's missing from the campaign."

I bit my lip and watched his face as he reacted to what I'd

said. It was a risk to even suggest he bring his family into the marketing. I didn't know if he'd be open to talking about Noah or using his story in the branding. We'd have to be careful in how we approach it.

"Your annual fundraiser for the Leukemia and Lymphoma Society is coming up soon, right?" He nodded. "We tie it together. Maybe do a contest for a family going through what you all went through. Let them pick their own family bonding adventure."

His face lifted at that. There was a hint of a twinkle in his eyes as he said, "Sadie, that's brilliant."

"Yeah?"

"Yes, it's perfect. I've always wanted to share Noah's story, but I'll need to run it by my family."

"That's a good idea. When do you do your annual sky dive?"

"It's next month, why?" he asked.

"Do you think they'd be open to having it filmed?"

He shrugged. "We can ask. Let's add this to our weekly touch base agenda."

I bobbed my head in approval. I settled back onto the couch beside him and snuggled against him. "Okay, back to not talking about work."

seventeen

"ARE you sure you have the address, right?" I asked Ava as she pulled into the driveway of a small ranch house in Crieve Hall, a neighborhood in South Nashville. The modest single-level home sat off the road and boasted a two-car garage and a carport. I could clearly see Tripp's Jeep parked in the carport, but nothing about this house screamed that Tripp James lived there. It was simple and not at all modern. In other words, it was nothing like the Take the Leap office, and it definitely didn't look anything like the sleek condo where his official CEO portraits had been taken.

"Yes, I'm sure," Ava said, glancing at her phone to confirm the address.

I asked, "Is the usual gang going to be here today?"

During our weekly meeting, Tripp had insisted we have two practice sessions in the kayak before he'd let me in the water, and he'd offered up his house and pool. One day on dry land, getting used to the boat, and another day in his pool, learning how to get out of sticky situations. In other words, he wanted to make sure I didn't drown while they were filming us. I appreciated his concern, but as with all the other challenges, I just wanted to get this one over with. I'd never been a strong swimmer, and wasn't usually a fan of water activities. I loved going to the beach, but it was mostly so I could sit under an umbrella, drink a fruity cocktail, and read a book. But, I'd done what I could to get ready for this excursion. I had a helmet, a life jacket, and a new bathing suit and outfit. Thankfully, it had been a work expense, so I didn't have to cover the ridiculous cost. I'm pretty sure the guy at the sporting goods store oversold me on a few things once he realized I had no clue what I was talking about.

"You ready to go kayak in the grass?" Ava asked.

"No, but at least I won't be getting wet today." It was spring in Nashville, which meant one day the weather would feel like summer was a promise away, and the next winter would be raging for a comeback. Today was somewhere in the middle. Definitely not the kind of weather that beckoned me to the pool.

We got out of the car and headed toward the backyard, as Tripp had instructed. We found Liam, Kyle, and Tripp set up in the backyard. There were two kayaks and the same camera setup we'd been using for each of the challenges. As soon as I saw the kayaks on the ground, I was immediately grateful that this adventure didn't involve any extreme heights. Just me strapped into a plastic boat I had no idea how to steer or even get in. It did look easier to manage than the massive basket on the balloon.

"Hey, we made it," Ava said, announcing our presence. The Take the Leap team all turned to look at us. I was certain I looked ridiculous carrying my helmet and lifejacket, but I'd been told to bring them.

"We're just about ready," Liam said, "We want to make sure to get plenty this time around."

"Today, I'll be handling your training. But weather permitting, we'll have a trained kayak instructor assisting in the pool tomorrow," Tripp said.

I shivered thinking about the pool. I glanced across his massive backyard. The pool was in the center and fenced in. At least it looked like a decent size. Big enough for one kayak.

"Don't worry," Tripp said, following my gaze, "it's heated."

"Thank goodness." I breathed a sigh of relief. "Today, we're just sticking to land, right?"

"That's the plan. We'll work on proper positions, getting comfortable in the kayak, and paddling. But first, did you decide if you want to attempt a solo trip? Or do you want to stick to the two-seater so we can go together?"

My desire to stay afloat and my heart answered before my protective brain could kick in. "Two-seater." The smarter option would be to go solo and keep my distance from Tripp, but that wasn't the safe choice. Sure, I'd have a few days of training under my belt before we got into the river this weekend, but the thought of floating down the Cumberland River by myself was far too terrifying even to consider.

Liam announced he was ready with the cameras and asked for my helmet. After not getting much footage of Tripp during the zoo outing, the entire team decided that I'd always have a camera on just in case the footage of me wasn't good enough. Well, to be fair, they hadn't said *good*. They'd just said it wasn't enough. The *good* was inferred.

He handed the helmet to Tripp, who inched closer to me and helped me strap it on. He gently shook it to ensure my head didn't wobble. "Good. Tight and safe. We should probably go ahead and practice with the life jackets."

"Seriously?" I glanced down at the oversized Savie sweatshirt I'd worn for the occasion. Anytime I could get our brand out there, I would. I wasn't sure the life jacket would fit comfortably over the sweatshirt.

"Do you have a t-shirt on under that?" Ava asked. I shook my head. "We could trade?"

I laughed. Her extra small shirt would not fit over anything but my extra small chest. "We can try to make it work."

Right as I said that Tripp said, "Here, take my shirt." Before I could protest, he peeled off his shirt and handed it to me. I couldn't look away. My gaze locked on the tattoos on his chest and arms, where it lingered for way too long before following the tiny trail of chest hair down to his very well-defined abs. When I reached the button of his jeans, I blinked and tried to act like I hadn't just ogled my client. We were in work mode today, not get to know each other with our clothes off mode.

Taking the shirt, I turned to face away from the group to hide the embarrassment that had crept over my face. I felt Ava move to stand behind me. "Wipe the drool off your mouth," she whispered into my ear. I nudged her back with my elbow.

I removed my helmet and quickly swapped my sweatshirt for Tripp's t-shirt. It smelled just like him, and I had to resist the urge to keep my face buried inside of it. While I changed, I dug deep into my consciousness and tried to conjure up the most unappealing images I could think of. *Snakes, bears, clowns. Snakes, bears, clowns.* I repeated the words over and over until I felt my body and face cool. When I turned around, I met Tripp's stare. If I didn't know better, I might think he was looking at me just as I'd looked at him. I glanced down to make sure I'd put on the shirt correctly. I had.

"Why is he staring at me?" I asked Ava in a hushed whisper.

"Sadie, you're wearing his shirt. And you're wearing it pretty darn well."

"Either that or I look ridiculous."

"Nope, definitely not that." She gave me a gentle shove toward him. He held out the life jacket, and I put it on.

"Don't let me forget to change before I leave so I can give this back to you."

"Keep it," he said, his voice thick. He stood closer to me as he put the helmet on again. I could feel his breath on my face. "It looks better on you."

"All right, now that everyone is comfortable, except those of us watching this, can we get moving before we run out of daylight? You guys can make swoony eyes at each other later," Liam said with a laugh.

I started to protest. I wasn't making swoony eyes, whatever that meant, and neither was Tripp. But Liam was ready to move on. He turned on both of our cameras and got into position beside Kyle while he reminded him to hold his phone steady while filming.

Tripp led us to the two-seater kayak. I climbed into the rear seat.

"You'll sit in the front," he said. I turned back to him, confused. There was absolutely no way I'd be leading us anywhere. "I'll sit behind you and follow your paddle strokes. I'll also steer."

"Got it." I pivoted and moved into the front seat. Liam handed me a paddle.

I waited for Tripp to climb in behind me, but he stood in front of the boat. "I'm going to show you how to hold the paddle, okay?" When I nodded, he carefully placed his hands on mine. He paused and waited to make sure I was comfortable with the contact. I ignored my instinct to move away from him and held still. He positioned my hands facing out and slid my right hand further away.

"You want to have your hands about shoulder-width apart. Loosen your grip a bit," he said, "Your knuckles should line up with the blade here. See this curved part? That's the back.

When you paddle, you want this long edge to face up." He ran his hand over the longer edge of the paddle to show me.

I rotated the paddle in my hands and held steady, determined not to drop the paddle or lean away from him. "Like this?"

He smiled and released my hands. "Just like that." He moved to the rear of the kayak, leaned over me, and wrapped his hands around my wrist. "You'll start the stroke by dipping your right arm like this." I tried to relax my arms as he guided them through the fluid motion of a paddle stroke. He did this a few more times before releasing me. "Your turn."

I attempted to move my arms in the same motion he had, but it felt clumsy. Rather than step in and move my arms for me, he slid into the kayak in front of me and moved his arms and shoulders in the proper motion. The muscles along his back flexed. I held my breath and watched him move his arms up and down. The flow of his arms had a soothing rhythm to it. I copied his movements. After a few minutes, he stood and moved to the rear of the boat. He asked Liam to hand him his paddle.

"If you fall out of rhythm, don't worry. I'll follow your lead."

We spent the next hour going over the different paddle strokes and how he'd control the direction and speed of the boat. We'd be at the mercy of the wind and the current, but he'd be the one guiding us down the river. He didn't have to say the words, but I could hear them in every sentence he spoke to me.

I've got you.

eighteen

I SLEPT in Tripp's shirt last night. I didn't admit this to Ava. I'd have hidden the truth from myself if I could have. Despite having worn it all day, it still smelled more like him than me. When I got up for the day, I carefully folded it neatly and placed it on my dresser. I wasn't ready to wash it yet. When I put on the new bathing suit, kayaking-friendly swim pants, and t-shirt, I was almost tempted to throw his shirt over the top. But if I was going to be falling into the pool today, I didn't want to be wearing baggy clothing. At least that's what the salesperson had told me.

We arrived at Tripp's house just before noon. Once again, the Take the Leap team was already there, along with an unfamiliar face. A very beautiful face that seemed to be very intent on standing very close to Tripp. I tried not to glare at her long, lanky frame and perfectly shiny brown hair that was elegant even in a simple ponytail. Unlike me, she didn't look out of place standing next to him. Jealousy wasn't a feeling I was familiar with, and I wasn't a fan of the bitter taste it left in my mouth.

"Ready for day two?" Liam asked as we joined them.

"I'm not sure ready is the word I'd have chosen, but sure let's go with that. Hi," I said and held out my hand to the stranger. "I'm Sadie Barnes."

"I know," she said with a friendly smile. "I've been enjoying the new content you've been creating for Tripp. It's been fun to watch."

I searched her words for any hint of mocking or clue that she was silently laughing at me, but her words felt genuine.

"Sadie's been great to work with," Tripp said, "and Ava, too."

"I'm Olivia, the kayak instructor. I've worked with Tripp and his team on a few different outings. I even taught this one everything he knows." She playfully bumped her shoulder against Tripp's. I chewed the inside of my cheek to avoid saying or doing anything that might show what I was feeling, which was another wave of intense jealousy. *Get it together*, I silently scolded myself.

"Nice to meet you," Ava said. "So, what's the plan for today? Will you be in the pool with her?"

"Yeah, so, based on what Tripp told me, they'll be in a two-seater open sit-on kayak, right?" I nodded. "But, if you're okay with it, I'd like to teach you some of the basics in the single sit-in kayak."

I opened my eyes wider. "Like the one that you're stuck inside?" The words caught in my throat. I tried to swallow back the fear. "Is that really necessary?"

Olivia's face softened. "For your specific trip, no, but I want to make sure you know everything you need to know before I set you loose on the river. I'll be in the water with you the entire time. We'll first work on getting in and out of the kayak. Once you master the sit-in, the other one won't be so scary. And even though you probably won't need it, Tripp and I both agree that learning how to do a self-rescue will be beneficial."

"What exactly does that mean?" Panic seized my entire body. The idea of a self-rescue kind of made sense to me, especially since I was fluent in self-preservation, but rescue implied I was already in danger. I preferred to prevent the danger from ever occurring. I stared past Olivia and at the pool. The kayak was already sitting on the edge, waiting for me. "Like, upside down? Underwater? Can I just go inside and cuddle with Tripp's cats while you all do this without me?" I was looking forward to meeting his dynamic feline trio, and I'd take any excuse I could use to get out of this training.

She bit her lip and nodded. "I promise you I will not push you past your comfort point. If you need to stop at any time, we'll shift our focus."

I wanted to say no, but even though I'd just met her, I felt like I could trust her. "Okay."

"And I'll be there too. I'll stay out of Olivia's way so she can do what she does best, but I'll be right there with you."

"And you have all of us here, too," Liam said, "all of us are fully trained kayakers. I'm also a certified lifeguard."

My face must have shown the sheer panic and shock buzzing inside my veins because Liam immediately backtracked. "I mean ... not like that ... you won't need that because you have all of us here to make sure nothing happens." He looked to Tripp for help, his eyes wide and pleading.

Tripp inched closer to me and placed his hand on my shoulder. "He's right. We're all here to make sure you learn how to handle the kayak, the paddles, and the water. Are you okay?"

I shook my head. "Why is he being nice to me?" I asked, pointing at Liam. "It's freaking me out."

Tripp's eyebrows raised in confusion, and then he started laughing loudly. The rest of the group joined in.

"No, seriously. He's always the first to make fun of me or

laugh when I get scared. Now he's offering to make sure I feel safe? Something's fishy."

"Sorry," Liam said, "Watching back the footage and editing everything made me see what a jerk I was being. I still think you're ridiculous sometimes, but I promised Tripp and Ava I'd try to be nicer and more understanding." He actually sounded remorseful.

"I threatened to break his nose if he laughed at you again," Ava said. She held up her fists and bounced like a boxer ready to pounce. Liam held up his hands and stepped back. My lips curved into a thin smile. I appreciated the gesture and Liam's attempt at playing nice.

"It still freaks me out."

"If it makes you feel better, I'll randomly point at you and laugh."

"Thanks, I'd appreciate that."

"All right, enough stalling, time to get in the water, Sadie." Olivia clapped her hands and led us all toward the pool. "I see you've got the appropriate clothes on. Not too loose. Do you have your gear?"

Tripp held up the helmet and life jacket I'd left here last night. She nodded in approval, and he helped me get everything buckled and strapped.

For the next hour, Olivia showed me how to get into the kayak and then into the pool. I felt like I'd had the move mastered but she had me practice over and over until I was sure everyone else had fallen asleep, me included. She was so matter of fact and straight to the point, that I couldn't even throw in a joke or two to keep things interesting. Straddle the kayak. Sit on the back of the cockpit. Straighten legs and slide in. Use the paddle to balance and push into the water.

On my first attempt, I tipped too far to the right and flipped straight into the water. I screamed as the boat rocked to the side and I took in a mouthful of water. My legs and arms flailed every which way. It took me one too many seconds to get back above water.

"Sadie!" Olivia scolded me in a sharp tone once the kayak was righted. I stopped squirming and stared at her. Her lips were pulled into a tight line. She shook her head at me. Apparently, wigging out was not the proper response. "Every time you panic, you set yourself up for the potential of something worse happening. Before you lose control of your emotions, you have got to get yourself out of harm's way. Understood?"

I nodded. "Sorry, can we try again?"

I only tipped over three of the ten times I did the entrance. But after the first, I didn't freak out. At least not externally. On the inside, it felt as those I had a mild heart attack with every flip. Each time, she and Tripp quickly righted me, so I wasn't underwater for more than a few seconds.

"Good," Olivia finally announced after my tenth plunge into the pool.

She took hold of the nose of the kayak and guided me out to the middle of the pool. We spent a few minutes on how to hold the paddle. I remembered most of what Tripp had taught me yesterday, but Olivia was much less forgiving in how loose or tight my grip was. If it was too tight, she'd tap my fingers until I loosened my hold to her satisfaction. If I was too loose, she wrapped her hand around mine to show me the proper grip. Compared to Tripp, her hands were soft and smooth. But at least they didn't send a rush of hormones through my body.

"Now we're ready to learn how to self-rescue. I'm going to show you the motions above water, and then I'll demonstrate, okay?"

"Sure." I was anything but ready for this portion of the training, but it had to happen. Olivia got out of the pool and pulled a second kayak into the water. I glanced around the pool and found Tripp, Liam, and Ava all staring at me with complete focus. Ava chewed her thumbnail while Tripp wrung his hands in his lap. Liam just sat completely still and watched with curiosity. I imagined he was waiting for my mental breakdown. I'd had two in front of them, so a third was likely.

Before she moved on to showing me how to do a wet exit, she gave tips on how to right the kayak to keep it from capsizing. It all came down to finding balance and steadying the boat. I sat motionless and listened with rapt attention as she went over the steps. I memorized each movement.

When it was my turn to demonstrate, I repeated her steps out loud. "Lean forward. Slide hand along the cockpit. Find the grab loop and pull. Hands on the side of cockpit. Knees together. Push forward."

It sounded easy enough. The movements felt natural above water. I practiced a few more times while she got into her kayak. While it seemed easy enough, I was 100% certain I wasn't going to be able to do any of this the minute I was upside down.

"Can one of you tip me over?" she asked. Tripp volunteered and stepped into the pool. He gave me a quick wink before making his way to Olivia's boat. "Ready when you are, Trippster. Don't go gentle on me." There was more than a hint of flirtation in her voice, but he didn't blush or react. Instead, he grabbed the edge of her boat and flipped her over in one swift move. Then he looked toward me and smiled as if to reassure me of something.

I tried not to be distracted by whatever silent message he was sending me and focused on watching Olivia slide out of her kayak. It happened too quickly for me to actually take note of what she'd done. She was underwater for less than ten seconds. She popped back up and splashed water toward Tripp. "I told you not to be gentle. I didn't say to try and drown me." I was worried she was angry, but she started laughing. "Did you see any of that, Sadie?"

I shook my head. I'd seen her boat tip and then her pop out of the water. I didn't want to ask her to do it again, but I needed to watch without Tripp distracting me.

"On the count of three this time, okay?" Tripp nodded sheepishly. She counted down and when they hit three, he grabbed the edge of her boat and flipped her over. This time, he did it slowly, so the water stayed calm. I could see her hand reach for the loop and pull. I watched her arms brace against the side and then she leaned forward and slipped out. I had to admit, it looked easy.

"I think I got it that time. I won't make you do it again," I said once she resurfaced. Tripp tapped the top of her helmet and started to climb out of the pool. "Wait, aren't you going to stay?"

The question was out of my mouth before I realized what I was saying. But watching him leave me alone in the water sent a shrill of panic up my spine. I knew Olivia was more than capable of teaching me, but I'd yet to do any of the scary stuff without him right by my side. I wanted him there ... no, I needed him. The realization slammed into me like a hurricane, knocking my breath away. I tried to backtrack and erase the deep feeling of need that filled my entire being but couldn't. I'd felt what I felt and there was no going back.

"Sure, I can stay," he said and slipped back into the pool. "I'll stay out of your way, though. I'm just here for moral support, okay?"

I nodded and asked Olivia to go through the motions with me one more time before agreeing to be flipped upside down. When it was time, I looked toward Tripp and met his gaze. His face was the picture of confidence. It was the last thing I saw before my eyes, nose, and mouth filled with water. I hadn't thought to take a deep breath or do anything to prepare my body for the flip. But I didn't panic. I quickly replayed the steps Olivia had taught me. I leaned forward and felt for the loop. When I pulled it, I pushed my knees together and slipped out of the boat. My lifejacket did its job and pulled me to the surface.

When I popped out of the water, Liam and Ava jumped to their feet and cheered.

Tripp swam toward me and wrapped his arms around me. He shouted, "You just did that! Holy crap, Sadie, you did it! You didn't panic or anything. You did exactly what you were supposed to and got out like a pro."

I leaned into his embrace. When I felt his cheek brush mine, every ounce of tension I'd been holding onto released.

"I did it."

"Well," Oliva said, beaming with pride, "you had a good teacher. I think we do that a few more times then move on to the kayak you and Tripp will be in this weekend."

I couldn't respond. I was too busy letting my thoughts and body get lost in the feeling of Tripp's arms around me. I wasn't sure what scared me more, letting go of him or admitting that I didn't want to let go.

nineteen

I SHOULDN'T BE this nervous. I'd already spent countless hours with Tripp. We'd held hands and canoodled on my couch. I'd even been at his house less than twenty-four hours ago for our last kayak practice. But we'd yet to have what most would consider a proper date. Nerves were to be expected, right? I wiped my sweaty palms on my jeans and wished I'd chosen less restrictive clothing. I hadn't realized I'd be sweating this much—it wasn't hot out, and the date hadn't started yet.

My hand hovered in the air, ready to knock on his door. I hesitated; my mind filled with doubt. Come on, Sadie, you can do this. I took a deep breath, trying to steady my nerves, and finally knocked. To my surprise, Tripp pulled the door open before I even finished the first knock.

"Hey," he said with a wide grin. "Come in." He stepped back and stumbled over an orange cat that had to weigh at least twenty pounds.

"Oh," I said, returning his smile, "I didn't realize I'd be meeting the dynamic trio tonight. Are you sure we're ready to take that step?"

"Absolutely. If they could talk, they'd tell you it was nice to *finally* meet you after hearing their human pine over you for months." It was hard to ignore the adorable blush that painted his cheeks, my new favorite shade of pink.

"Well, don't believe everything you've heard. Is this floofy man, Detective Stabler?" I knelt down to give Elliot a quick ear scratch, but when I tried to stand, he nudged my leg, nearly knocking me over. I obliged his request and continued giving him my undivided attention.

"The one and only, yeah. Derek is around here somewhere, and I'm pretty sure Taylor is camped out by the back door, hoping I'll drop a hot dog or burger."

"Your cats eat hot dogs?" I asked, standing back to my full height. All five-foot-one of me. I propped my arms on my hips in mock disappointment. "I don't think that diet is PETA-approved."

"Only when I'm not looking, or Zoe is here. She's always giving them human food. She claims it's her right as their auntie."

"As a dog aunt, I can confirm. It's my job to spoil Tommy Pickles, Seth's dog." Tommy and I had a love-hate relationship. I loved him, and he loved me, but my allergies hated him and me. Anytime I visited my brother's place, it was also with a healthy dose of allergy medication. Thankfully, feline dander didn't have the same effect on me. If our home didn't double as our office, Ava and I would have our own brood of pets.

I followed Tripp through the house as he gave me a quick tour. It wasn't a big house, but he still kept a spare room for each of his sisters. Apparently, he was their landing pad after bad breakups or tough workdays. I guess I wasn't the only one who found refuge and safety with him. Every detail I learned about him, and his life made me crave more. I wanted to drink from the well until it ran dry.

We ended up in the kitchen. I leaned against the cool quartz countertops and took in the open space. His entire house was well-decorated and modern, but it was also well-loved and clearly lived in. The essence of him was everywhere. Each piece of art or furniture reminded me of him. It even smelled like him.

"So, what culinary delight are you making me tonight?" I asked. I'd suggested a few restaurants, but he'd wanted to keep this first official date lowkey. I wasn't one to turn down a home-cooked meal.

"Don't get too excited. It's nothing fancy, but I make a mean burger. So, burgers, hand-cut fries, and a salad featuring vegetables grown in Lydia's backyard garden."

"How'd you know burgers are my favorite?"

"Lucky guess," he said, grinning, "and you order one almost every time we get food at the office. I snagged a few fresh onions and tomatoes from Lydia, too."

A warm glow radiated from my core. I loved how he paid attention to the small details, like what I ordered at restaurants or that he had my favorite Taylor album playing on his sound system.

We settled into a comfortable rhythm of conversation while he expertly maneuvered his kitchen. I'd offered to help; but he handed me a glass of wine and told me to sit and relax. I'd never had a man cook for me before, but then again, I'd never met a man I'd let cook for me. No one had ever made me feel as comfortable as he did. Any nerves I'd had when I arrived had faded away. I wish there were a way to bottle up this contentment that washed over me every time I was around him. I'd take a sip anytime doubt and fear started to rear their ugly heads again.

We ate in the backyard as the sun started to give way to the moon. The fairy lights and sunset-painted sky made the meal far more intimate than it had any right to be.

"Thank you for all of this," I said, finishing off the fries on my plate. "I don't have many dates to compare it to, but let's just say I wasn't expecting to feel this relaxed."

"Really? I find it so hard to believe that you don't have a line of boys waiting to wine and dine you over burgers."

Laughing, I said, "Even if there were, I wouldn't have said yes. I found it much easier to avoid the things I fear rather than face them. You can't miss what you've never known. But I think I might be learning that some things are worth the rush of fear."

A frown tugged his lips down. "What else have you missed out on?"

"What do you mean?"

"You said you can't miss what you've never known, but surely you know the things you've missed."

I considered his question again. The answer was like a gun loaded with all the what-ifs and could've beens that I'd tucked into a safe I never intended to open again. "I guess I've never thought of it that way before."

"It's okay if you don't want to answer."

I shook my head. It wasn't that I didn't want to. I was afraid to crack into those memories. I cleared my throat and asked, "You know how I feel about elevators, right?" He nodded. "Well, in college, I landed an amazing internship with a former United States Senator who'd just lost his bid for the presidency. I used to want to go into politics."

His eyebrows raised in surprise. "Politics? Interesting."

"I wanted to be a lobbyist. It was a short-lived dream. Anyway, I showed up for my first day and realized the only way to get in the building from the parking garage was this janky, terrifying elevator that was slower than Christmas. The stairs weren't an option. I quit after the first day, so I didn't have to get in it again."

"Do you regret quitting?"

"I did at first. I was too embarrassed to tell anyone the real reason I quit, so I made up some excuse about it not being what I expected. Now? Not really. I'm happy with how my career has turned out. Politics would've eaten me alive."

"I won't lie. I'm thankful you took another route. I'm also really glad you pushed through and rode the elevator up to our office that day."

"Me too." I pushed back my chair and stood, ignoring the fear that bubbled in my stomach as I walked toward him. He opened his arms, and I slid inside them, curling onto his lap.

"And you're working on your elevator fears. I've seen you handle the one in our office like the boss you are."

I had to laugh. I'd only been in the elevator with him once, and I'd been quick to press the buttons so we could all get out quickly. There'd been five of us crammed into the space. But he was right, my heart no longer raced when the doors closed. "I guess that's true."

"What else is on that list."

"Camping. I went once when I was a kid but missed out on the campfire, s'mores, and roasting hot dogs because I'd gotten too scared to stay all night."

"You've never been camping?" I shook my head. "Well, why don't we make that one of the less extreme challenges? I've got a free weekend next month, and I've been trying to lobby the team to add camping to our line up."

I thought about it and listed all the reasons this was a terrible idea ... I hated bugs and the outdoors, and I wasn't sure I was ready for an overnight excursion with Tripp and the content team. But, on the other hand, it could be fun. *Fun?* Did I just think camping might be fun? Weird.

"Sure, I think that could make for some great content."

"I'll have Liam work on the plans," he said. "But there's something you need to know before we go camping."

Intrigued, I raised an eyebrow.

"I'm not completely fearless."

I clutched my hand over my heart. "What?"

Laughing, he said, "If there are any spiders anywhere near the tent, you're going to have to take care of it."

"Hmm. Well, as long as it's a small spider, I think I can do that." I pictured him hiding in the corner of the tent cowering in fear of a Daddy Long Legs. The image made me smile. "Do you want to hear one of my most ridiculous fears?"

"Sadie, I just confessed to having arachnophobia, it's the least you can share." He smirked that half smile that made my knees go weak.

"Have I mentioned my fear of bridges?"

"Aside from the one we bungee jumped off of? No."

"When I was little, anytime we'd go over a bridge, I'd get super quiet and stare out the window. Gran thought it was because I loved bridges and was fascinated by the cool, old ones. She used to plan road trips to find the oldest and most interesting bridges. It was a whole thing that she did because she thought I was having the time of my life on those rickety things. When I started driving, she noticed I would take the long way home and drive around the lake rather than over it. She asked me why, and I told her it was because I *hated* bridges. She was horrified and wouldn't stop apologizing."

Tripp covered his mouth to stifle a laugh. "The whole time, she thought she was giving you an amazing experience, but nope."

"That was my first lesson in how important communication was. Though, I still keep some of my fears close to the vest. People love to make fun of phobias or try to push and test them." I bit my lip as I thought of Liam and how quickly he'd grown frustrated with me at the trampoline park.

Tripp read my face and frowned. "I hope I didn't push any of this on you. I want you to tell me when you're scared or worried. I won't make fun of you."

I closed my eyes and rested my head back on his shoulder. "I'm kind of like the Hulk when it comes to fear. That's my secret. I'm always scared."

"Even now?" His fingers trailed up and down my arm. The touch was excruciatingly gentle.

"Especially now," I whispered. I placed my hand over his hand and tucked my fingers under his. "I don't want to be, though."

There wasn't anything else to say. Neither of us moved. I stayed curled in his lap, tucked safely in his arms, as the sun set, and darkness took over the night sky. The crickets and frogs sang their mating call, and the world carried on as if mine hadn't completely shifted off of its axis. No matter how this ended or worked out, nothing would ever be the same for me. That was what scared me most. The longer the silence lingered, the heavier my fear became. Unease crept in, and I shifted out of his arms.

"Tripp?" I asked, breaking the silent reverie between us. "Are you sure this is a good idea?"

A deep sigh escaped his lips. "Honestly? I don't know, but everything about this feels right."

"I know." He felt like home ... safe, secure, cozy, and warm. I settled deeper into him, and he pulled me in closer.

twenty

I HAD a few days to rest and recover from the kayak lessons and my dinner date with Tripp, but it wasn't nearly enough. There was still the day-to-day business of Savie to tend to and incessant thoughts of him to keep me nice and distracted.

By Friday, everything inside of me was a tangled mess. I was in trouble, and I knew it.

It wasn't like I'd never had feelings for anyone before. I have, but I never had feelings too strong to ignore. I could usually go on a few dates, make out, or whatever, and then move on. Once I got the kissing and physical attraction out of my system, it was easy to kiss and forget.

I'd never had anyone completely invade my thoughts and heart the way Tripp had. He was all I could think about. I couldn't even get away from him in my sleep. Every dream was filled with him.

Ava could tell I was distracted, but she wisely didn't say anything. She let me walk around in a fog and made sure I didn't completely lose myself. I doubt she had any idea how far gone I already was. I'd managed to keep my date night with Tripp a secret for the past day and a half, but I wasn't sure I'd be able to hold it in much longer. She needed to know. We went through our usual end-of-the-month budgeting meeting. Thanks to Take the Leap, we'd been able to end in the black for the third month in a row, which made the risk of entering a relationship with Tripp even higher.

Thankfully, we'd had a few new leads on clients because of our work with Take the Leap. Their social media team had graciously tagged our business page in every social post and gave us shout-outs whenever new content went live. There should've been more than enough work to keep me preoccupied. But anytime there was a lull, or I let my mind wander, my thoughts drifted back to him. If I dared to close my eyes longer than a blink, images of his face inches from mine in the pool flooded my senses. I could still feel his arms around me.

I stared at the request for proposal in front of me and read the introduction sentence for the hundredth time. Of the five new client leads, Ava volunteered to tackle three, and I took the last two. The first one I reviewed wasn't a good fit for us, so I passed on their request for a proposal and recommended a few other agencies in Nashville that were better suited for their industry. The last one was from a woman-owned coffee shop that was looking to expand into franchising. I was excited and intrigued by the prospect of being the marketing agency that could help launch them into the next phase. They already had a solid hold on the market in their neighborhood, and their projections for growth were promising.

I found myself wondering if Tripp had ever tried their coffee or if I could introduce it to him. It seemed no matter what I did, every thought circled back to him.

I slammed my laptop shut and pushed my chair back. Letting out a frustrated groan, I dropped my head on the desk.

"Are you ready to talk about it?" Ava called from her office.

"No. Yes. I don't know." I kept my head buried in my arms,

and the desk muffled my words. Ava padded into my office, and the door frame creaked when she leaned against it. "What is wrong with me?"

"Like right now or in general?" I know she was trying to make a joke, but it fell flat. I didn't laugh or lift my head. I wasn't in the mood to play along. "I have two guesses."

"Go for it."

"My first guess is the thought of jumping out of a plane in a few months is stressing you out."

"Ugh. Don't remind me. But no." Skydiving was the furthest thing from my mind at the moment.

"Okay," she said, hesitating, "don't get mad, please. But I think you might be experiencing something more than a crush on Tripp."

My silence was all the answer she needed. Just hearing his name made my heart flip-flop. Plus, I hadn't told Ava about our dinner date or the couch cuddles. I peeled my head off of the desk. "Um, about that."

Ava's eyebrows shot up. I had her full attention now. "What?"

"You know how you slept over at Heath's on Thursday after our last Kayak practice?" She nodded and eyed me suspiciously. "Well, Tripp and I kind of sort of had a date."

"You what?"

"I went over to his house, met his cats, and he cooked me dinner. We might have cuddled a bit."

"Ohhh! A cuddle? The scandal!" She slapped her hand over her mouth in mock horror.

"Technically, we've cuddled twice now," I admitted sheepishly. "And I wish it had been more than that."

"Sadie! Who are you? It's like I don't even know you anymore." She shook her head and giggled. "But tell me everything. I want all the details."

I groaned. I was supposed to be the one grilling her about her night with Heath. She was the one with the exciting dating life and line of suitors. I was the one who stayed home and got lost in romance novels and kept my escapades securely locked in daydream mode. It was odd to be on the other side of things. So, I gave her the highlights of our night.

"So, nothing too scandalous, right?"

"Have you ever done anything even remotely scandalous in your entire life?"

I considered the question and said, "Remember that time in fourth grade when I stole the scented markers from Mrs. East?"

"The ones you brought home and were too scared to use or sniff and brought back the next day?"

I grinned at the memory. I'd been so scared of getting caught and then expelled. "I was a common thief for twenty-four whole hours."

"Yeah, that doesn't count," Ava said, laughing. "I know you probably don't want to talk about feelings and all the mushy things, but I'm here."

"It's not that I don't want to talk. It's that I don't know what to say. I don't understand why this is happening."

"He's a decent guy. He's gentle, patient, and smart. And he's not exactly a troll."

I nodded. "He makes me feel safe even when I'm not even remotely close to being safe. He takes me seriously. I don't ever feel like he's mocking me. And did you see him when he took his shirt off?" An image of his bare chest and abs flashed in my mind.

"I did. I see all of those other things, too. The way he looks at you and hovers nearby when you're about to try something new—if you could see what I see, you wouldn't be questioning any of this."

"He's a client, Ava, and I'm too messy. You know me ... I don't do relationships. I don't do any of this. This is all wrong."

"What if it's not? What if he's everything you need? What if this is your chance to be happy?"

Her words slammed into me like a punch to the gut. I couldn't have blinked away the tears if I wanted to. Every one of those questions came with an answer loaded with trauma and a lifetime of disappointment. If things ended badly, I'd lose more than Tripp. Take the Leap was now crucial to our business and bottom line. We spent nearly every hour working on their account between the challenges, content creation, general marketing, and publicity. Even with the new client leads, we wouldn't be able to replace what we'd lose if they jumped ship.

"Can you look at me?" Ava asked softly. I rolled my head from side to side. No. I knew if I looked up, she'd see my red-rimmed, tear-stained eyes. Then she'd give me the look that would break me completely. Pity. "Sadie?"

Silence filled the space between us. She waited patiently for me to respond. I hated the way being emotionally vulnerable made me want to retreat into hibernation. Constantly being at war with yourself is exhausting. I didn't want to keep fighting, but I didn't know how not to. I'd been fighting for as long as I can remember. Like fear, it's second nature. I don't have to say what I'm thinking. My best friend read my face like a book.

"No, don't go there, Sadie. You are worth everything. You're worthy of love and deserve someone who truly sees and knows you. I don't care what your past says. People don't always leave, and if they do, it's not because of you. I know you, Sadie. I *know* you. I've been on the other end of your friendship and love for more than half my life. You are a kind, supportive, and loving friend. You're an amazing person when you finally let your walls down and bring people into your bubble. No one deserves someone like Tripp more than you."

Her words washed over me like a weighted blanket. I don't bother fighting the tears as they welled and finally released down my cheeks. She was at my side before the second tear fell. She leaned over me and wrapped her arms around me.

"I can't do this." The words came out broken. I sucked in a deep breath and tried to calm the swell of desperation flooding through me. "I don't know how."

"The same way you've tackled every one of these challenges. You take it one step and one breath at a time. You let him in little by little. You stop hiding behind your fears and lean into the things that make you happy."

"And if he runs for the hills as soon as he sees just how much of a disaster I am?"

"You're not a disaster. You're a human being who's experienced far too much loss and heartbreak," she said reassuringly. "Besides, I don't think he's going anywhere."

"I hope you're right," I said. I wanted to list out the thousand other what ifs that have been racing through my thoughts for the last few days, but I don't. Ava already knows, and verbalizing them will only give more power to my fears.

For the first time in my life, I told my inner scaredy cat to shut up and focused on what Ava was saying. If she was wrong, I could handle it. I was used to being heartbroken and disappointed. But if she wasn't wrong? The possibility of getting my own happy ending sparked something hopeful inside me, and I wanted to cling to it like a life jacket.

twenty-one

MORNING CAME FAR TOO SOON. I packed us a quick breakfast to eat in the car and brewed an extra-large mug of coffee for both of us. We had to meet Olivia, Tripp, and the rest of the team by eight. The plan was to get an early start to avoid the rain that was forecast for the afternoon. We drove to Shelby Park in silence. I sensed that Ava wanted to bring up the conversation we'd had yesterday, but I didn't have it in me. Melatonin-fueled dreams haunted my sleep. Every last one of them centered on Tripp. Some were amazing, and others were nightmares I wish I could forget. All of them were forever seared into my memory.

Ava parked her car next to Tripp's Jeep. "Anything you want to talk about before we embark on an hour-long kayak tour?"

"Nope. Nothing." I tugged my hair into a tight bun and flung open the car door. I paused, leaned back into the car, and said, "I'm sorry. I didn't sleep well, and I'm grumpy. I shouldn't be taking that out on you."

"I know. You were talking in your sleep last night."

"I was?" Oh, god. What had I said? I hoped it wasn't during

the dream where Tripp and I went on a tandem bungee jump in our birthday suits. Heat radiated from my core as I remembered the details of that dream. I fanned my face.

But Ava was frowning. "You were talking to your grandmother."

Oh. My heart clenched. The memory of that dream was equally vivid. "I'd dreamt that she got to meet Tripp."

"She'd have loved him," Ava said softly. She'd known and loved Gran almost as much as I had.

"Yes, she would've." I reached over and squeezed Ava's hand. "Do you think she'd enjoy watching me do all these challenges?"

"Are you kidding? Gran would've been out here with us." Ava laughed. She was right, Gran loved trying new things and exploring the world with Seth and me.

"Especially the hot air balloon ride." A flood of warmth calmed my nerves as I imagined Gran up in the hot air balloon snapping photos and imaging animal shapes in the clouds. "But, I think she'd have enjoyed this kayak trip, too."

Ava nodded. I swiped a tear away from my eye and took a deep breath to steady myself. Gran wouldn't want me to mourn her today. She'd want me to get out of the car and go explore the river with my friends and clients. She'd tell me to find my happy and lean into it. So, I climbed out of the car and made my way to where the team was waiting for us.

Tripp, Olivia, Liam, and Kyle gathered at the river's edge. They were already in their gear and ready to go.

"Are you going out too?" Olivia asked Ava. Concern filled her voice. Ava hadn't joined in on any of our practices, and I could see Olivia sizing her up to make sure she'd be able to manage a kayak.

"Yes, I've done this a few times. Liam said I could go with him."

"You're with me." Olivia moved toward us. When she got close enough to whisper, she said, "They've been fighting over who gets to sit with me for the last five minutes. Save me. Please."

Ava smiled and agreed. She left me and followed Olivia to the middle kayak. I stifled a laugh as Liam and Kyle watched the two women walk past them without so much as a good morning or hello.

"How are you feeling?" Tripp asked. I don't think he realized just how loaded that question was. I felt great about the kayak. We'd practiced enough that I wasn't even nervous. I was ready for this. Besides, there weren't any heights involved today. Just the risk of drowning, water snakes, and rogue river pirates.

"Great," I said. "But quick question ... are river pirates a thing?"

He laughed and shook his head. "Not in metro Nashville."

"Phew." I wiped my hand across my forehead and grinned up at him.

Liam approached and adjusted the camera on my helmet. "Be sure to turn around and get some footage of this handsome man's face, okay?" He turned to walk away before I could answer him.

I followed Tripp down to the riverbank. Olivia went through the safety guidelines while we all settled into our kayaks. Once we were ready to push into the water, Tripp confirmed I was set as well. I answered with a quick nod of my head and checked my grip on the paddle. This morning, those two days of practice had felt sufficient enough, but now that the nose of the boat was heading into the water, I began to doubt myself. I double-checked the paddle position and then turned back to Tripp. His warm smile immediately soothed my initial round of nerves. He always smiled like that when he knew I was scared.

"Don't worry, I'm not going to panic today. You and Olivia did a great job preparing me. But," I added, blushing, "am I holding this right?"

"Perfect." He leaned forward and pushed us fully into the river. I settled into my seat and shifted until we felt balanced. Then we were off.

We floated down the river in silence for what felt like an eternity. I didn't have to talk to him to know he was there. I felt his calming, confident presence. Every so often, his foot would brush against my back as if he were saying, *I'm still here.*

It was still early enough that the morning fog hadn't completely burned off the river. We floated into the thick grey mist. I couldn't see the others, but I could hear the soft chatter of their conversations. If I let my imagination run wild, I could almost pretend that Tripp and I were out here alone on a romantic morning date after a perfect night together. I bet he was the type that woke up ready for good morning kisses regardless of how bad your morning breath was. He also seemed like the kind of guy that would bring you breakfast in bed for no reason or let you sleep in while he went to get your favorite coffee and just because flowers. I quickly shut down that train of thought and focused on making sure my paddle strokes were smooth and well-paced.

I wondered if we were getting enough good footage. I knew the fog would limit what Liam would capture, so it was up to our head cameras to fill in the gaps. As much as I wanted to turn around and stare at Tripp, I wasn't sure my heart could take it. I'd barely looked at him when we'd gotten here this morning. Every time I did, a flash of one of my dreams clouded my vision. I took a slow, measured breath and mentally counted to ten before turning toward him.

"This is much calmer than I was expecting," I said.

"Were you expecting rapids and waterfalls?"

I shrugged. "Or water snakes and gators."

"Gators in Nashville?"

"Maybe one escaped from the zoo."

"I suppose that's possible."

"I bet there's one lurking up ahead, just chomping at the bit for one of us to fall in."

"I'll let them eat me first, deal?"

"No!" I said too quickly. Fear gripped my chest as I pictured him being eaten by an escaped alligator. "Let's throw him Liam."

"I heard that!" Liam said from the boat next to us. "And here I thought we were going to be friends. But no, you're ready to sacrifice me to an imaginary gator. Rude."

"Sorry. I'm still weirded out by this new and nice version of you." For a split second, I forgot we were on a kayak in the middle of the Cumberland River. I leaned to the side to whisper conspiratorially to Liam, "I'll only let him eat an arm. Then, I'll whack him with my paddle." Still leaning toward him, I tilted the paddle to show him I meant business.

A shout from Tripp pulled my attention back to the kayak and the river. But it was too late. We were already tipping to the side.

I forgot everything I'd learned earlier in the week and flung the paddle away from me as I tried to steady myself. It didn't work. The kayak pitched to the side and threw both of us into the water. I flailed my arms, and my wrist slammed into the edge of Liam and Kyle's boat. A sharp pain shot up my arm. Before going underwater, the last thing I saw was their kayak rocking to the side.

I kicked my feet to push back up. Tripp swam toward me and pulled me to him.

"Are you okay?" Panic seized his face as he searched mine for any sign of injury.

"I think so." I coughed. Once again, I hadn't closed my mouth before plunging below the surface. I helped him right the kayak, wincing from the pain in my wrist. I didn't say anything but shifted the weight to my left hand.

Tripp hoisted himself onto the kayak and reached to help me up. I shook my head. I could do this without him helping and risking flipping us back into the water. I put my hands on the edge of the boat and pulled myself up. Pain throbbed in my right wrist. I tried to ignore it until I was out of the frigid water, but it was almost too much. When I finally got on the boat, I glanced down at my wrist. *Crap.* It was already swelling.

Olivia had retrieved my paddle. Her gaze followed mine down to where I was cradling my arm. She handed it to me and asked, "Was that your wrist I heard cracking against their kayak?"

Nodding, I replied, "Yes. I think it might be sprained or something."

She shot a worried look toward Tripp. With the other two kayaks on either side of us, keeping us steady, he leaned over my shoulder. His arms came around me as he gingerly lifted my hand away from the wrist I was trying to hide from him. "We need to get her to the doctor. Olivia, will it be faster to turn around or keep pushing forward?"

She took a moment to survey our surroundings. "I think we keep pushing forward. The current working with us will help us get downtown faster. Do you think you can still paddle?" she asked me.

I tried to hold the paddle with my injured hand. I couldn't grip it tight enough to hold it steady. Pain shot up my entire arm. I gasped, unable to pretend that hadn't hurt. "I don't think so."

"I can paddle for both of us. Liam, give me your keys. Olivia will take the rest of you back to Shelby Park while I take Sadie to the hospital."

Liam handed his car keys over to Tripp while Ava protested. "I'm going with you."

Tripp didn't argue. He just said, "Then you better be able to keep up." To me he added, "Hold your paddle flat across your lap. Don't move your wrist."

I didn't argue. The concern in his voice and the fear in his eyes scared me. My wrist hurt and was swelling, but it wasn't like I was going to need it amputated or anything. It was probably nothing more than a sprain or a small fracture. I dipped my hand into the water; the cold soothed the ache. The rest of my body shivered in response. My clothes, sopping wet with river water, clung to my skin. I wondered if I'd ever feel warm again.

"I hope his truck has heated seats." I tried joking, but Tripp was all business. His jaw clenched as he started paddling. I watched his muscles beneath his river-soaked shirt. They flexed with every stroke of the paddle. He kept his eyes trained on the river ahead of us with a look of sheer determination. It was almost as if he were angry.

"I'm sorry," I said and turned away from him. This was entirely my fault. If I hadn't been too comfortable in the kayak, I wouldn't have leaned over to tease Liam. If I'd paid closer attention to Olivia's instructions, I might have fallen into the river with more grace. If I were him, I'd be angry at me too. Not only was he freezing and soaking wet, but now he had to rush through what was supposed to be a relaxing float trip and spend his afternoon with me in the ER. "You can drop me and Ava off at her car. She can take me."

"No." His sharp tone startled me. "I'm not leaving you."

twenty-two

"I'M SUCH AN IDIOT." My teeth chattered from the cold. I leaned deeper into the leather seat of Liam's truck. "And a klutz. Who breaks their wrist on a completely calm and boring kayak float? Me."

Thankfully, his truck did have heated seats. That, combined with Olivia's dry clothes and blanket, had been a welcome surprise. While Tripp warmed up the truck, Ava had helped me out of the wet clothes. She was careful to keep my wrist elevated and make sure no one else caught a peek at me while I changed.

"Don't blame yourself," Tripp's voice was strained, his teeth clenched against the cold. "This isn't your fault. We should've picked another weekend and done more practice. The fog didn't help anything." He was still wearing the same clothes, soaked to the bone from the river's unforgiving water.

I didn't respond. I turned and kept my gaze fixed on the world passing us by outside the truck. Thankfully, we weren't too far from Vanderbilt. He dropped us off at the emergency entrance and promised to meet us inside once we parked.

Inside the ER, Ava dug through my crossbody bag to find

my ID and insurance card. Since the swollen wrist was my dominant hand, she also filled out all of the paperwork. I cradled my wrist in my arm and tried to ignore the throbbing pain. Every heartbeat sent a shock of pain from my elbow to the tip of my finger. I tried my best to hold as still as humanly possible.

"Date of your last menstrual cycle? Oh, wait. It was last Tuesday, right?" It was embarrassing how well she knew me. "You're definitely *not* pregnant, am I right?"

"Hah. Nope."

Before she could move on to the next section, a tall brunette woman dressed in scrubs called my name. We'd barely finished checking in, and the waiting room was packed. Based on what the intake nurse had said, it should've been at least an hour before we got to see the triage nurse. I glanced up in confusion as the woman approached us. When she got close enough, I read her name badge: Dr. Kelsey James. Since when did doctors retrieve patients from the waiting room?

"Sadie?" she asked and peered down at my wrist. She gently took it into her hands and applied a tiny bit of pressure. Another wave of pain shot down my arm. I gasped. "I'm Dr. James. Tripp called me, panicking and demanding that I come to see you at once."

"Sister?" Ava guessed. Dr. James nodded.

"Let's get you back and get some X-rays, okay?"

"Do I need to finish checking in?"

"No, bring the paperwork with you and finish in the back."

"I'm okay to wait like everyone else."

"When my baby brother calls and begs me to help the girl he's been obsessing over for weeks, I pull all the strings I can. Besides, it's been surprisingly quiet today. Now, let's get back there before Tripp shows up and ruins all the fun."

"Too late," Tripp said. He rushed through the security

entrance, barely pausing long enough to empty his pockets. His shoes squeaked across the linoleum floors. "Thanks, Kels."

"Bummer. I was going to tell her all your embarrassing stories. Believe me, there are plenty."

I stood between them both, stunned. He'd told his sister about me? Enough for her to say he was obsessing over me? I tried to process this information but couldn't. Ava nudged me forward when they started toward the doors. I followed close behind, still unable to speak. Tripp filled his sister in on as many details as he could.

"The swelling went down a little. She dunked it in the river while we kayaked back. I think that helped. But it's tender to the touch and bruising."

"Smart move. The cold water likely helped control the swelling. We'll put you in room 115, but first, I'll take you down to imaging. Do you want to go with her?" she asked Ava.

"I will," Tripp answered before Ava could. "That way, you can finish the paperwork."

"Right, of course." Ava gave me a knowing glance before disappearing into the room. I rolled my eyes and focused on the pain in my wrist. It had been intensifying since we'd left the river. The cold water had helped, but now it pulsed with pain. As much as I hated hurting, it was easier to focus on the pain than it was to obsess over the fact that he'd been obsessing over me. Pain, I understood. But I didn't have the emotional or mental capacity to think about what Tripp had told his sister.

The X-ray confirmed I had indeed fractured my wrist. Thankfully, it was a small hairline fracture that should heal without surgery. I hadn't even been considering the possibility of surgery. All I'd need was a splint and to rest it for three to four weeks. I shouldn't need too much rehab time. Dr. James prescribed a strong painkiller and showed me how to take care of the splint. Tripp took notes on his phone and promised to share them with both Ava and me. He hovered while they put the splint on as if he were supervising the doctors. He stayed glued to my side the entire time.

"My nurse will call to make a follow-up appointment."

"Great, thank you," I said, my words slurring as the pain medication kicked in. I was going to sleep well when we got home…maybe even before then.

I was acutely aware of Tripp holding me up and helping me into the truck. He drove us home, helped me up the stairs, and carefully placed me in the bed. Then, I don't remember much. My sleep was hard and dreamless. It was nearly dark when I awoke. Groggy, I sat up. The pain in my wrist had returned, but it was a dull ache that I had a feeling would linger for a few days. As much as I appreciated the numbness from the strong pain medication, I wasn't a fan of how heavy my eyes were hours later.

"You're awake," a deep voice said from my reading chair. Tripp.

"How long have you been here?" My throat was dry. He stood and handed me a water bottle along with another pill.

"Long enough to know you have the most adorable little snore."

I laughed weakly. I did snore, but it was anything but adorable. "You must find freight trains adorable, then." I tossed the medicine into my mouth and took a gulp of water.

"Only ones packed inside hazel-eyed, petite women. How's the wrist?"

"A little sore, but better than it was. You don't have to stay. As soon as this medicine kicks in, I'm probably going to pass out again."

"I know. I want to."

Maybe it was the pain medication, or maybe it was the

pure rawness of his voice, but I had an overwhelming need to go to him. It started deep inside me as a whisper but grew stronger every second I waited to act on it. I sat up and immediately regretted the quick movement. My head spun. I laid back down. Tripp was up and beside me before my head hit the pillow.

"Easy."

"Sit with me?" I asked. The bed shifted under his weight. He sat perched on the edge of the bed, but he was still too far away. "Lie with me?"

He hesitated long enough for me to wonder if I'd gone too far. I was about to take back the invitation when he settled back onto the bed and beside me. He slipped one arm under my shoulders, and I curled toward him and rested my arm across his stomach. He gently ran his fingertips over my arm between the splint and my shirt sleeve. Neither of us spoke. His chest rose and fell with the rhythm of his steady breath. I nestled deeper into the crook of his arm. He'd changed out of the river clothes. He smelled of fresh linen, but a hint of the river and outdoors still clung to his skin. I breathed in deeply to memorize the scent.

"So, you told your sister about me?" I asked.

"All of them, yeah."

"What did you tell them?" I both wanted to know and didn't want to know. My eyes were already heavy with sleep.

"I think you know the answer to that." He pressed a soft kiss to the top of my head. As his lips lingered, his breath made my hair dance. I tilted my head back and met his gaze. The intensity in his eyes told me all I needed to know. It was as if they were peering straight into my soul. I drank him in, taking every drop I could get.

"So, I'm not imagining all of this?" I asked.

"No." This time, his lips found my forehead. He kissed a

trail of tiny kisses along my hairline but stopped before he reached my cheek. He pulled back and stroked his fingers down my cheek and over my lips. Desperate to touch him, I lifted my hand and ignored the tug of pain in my wrist. He gently pushed my arm back down. His fingers stroked my arm just as he'd done before. He placed one last kiss on my forehead. "Get some sleep, Sadie."

"I'm not tired," I mumbled, barely able to keep my eyes open. My eyelids fluttered. I forced them open and pleaded with him. "Don't leave, okay?"

"Never."

I settled back into the crook of his arm and let the heaviness take over. I couldn't have stayed awake and analyzed this entire moment if I wanted to. That was a worry for tomorrow. Tonight, I'd enjoy the comfort of him beside me.

twenty-three

SUNDAY MORNING, I awoke to an empty bed and a note from Tripp. Disappointment settled into my veins. He left. *I'll be back soon. I promise.*

I stretched my arms over my head and nearly gagged at the smell that flooded my nose when I took a deep breath. *Was that me?* I pulled my arm up to my nose and sniffed. Yup. That was definitely me. I smelled like stale toilet water. After taking a quick shower, careful to keep my splint dry. I threw on a clean pair of pajamas and head out into the living area. I knew without a doubt that Ava would be waiting for me. I could count on her.

"She lives!" Ava said cheerfully when I walked out into the living area.

"Barely. What time is it?"

"Noon. Lunch will be here soon. We ordered your favorite." We? Was Seth here?

"Good, I'm starving." I was tempted to ask her if she saw Tripp sneak out, but I wasn't ready to tell her about last night. I wasn't even sure if it really happened or If I'd just dreamt the whole thing, which was a sad possibility. But at least if it were a dream, his disappearance wouldn't sting so much.

"Do you need anything? Pain meds? Diet Coke?"

"Water and an ibuprofen. I don't want to pass out and miss another day." That was a lie. I very much wanted to pass out and sleep the day away. A heavy grogginess settled over me.

Before Ava could answer, the strong scent of spice and Thai food wafted up the stairs. My stomach growled. I followed the scent to the stairs. Tripp held out the bag of takeout. I met his gaze and smiled.

"Hey," he said, greeting me with a broad smile that reached his eyes.

"Hi."

"Food," Ava said and grabbed the bag from his hand. "You two can keep making eyes at each other, but I'm hungry." I didn't have the energy to argue with her, and I didn't have a case to argue. She was right. I was making eyes at him, and he was returning them right back to me. It ignited a tiny spark of hope.

Ava sat at the far end of the sofa, leaving Tripp no choice but to sit beside me. He scooted close enough that our legs were touching. Instinct made me want to pull away, but I didn't move. Fear crept into my bones. Everything inside my brain told me to run and ignore this overwhelming desire I had to be near him. The desire won. I let my knee fall to the side and against him. We ate our lunch and watched the show Ava had on. It was her favorite reality show, which I hated. But at least it provided enough distraction to limit conversation. I wasn't sure I was even capable of forming complete sentences with him so close to me.

The pain in my wrist had dulled almost completely, but it still ached enough to distract me. I wondered what this meant for the challenges we still had to complete before the final skydive.

"So, what are we going to do about the remaining challenges?" I asked. I held up my wrist. "This thing doesn't exactly scream, *join our adventures, they're totally safe.*"

Tripp sighed audibly. "Let's not worry about that, now, okay?"

"What about the content?" We had another week or two of buffer content before the kayak video had to go live. After that, we'd be behind. "Can we even use the footage from yesterday? I doubt my klutz move will make for a great advertisement."

"Liam can work his magic. We got plenty of footage during the practice sessions and before the kayak flipped. What we have will be great. It always is." He sounded confident, but I felt anything but confident. His words did little to reassure me. Sure, we'd built a great rapport with Tripp and his team, but a pause in the campaign wasn't something we'd planned for. In hindsight, we should've. I wasn't exactly known for my grace.

"I really mucked this whole thing up. I'm sorry guys." I hated how much the success of the campaign depended on me. "Maybe Ava can do some of the challenges, instead?" Just saying that broke my heart a little. Two months ago, I'd have gladly handed the challenges over to her, but not now. Now I was starting to enjoy the new experiences. And all the time with Tripp. I did not want that to end.

"Stop it, Sadie, please. Things happen. We will figure it out, but it doesn't have to be today. Okay?" Ava exhaled in a huff. "What we aren't going to do is wallow and worry up problems that don't exist yet. You're going to let your wrist heal, and we'll make things work however we have to."

"We're in this for the long haul," Tripp said. "I meant it when I said I wasn't going anywhere."

"Well, we do have the fundraiser to consider," I said. Ava

looked at me with furrowed eyebrows. "Remember for the Leukemia and Lymphoma Society?"

"Oh, right. We discussed it briefly at our meeting last week." Tripp and I had pitched the idea to do some content on his family and the story behind Take the Leap, but we'd gotten distracted by the weekly app download reports. "What's the plan there?"

"My sisters are on board with us filming our annual skydive, which is next weekend. Liam will be out of town, so maybe you two could come along and help film."

"Next weekend?" Ava asked. "Next weekend is Mom's birthday."

"You can't miss that. I can cover it, I think," I said, not sounding at all confident.

"You can?" Ava shot me a look of pure disbelief.

"Sure, why not? I'm great on airplanes without safety equipment."

They both laughed. Tripp patted my knee and said, "There is more than adequate safety gear on the plane, I promise. I think it might also be good for you to see what it's all about before we start preparing for your dive."

I wasn't entirely sure I believed him, but I didn't argue. "Great, then I'll work with Liam to make sure I have everything I need. We should probably make sure you and your family all have cameras, too. We'll want plenty of footage and candid images and commentary."

With that settled, we fell back into a comfortable silence as we ate. After we finished, Ava gathered our empty takeout containers and brought me fresh water. "Are you good if I keep my date with Heath? His friend's band is playing at Brooklyn Bowl."

"Yes, go. I'll be fine."

"I can stick around, too," Tripp said. He turned toward me

and added, "And before you tell me I don't have to stay ... I *want* to stay."

I pushed aside the itch to argue with him. Pushing people away was second nature to me. It was hard to admit that I not only wanted him here but also needed him.

"Okay, I won't." I settled into a cozy nook between him and the arm of the couch. He draped his arm over my shoulder and pulled me closer.

"Yup, you'll be just fine without me." Ava excused herself and went into her room to get ready. When she re-emerged ten minutes later, we'd already switched to a different show, picking up where we'd left off on *Big Bang Theory*. She patted my head before leaving and said, "Don't do anything I wouldn't do."

Then we were alone again. This time, I wasn't drowsy. Every nerve ending in my body was fully aware of Tripp's presence beside me. I half expected to feel my fight or flight response kicking in like it usually did anytime someone got too close to me, but it didn't. My heart didn't race with panic, and I didn't feel the need to come up with an excuse to kick him out. I barely recognized this version of myself. This realization scared me. This was entirely unfamiliar territory.

"Are you comfortable?" Tripp asked.

"Yeah. I think so." Hesitation filled my voice, and he picked up on it. He shifted to move away from me. "No, please don't. It's just that—" I wasn't sure how to finish that sentence. How could I explain to him that even though I wanted him here and very much liked his company, I didn't know what to do with that information.

He leaned forward and placed his hand on my cheek, gently turning me to face him. "Does this make you uncomfortable? Me being here?"

"No," I answered quickly. Too quickly. I pulled back and

buried my face in a pillow. "I don't know, Tripp. This is all new to me. I've never met anyone that made me feel the way you do. I don't know how to do all of this."

"All of what?"

"Feel things." I glanced at his face and immediately dropped my gaze to the floor before I started rambling. "These last few weeks have pushed me so far out of my comfort zone that I don't think I'll ever find that comfort zone again. And the thing is, I don't hate it. The kayak yesterday? That was fun. I was having fun. Maybe because Olivia really helped prepare me, or maybe it was just freeing to do something I'd never done before. I don't want to jump off a bridge again anytime soon, but trying all this new stuff is changing me. You're changing me. I thought I wasn't capable of feeling like this. Like, I want to both run to you and away from you at the same time."

I was rambling. Words tumbled out of my mouth before I could stop them. His hand rubbed soft, slow circles on my back, soothing me without a word. He didn't say anything, but I knew he was listening. There was something about him that made all of my knots untie and want to reveal themselves to him.

"But mostly, I want you to hold me like you did last night and never let go. I don't want to fall asleep. I just want to be near you, and that is terrifying. I mean, you're my client, and a big client at that. What if I screw this up? I mean, not if, but when. Because I will. I always do. I'm not the girl who stays. Even if I want to, I don't think I can. Then what? I lose you as a client, a friend, and whatever this is? I can't handle that. I can't handle any of this."

Tears welled in my eyes. They broke free before I could stop them. "I'm sorry. I'm such a mess. You can leave if you want to. I wouldn't blame you if you did." I'd meant it, but as I said it, a sob so large it nearly choked me rose in my throat. I tried to hold it in but failed. "Ugh! Why am I like this?"

Tripp didn't move. He kept his hand on my back and stayed right by my side as I tried to work through whatever this was. "I'm here as long as you want me here, Sadie."

I curled into him and rested my head on his chest. He continued rubbing my back. "I want you here." And I did. I didn't want him to leave, no matter what I said or felt. Something inside of me shifted. The longer he stayed, the safer I felt with him. That should've scared me, but it didn't.

We stayed like that through three episodes. Then the doorbell rang, and my sense of contentment vanished as soon as I heard my brother's voice announce his presence. He had a key, so the doorbell was a courtesy.

"Sadie?" he yelled up the stairs. "Don't be mad, okay? Dad's here."

twenty-four

MY HEART STOPPED, and a lump rose in my throat. I couldn't have responded if I wanted to. *What are they doing here?* I understood why Seth would show up. I sent him a text about my wrist from the hospital yesterday. I'd assured him I was fine, but my brother couldn't resist an opportunity to check up on me. But Brett? Why was he here? Had he really come all the way from Kansas City? I never should've given my brother a key to the house. If I hadn't, he'd be stuck on the other side of the door, and I could ignore him.

Two sets of feet clomped up the stairs. I shifted away from Tripp and stood. He leaned forward and stood up beside me. My body tensed, ready to either fight or run. My bedroom door had a lock. I could easily lock myself away in there for a few hours. I'd had plenty of food, so I wouldn't be hungry until at least dinner time. I'd settle for bathroom sink water if it meant I could avoid spending any time with Brett. I glanced toward the bedroom and back at Tripp. I couldn't leave him out here on his own. Could I? Surely, he'd understand. Besides, Seth and he were friends. Well, at least they knew each other on a professional level.

Before I could make up my mind, my brother and Brett were at the top of the stairs. Brett's gaze went straight to my splint. There was a visible sigh of relief when he realized it wasn't terrible. Based on the look of terror on his face, he'd been expecting much worse. Satisfied I wasn't about to lose a limb, he turned his attention to Tripp. He was there beside me. His hand reached for me, interlaced his fingers between mine, and squeezed. He wasn't even considering abandoning me. That knowledge alone made me grateful I hadn't retreated to my bedroom. Seth caught my eye and raised an eyebrow as he glanced between Tripp and me. I hadn't spoken to my brother in a few days, so he was not up to date on whatever this was with us.

"Sorry to show up unannounced," Seth said. "Hey, Tripp. I didn't expect to see you here." If I didn't know any better, I'd say my brother's voice had a hint of protectiveness. Interesting.

"He's been here since last night," I said. Seth cocked his head to the side and stared me down. Brett shifted his weight between his legs and glanced between Tripp, Seth, and me. His mouth was creased into a tight line, like he didn't know whether to frown or scowl. "Just to make sure I'm okay and keep me company while Ava is out with her boyfriend."

"Ava has a boyfriend?" This time, I couldn't decipher what I was hearing in his voice, but I could dissect that later. The more important question had to do with the man standing beside my brother.

"What is *he* doing here?" I asked. I didn't bother hiding the disgusting taste that question left in my mouth.

"I called him after you messaged about the accident."

"Accident? I have a tiny hairline fracture on my wrist. Hardly worth his time."

"I'm right here, Sadie," Brett said. "You can talk to me, you know."

"Can I?"

"Yes, of course. You're my daughter. You can call or text me any time. I'm worried about you. It's not just the wrist but everything I've seen on social media recently. The bungee jumping? Hot air balloon rides? I mean, I barely recognize you. All of this seems like a cry for help. It's so out of character for you."

Tripp stepped forward and opened his mouth to speak. I tugged his hand to pull him back. While I appreciated his desire to speak up for me, I could handle my father. "No, Brett, it's my job. And even if it weren't, you are the last person on earth who gets to decide what is and isn't out of character for me."

Seth sighed and shook his head at me. "I think what Dad is trying to say is —"

"No, Seth, don't defend him. You know exactly what I am doing and why."

"Maybe, but you're different."

"Maybe I am, how is that a bad thing? How is it any of his business? None of this," I said, waving my uninjured hand around me and Tripp, "has anything to do with you."

Tripp's grip on my hand tightened. "I get that you're worried about your sister, man, but maybe this isn't the best time to be springing more surprises on her."

"Stay out of this," Seth snapped at Tripp.

I held up my hands. "No, please don't take your frustration with me out on him. This has nothing to do with him, but he's right. Now isn't the best time. You can't just show up with Brett like this."

"We're family."

"We are." I pointed between Seth and me. "You're my brother. He's a distant relative." Tripp squeezed my hand again.

"No, you're right," Brett said. He handed me a gift bag. "Mel sent a care package. She broke her dominant arm a few years ago, and these are all the things that helped her maintain her independence while healing."

I reluctantly took the bag and peered inside. "A bidet?" Heat flushed my cheeks. Despite the instant embarrassment, a giggle rose in my throat. "I hadn't even thought about ... that."

I couldn't hold the laughter back. Curiosity got the better of me, and I set the bag on the table to inspect the rest of the contents. Mel had managed to pack a bidet, a back scratcher, an eBook reader stand and a remote control, along with all of my favorite snacks into the gift bag. There was even a gift card to our local independent bookstore.

A strange burst of warmth flooded my body. She'd pulled all of this together and sent it with Brett on a plane in less than twenty-four hours. She'd done it for me, the ungrateful step-daughter who always treated her like a parasite.

Tripp's warm hand pressed against my back.

"I don't know what to say," I admitted.

"I'm sorry would be a great place to start," Seth said.

"No, you don't owe anyone, especially me, an apology," Brett said.

"Tell her thank you for me, please." I carried the bag into my bedroom and closed the door behind me. I sank onto the bed and closed my eyes. Placing my hand over my chest, I tried to calm my racing heart. Between the conversation with Tripp earlier and all of this, the swell of emotions threatened to undo me completely. I wasn't going to let that happen, though. I'd cried enough tears over my dad. I'd vowed never to let him break my heart again a long time ago, but this was a new kind of ache, and it was still too much. I drew in a deep breath and steadied myself. I couldn't leave Tripp to fend for himself.

I'd only been gone a minute or two, but when I returned,

the three men were sitting on the couch, watching something on Tripp's phone. Did they become best friends already? Was Tripp taking their side? Not that there was a side to choose in this situation, but if there was, I knew without a doubt that he'd choose me.

"What are you watching?" I asked.

"Oh, I was showing them some of the footage from the kayak practice."

"He was bragging about how awesome you were at the wet exit. I'm impressed, sis. You even look like you're enjoying yourself." Seth had been on a few kayaking trips over the years, granted his were usually a bit more exciting than a float down the Cumberland River.

"I was," I admitted. "Of all the challenges so far, the kayak has been my favorite. Despite this." I held up my arm.

"Does it hurt?" Brett asked.

I had to give him some credit; despite my very intense efforts to shut him out, he kept trying. He stood and walked toward me. I fought the urge to pull away from him. I glanced at Seth and Tripp sitting on couch. Tripp raised his eyebrow as if to ask if I needed him, I shook my head. No, I could handle my father.

I let him take my wrist into his hand gently so he could inspect it.

"Not right now, but it did. They said it should heal within three or four weeks. So, I won't be out of commission for long."

"Already ready for another adventure?" Seth asked.

"Yeah, I am." The honest answer surprised me. It shouldn't have. Something had changed between the hot air balloon and the kayak. I couldn't describe the feeling exactly, but it was as if I'd found a long-dead part of myself. I'd never pushed myself as much as I had these last few months. I'd just accepted the status quo and hadn't let myself imagine a life that didn't involve constant fear. I didn't hesitate at the elevator when we visited Tripp's office. I'd even gone up a few times without Ava.

"I'm sure this isn't the best time to say this, but I need to say it someday, Sadie. Why not today?" Brett asked. He drew in a slow, measured breath as he stood and walked toward me.

I looked at him in confusion. "What?"

"I've made a lot of bad decisions in my life regarding the two of you. I know I can't undo any of it, but I wish I could."

"Please, don't," I said. I wasn't ready for this speech. I'd dreamt of it often as a child—the day my dad finally admitted he'd made a mistake walking out on us. The day he begged for my forgiveness and told me how much he loved and missed us. "Not now."

"Can you let me finish?"

"No, I can't. I'm sorry." I needed to set this boundary almost as much as I needed to hear him say the words. "Not when you're here because I got injured, and not when it's from a place of guilt. I'm not here to make you feel better about abandoning your family. I appreciate you coming, and the gift from Mel was very thoughtful, but I'd like you to go. I'm not sure I'm ready for any of this. Not yet anyway."

Dejected, his face fell. He stepped back, putting more distance between us. But he didn't fight me. He respected my wishes. "I'll wait in your car, Seth."

"Wait, Brett, thank you for showing up today. I'll call you soon, okay?" He was trying and watching him turn his back to leave nearly broke me. He'd dropped everything to be here for me. I could see the pureness of his intention, even if I wasn't ready to welcome him with open arms.

"I know I haven't always been there, but I promise I'm going to be here as much as I can," Brett said.

"I'll call you, okay?" I watched him walk back downstairs and waited for the door to close before turning to Seth. "You can't just show up with him like this. I know what you're doing and why, but you can't force me into forgiving him. Even if you could, it wouldn't automatically heal every broken thing. And it's not fair to me or to him."

"I'm still going to try. I can't give up on us."

"I don't want you to." And I didn't. I appreciated his desire to have a whole family after we'd been broken for so long. He gave me a quick hug before turning to go.

He gave Tripp one last look that said *I'm watching you.* I rolled my eyes. He played the role of protective brother a little too well sometimes.

twenty-five

I STOOD on the tarmac at the small airport and glanced at the chaos around me. The second I climbed out of Tripp's car, I fell into a stunned silence. His sisters, all three of them, rushed toward me. The cacophony of their voices sent a shrill of panic through me. I didn't have time to melt down or give into the attack. Kelsey inspected my wrist and peppered me with questions about how it was healing. His youngest sister, a bubbly girl with the softest, sweetest voice I'd ever heard, demanded to know what a "hottie" like me was doing with her loser brother. Tripp rolled his eyes and whispered her name into my ear, "That's Zoe. She'll talk your ear off if you let her."

I silently pleaded with him to please save me. He shrugged as if to say he had no control over his sisters. He'd warned me this would happen.

Lydia, the middle sister, stood off the side, yelling at her sisters to give me space to breathe. "Come on, guys, you're going to scare her off. And Lord knows this one won't bring another girl around ever again."

Zoe grabbed my arm and tugged me toward the plane, which I'd been avoiding acknowledging. "She's right. He never brings girls around. We'd just assumed it was because he was too lame to catch a decent girl. Way to prove us wrong, William Edward."

"William Edward?" I asked and glared back at Tripp. "Who's William Edward?"

Zoe giggled. "He hasn't told you his full name?" When I shook my head she tsked at her brother in disappointment. "William Edward James the Third. We call him Tripp for obvious reasons."

"Right, because he's the third."

"That and he has three first names," Kelsey said. "When he was little, he got in trouble so much that mom was always yelling 'William Edward James,' and he got confused about what his name was. He'd tell everyone something different. We started calling him Tripp, so his brain wouldn't overload." She rubbed the top of his head affectionately.

"Are Mom and Dad coming today?" Lydia asked.

Tripp shook his head and said, "No, but they're going to meet us at the drop point."

"Are you jumping with us today?" Zoe asked, wrapping her arm around my shoulder.

"Nope. I still have a few months before I leap to my death." All three sisters laughed. Tripp didn't join them. His eyes flicked down toward my wrist. His lips turned down, and he looked away quickly. "I'm here to help grab content for the feature we're doing on Noah and what inspired Tripp to start Take the Leap." I held up the small camera Liam had lent me.

With that, the James sisters were ready to chat. I held up the camera and tried to keep up with their conversation.

"That first jump was my idea," Lydia said as she smiled at her brother, "Tripp almost chickened out at the last minute. But he ended up falling in love with the sport."

"I was terrified for the first dive. Kelsey had to keep

reminding we were doing it for Noah," Tripp admitted. "As soon as I felt that first hint of weightlessness, I was hooked. Those first few seconds of free falling cleared my mind, and it felt like I was able to breathe for the first time since Noah was diagnosed."

My heart squeezed at the soft smile he offered the camera, and me.

"Mom and Dad tried to talk us out of it, too," Zoe said, laughing. "We lied to them, remember? We told them we were going to buy Noah a new video game."

"That's right," Kelsey said, "I completely forgot about that. They didn't know we'd done it until we showed the video to Noah."

"I thought they were going to kill us!" Zoe shook her head.

"Until they saw how happy the video made Noah," Tripp said quietly. "I'll always have that final memory of laughing with him as we watched the video. Every time I dive or do something new with Take the Leap, I swear I can still hear his little giggle."

For a moment, I think we all forgot we were filming. I wasn't sure if I should be wearing my marketing hat or my girl-friend, er, friend, whatever I was, hat. We were getting content gold, but all I wanted to do was drop the camera and hold him. I opted for something in the middle and held out my hand to him without putting down the camera. He took my hand, and I rubbed my finger over his knuckles.

"I think Noah would've loved everything you've created and done with Take the Leap," Kelsey said. She placed her hand on top of mine. Lydia and Zoe added theirs to the small pile. "I know I do."

We kept our hands stacked for a few more seconds until the pilot approached us to let us know it was almost time. While Tripp reviewed the flight plan with the pilot and the

James siblings got into their gear, I stood aside and drank in every drop of their family bond. I'd always wondered what it would've been like to have sisters or a big family. It was a ridiculous fantasy, but I would often daydream that my mother had lived, and they went on to have more kids. Always another boy and girl. Even in my delusion, I kept the gender scales balanced. I never knew whether they'd planned to have more, and I didn't ask. The truth wasn't nearly as fun as my imagination.

"Are you sure you want to go up?" Tripp pulled me aside to ask. "You can still get a ride over to the drop site. Mom and Dad both promised to be on their best behavior."

As tempting as it was to have an out, I wasn't ready to meet his parents just yet. The plan was to go up, watch them jump, then return to the airfield. I'd drive Tripp's Jeep back to the landing zone and pick him up. Then I'd meet the parents over lunch. I was still surprised he'd invited me along today. Neither Kelsey nor Lydia brought along their spouses. Doubt built inside me. I swallowed back the lump in my throat and asked again, "Are you sure it's okay that I'm here? I know how special today is for you all."

He'd spent the drive out here talking about Noah. He spoke about him in the present tense, as if he were forever alive and five years old. "Yes, I want you here."

I let that be the final answer. His sisters seemed fine with my being there. Maybe I was a welcome distraction from the painful memories this day inevitably brought back to life. I'd happily take on that role.

"So, who has the most embarrassing Tripp story?" I asked when his sisters approached us.

"Never mind," Tripp said and pulled me back.

"Nope, too late. I'm here, and I'm not missing any opportunity to gather as much dirt as possible."

Zoe nodded with an approving smile. "I like you, Sadie." She then launched into a story from when Tripp was a teenager. I tried my hardest to focus on her words, but he was the only thing I was paying attention to. With each story they told, and they had plenty, he just shook his head and laughed along. He'd drop in a fact correction or new detail if they left something out, but he let them go on and on about all the dumb and embarrassing things he did. By the time the plane roared to life behind us, I'd almost completely forgotten the real reason we were here. The engines reminded them as well. The storytelling stopped, and they naturally navigated toward each other. Tripp reached for my hand and pulled me into their circle.

"Happy birthday, Noah Bear," Zoe said. They bowed their heads.

I joined them in their moment of silence. I squeezed Tripp's hand. He'd spent so much time comforting and reassuring me that it was nice to return the gesture. He leaned in and rested his head against mine. "I've got you," I whispered to him. A tiny smile tugged at his lips. I'd never said those words to anyone before. Until Tripp, no one had ever said them to me, either. For three simple words, they carried so much intimacy and power. Even when he didn't say them out loud, I knew he was thinking them. I wanted him to know I was here, too.

As I boarded the plane, my throat tightened. It felt as if my knees were about to give out. I drew in a slow, deep breath to steady myself. I'd never been on a plane this small. If I flew, I always made sure the plane was a massive one with at least two engines and multiple emergency exits before I booked the flight. This plane appeared to have none of those things. It had propellers on each of the wings. There weren't seats with tray tables or friendly flight attendants smiling to reassure me.

I closed my eyes and took a deep breath. I held it in while I counted to ten. I could do this. I was just going up. I wasn't jumping. I was there for Tripp, not for me. He waited patiently beside me as I gathered the courage to board along with them. Tripp helped me into the plane and to the bench seat furthest from the door. When I'd agreed to come along, I insisted I have a seat and a seat belt. That, for some reason, gave me enough of a sense of safety that I'd agreed. Now that I was actually buckling into the seat, I was having serious doubts. The seat folded like a movie theater chair, and the seat belt was flimsier than a car's. He handed me noise-canceling headphones. I slipped them on as he took his seat beside me.

Lydia, Zoe, and Kelsey sat closest to the door on the other side of Tripp. The plane had another row of seats on the side by the door. A flight instructor and another employee of the skydiving company sat there. One of them would be jumping before the James family, and the other would stay on board with me and the pilot while we landed. I hoped he had a role that went beyond making sure I didn't lose it when Tripp jumped.

Once the door was closed and the plane taxied down the runway, Tripp rested his hand on my thigh. I placed my hand on top of his and interlaced our fingers. It was too loud to talk, so I let that simple gesture be enough. Even through his gloves, I felt the warmth of his skin. I dropped my head back against the wall and closed my eyes when I felt us leave the ground. This was the worst part of flying for me. The moment it was too late to back out. The moment I lost any control I might have had. My stomach dropped. I held on to my seat with the hand that didn't have a death grip on him. The small plane rattled and shook as we climbed higher into the air. We'd only be climbing to 10,000 feet. Only. Which meant the flight would be over in a matter of minutes. I focused on my breathing. Four seconds in. Hold for four. Out for four. Hold for four.

My legs bounced up and down. Tripp tightened his hold on my leg.

Then, it was time. I forced my eyes open long enough to watch Tripp and his sisters unbuckle and exit their seats. They jumped in age order—Kelsey, Lydia, Tripp, and Zoe. I watched in awe as they moved, without fear, to the open door. Tripp kept his eyes locked on mine until it was time for him to jump. As he turned to go, he gave me one last smile.

Then he jumped. I gasped. I'd known he was going to drop from the door and then be gone but watching him fall into the open sky shook me. My heart raced, and it took me a moment to catch my breath.

By the time I'd grounded myself again, we were back on the ground and headed to catch up with Tripp. I'd already met his sisters, but the idea of sharing a meal with his parents, wrecked my nerves. Especially knowing just how emotionally charged this dinner was likely to be.

I shouldn't have been worried, though. His mother greeted me with a warm hug and his dad's smile was just as bright and welcoming as Tripp's. I could tell immediately that he'd gotten his sense of loyalty and compassion from the two of them. What had it been like to grow up with two loving, kind parents?

twenty-six

AT THE RESTAURANT, a family-owned Mexican bar and grill, I sat between Tripp and his mother, Carly. Like me, she was a petite woman. Tripp definitely got his height from his dad. I'd been expecting to feel like a third, or seventh, wheel, but they went out of their way to include me in the conversation. I did my best to channel every ounce of extrovert I could.

"So, Sadie, Tripp tells us you have a twin brother?" His dad, Robert, asked over chips and queso.

I took a sip of my margarita and nodded. "Yes, Seth. He's actually working with Tripp and his team on an app for the company."

"The quiz you told me about?" Carly asked.

"That's the one. Seth's been a Quest member for a few years, and the app was actually his idea. He's also the one that suggested we give Sadie and Ava's agency a shot."

I glanced up at him and furrowed my brow. *He had?* Seth had been the one to tell us Take the Leap was looking for a new agency, but I didn't know he'd played a role in encouraging Tripp and his team to invite us to pitch them.

Tripp reached under the table and squeezed my hand. "He basically told us any campaign that didn't involve Savie Media would be a massive flop," he said.

Wow. "He's a pretty good brother."

"So, is he your only sibling?" Zoe asked. I nodded. "What's that like. Was it quiet growing up? I bet it wasn't chaos like our house."

"I don't know, I'd bet my Gran would say we were anything *but* quiet. Seth and I have pretty different personalities, so we were always arguing and fighting over something. She used to joke and threaten to send us to marriage counseling."

Carly let out a loud, bellowing laugh. It surprised me to hear such a boisterous noise from the tiny woman. "Now that's not a bad idea! These four would've benefited from some couple's therapy. If two of them weren't fighting, all four were."

I glanced around the table and took in the amused faces of Tripp and his sisters. "Let me guess, Tripp was the instigator and Lydia, the peacemaker."

Tripp playfully bumped my shoulder and shook his head. "No, that was Zoe."

"What?" Zoe asked in mock outrage. "Little old me?"

"Yes!" Tripp and Lydia shouted.

"You were always stealing my clothes," Kelsey said, pointing at Lydia, "and you, Tripp, cut the hair on every one of my Barbie dolls because I didn't take you sledding with me and my friends."

My mouth dropped open as I watched a guilty, mischievous grin spread across his face. "You didn't!"

I dropped his head in shame. "I did."

"Mr. James, I'm shocked and horrified."

"See," Carly said, crossing her arms over her chest, "couples therapy would've been brilliant."

From there, the conversation shifted to Noah and the role he played during his short life. They all wondered who he'd have grown up to be and even argued over which sibling would be his favorite. Each of them had an entire life dreamed up for him. I don't know how they could imagine him as a grown-up and not collapse under the unbearable weight of his loss, but they'd been all smiles as they shared their fantasies. The rare few times I'd allowed myself to ask the what-if questions about my mom had never ended well. What good would it do, anyway? She was gone before I'd even had a chance to meet or know her, and my father had never bothered to fill in the gaps. Gran had tried to keep us close to her parents but seeing us was too much for them.

It was nearly sunset by the time we headed back to Nashville.

"Your family is amazing," I said, facing him. "Loving and kind, I'm still in shock that you all were so normal and calm about jumping out of the plane. Like it was nothing, though it probably is like nothing at this point."

"I don't know if it will ever feel like nothing. I always get a rush when I feel the wind on my face right before I jump. It's exhilarating. If it ever becomes routine or boring, I'll have to find something else to do. But I've never done this just for myself. It's always been for him, which keeps the thrill alive."

"Thank you for bringing me along today. It was insane to see that, but I know how important today is for your family. I'm honored to have been included."

"I wanted you to experience this the way we do before you're the one diving. It's one thing to go through the training and planning, but it's totally different when you go up just to watch."

"Do you ever do that?" I couldn't picture him sitting patiently on the plane while everyone else jumped. He didn't seem like the kind of man who enjoys sitting on the sidelines.

"Sometimes. Usually, when we have first-time divers or if it's an employee or friend. I've found that having a familiar face helps relax people."

"You do seem to have that effect on me."

"I relax you?" he asked.

Among a thousand other sensations that I wasn't quite sure how to share with him, but knew I needed to. I couldn't continue obsessing over what was or wasn't happening between us. "When I'm about to do something scary, yes."

I glanced at him and caught his irresistible half-smile. Then, my hand grew a mind of its own. It reached across the space between us and landed on his leg. His muscle twitched slightly under my touch. He took hold of my hand and raised it to his lips. He placed a gentle kiss on the top of my hand. His soft lips lingered over my hand as if they couldn't bear the thought of being separated again. When he finally released his kiss, I brushed my fingers over his lips and down his cheek.

I sighed and dropped my head against the seat.

"Everything makes so much sense when I'm with you," I said, closing my eyes. "The old me would be fighting every single sensation I'm feeling right now, but I don't think I'm that person anymore."

"What do you mean?"

"I don't know what it is about you, Tripp James, but every time you touch me, it feels like a bit more of the walls I've spent years building are coming down around me. It's scary, but at the same time, it's freeing."

"Kind of like what I said about skydiving earlier?"

"Maybe, yeah? Except, I feel like I'm completely and utterly out of control, and it feels natural."

"That's pretty much what it feels like when I jump."

"So, you want the sky and the clouds to kiss you, too?" I asked. He lifted my hand to his lips again. I opened my eyes and turned to face him. My lips curled into a teasing smile. "But not there."

"We're in a moving car, Sadie, this is the best I can do right now."

"I'm pretty sure you can pull over at one of these small town exits."

"If I didn't have to get back to the office and get this footage to Liam before he heads out for vacation, I'd test that offer."

"He needs it today?" I glanced at the clock, it was nearly seven. Surely Liam would've gone home for the day by now.

"Unfortunately, he wants to review the footage before he leaves it with the team so he can give them direction."

"Oh, that makes sense," I said. He was still worried about how this story was going to impact the business considering their audience hadn't been too keen on the videos with me. I glanced at the GPS on his phone. We still had another hour to drive. I needed to change to subject before I lost complete control of my words and talked him into finding us a motel room. "Ava and I were talking to Liam about the next challenge."

"Oh? Did he tell you about my idea?" Tripp asked. He ran his fingers over the skin on the back of my hand.

"He did. I know we talked about camping, and we do still need to do some of the non-scary challenges, but I think we need to keep the momentum going. I felt so comfortable and ready for kayaking. I don't want to lose that confidence—not counting the fractured wrist."

"We should definitely consider the fractured wrist. You've got another week and a half in the splint. That won't put us too far behind."

"Maybe not content-wise but waiting any longer might have a negative impact on me. It feels like we've made good progress. Or, at least, it does to me." And it did. "I don't think I'll ever be the thrill seeker you are, but I'm beginning to see the appeal. A part of me—a very, very small part—wishes I could go back and do the hot air balloon or bungee jump again. I'd like to experience those without crippling fear and anxiety so I could get a taste of what it's like."

His smile widened as he considered this for a moment. "I'll follow your lead on this one, but we're okay to wait, too."

"I appreciate that, I do. But I'm not okay with waiting." I shifted in my seat, tucked my splinted wrist against my stomach, and wrapped my other arm over it. I didn't have to look at him to know he was staring at my injury. He'd been doing it ever since the incident. We'd be talking or walking together, and then all of a sudden, he'd drop his gaze down to my wrist and frown. A cloud would pass over his eyes before he shook his head and pulled his attention back to me. I couldn't decipher the look but knew it wasn't good. Staring out the window, I let the silence between us settle.

twenty-seven

CHALLENGE NUMBER four wasn't going to wait for my wrist to heal, even though I only had another week in my splint. Liam's urgent emails reminding us that our *fans* demanded more content had flooded Ava's and my inboxes. Thankfully, this time, I didn't have to blindly draw an adventure from the hat. Only one on the entire list had been deemed safe enough for me to do—a thrill ride in a stock car around a racetrack. This one felt pretty tame compared to jumping off of very tall somethings. At least until I'd watched video after video of NASCAR and racing crashes at the Nashville Speedway, which is where I was taking my joyride. I'd known better, but I couldn't help myself. Old habits die hard.

The worst part? Tripp wouldn't be with me. The car had room for two people: me and a professional driver, which he, sadly, was not.

Ava helped me into the fire suit. It was snug over my arm. "Does that hurt?"

"No, it feels fine." I was ready to be done with this splint. I was used to being treated like a fragile piece of glass, but this was something else entirely. "Are you sure this is necessary? None of the videos I watched had the passenger in a fire suit."

"Yes. For starters, *you* asked for the safest situation, remember? And it will look cooler in the videos."

"I asked before I realized this was basically a straitjacket."

"Is it too tight? Is it bothering your wrist?" She nervously tugged at the sleeves. "Maybe we should wait to do this."

I rolled my eyes. Freaking out was my job, not hers. "Stop fussing over me."

"I'm not fussing."

"No, *mother*, you're smothering me. You and Tripp, both." I grinned to show her I was only joking.

"It's only because we care."

"Well, care less, then."

"Not a chance."

"I'm never getting rid of you, am I?" I teased.

"You're stuck with me, and I'm stuck with you. At least you'll get in elevators without bribes now. My little girl is growing up." She playfully smooched baby kisses at me.

I gently shoved her with my non-injured arm. "Please stop, you're going to embarrass me."

"Naw. I bet you'll do a fine job of that on your own."

"Probably." I tugged the zipper of the fire suit up and shifted my body until it felt somewhat comfortable. I hated jumpsuits or any one-piece clothing. It felt so claustrophobic. Tight clothing, in general, made me want to crawl out of my own skin. I hated feeling trapped, which was another reason this particular challenge was one I'd been dreading.

I resisted the urge to continuously pull at the permanent wedgie as we walked to meet Tripp, Liam, and the rest of the team. Tripp was chatting with the driver. A serious frown line pulled his usual smile down.

"You're sure?" he asked.

"Sure about what?" I interjected. Now was not the time to be adding in new anxieties.

"Nothing to worry about." Tripp slung his arm over my shoulder. "I just wanted to make sure the vibrations and everything in the car wouldn't be too much for your wrist. Luke, your driver, has assured me they wouldn't let you in if they were worried."

"Why do I feel like you and Ava have swapped brains with me? You two are going to make me have a panic attack if you're not careful." I was only half joking. I'd never seen either of them act like they were even slightly worried. I'd only known Tripp for a few months, but I was confident this was completely out of character for him.

Luke turned to me, smiling, and said, "Don't panic or worry. This is my job, and we'll be the only car out there. We'll have fun."

I didn't doubt him. I knew the risk of anything happening was fairly minimal. I'd already broken my wrist in the most random, unexpected way. I hoped this would be the extent of my injuries during this whole campaign. The splint on my wrist was reassuring in a strange way. I glanced around at the usual Take the Leap crew and smiled to reassure them all that I was fine. There wouldn't be any breakdowns today. I knew this was true. I don't know how I knew, but I did. Down to my very core, I had this deep sense of contentment. I wasn't calm, exactly, but I didn't feel the usual surge of panic. My legs didn't twitch to run in the opposite direction. My heart didn't race. My palms weren't sweaty or shaky. Everything was okay. Optimism. Is that what optimism feels like? Weird.

Luke and the driving experience team went over the rules and expectations with me again. They showed me how to climb in and out of the car and told me what to expect. It would be loud and bumpy. We'd go around three times, and if I still felt all right, they could do two more laps for a total of five. We'd top out at 170 miles per hour.

"Pretty sure Sadie's never driven over 70," Ava said with a nervous laugh.

"I've gone at least 75 before," I said. "But as a rule, I am a rule follower." Breaking rules and laws gave me actual hives. "Maybe 76, but not on purpose!"

I picked up my helmet and followed Luke's directions to get it on and snug. I was getting used to protective headgear, but this helmet was massive. It pulled my head back, and it took me a few seconds to steady myself. Once it felt secure, I asked Luke to inspect it.

"Perfect, but you'll need to take it off before you get in."

"Right, I knew that." Tripp helped me remove the helmet. "Is Liam ready? I'm ready." I wasn't sure if I meant I was ready to do this or ready to get it over with. A strange mixture of nerves rattles through me. Excitement with a hint of fear. For the first time, the excitement was louder than the fear.

Luke climbed into the car first and got to work getting strapped in. I walked around to the passenger side of the car. Instinct had me reaching for the handle, but it wasn't there. Right. Climb in. Tripp rested his hand on my hip. "Need a hand?"

I shook my head. "I think I can do it, but maybe don't go far in case I lose my balance." With a nervous laugh, I lifted my leg over the window. I was supposed to brace my foot on the seat but couldn't reach it. Being petite wasn't going to do me any favors today. With my non-injured arm, I pushed on the edge of the window and lifted myself higher. I moved my right arm to grasp the other side of the window, forgetting the splint. Tripp stood behind me and gave me the boost I needed to get my second leg in. Sitting on the window, I slid into the car and settled into my seat. He passed the helmet through the window.

"You good?" he asked.

"I've got this," I said, grinning. I meant it, and pride filled my chest. This time, I had myself. Damn, it felt good to say that. The frown that had been on his face since we arrived disappeared.

"Yes, you do." He reached into the car and squeezed my hand.

Another member of the crew came around the car and tightened the harness that served as the seatbelt. Despite the lack of airbags, speed governors, and the usual comforts of a passenger car, I felt surprisingly safe. Probably because I was completely strapped to the seat and could barely move my head. But rather than focusing on the sensation that the car was closing in around me, I focused on the sound of Luke's voice in my ear. The helmets were outfitted with earpieces and radios so I could communicate with Luke, and his team could communicate with him. I knew we were the only car out here today, but it still felt like we were on the verge of racing forty other cars.

"Gentleman, start your engine!" I said, mustering as much pomp and circumstance as I could.

Luke laughed, reached forward with his gloved hand, and flipped the switch that made the engine roar to life. The car sputtered and shook as the engine fired, vibrating my entire body. I had the urge to unbuckle and climb out for a split second, but I didn't. I gripped the seat and locked my gaze out of the windshield.

He pressed the gas, and we lurched forward. We left pit road at a reasonable speed, but as soon as he reached the actual racetrack, he put the literal pedal to the metal. The force of the acceleration slammed my body back into the seat. The car's vibration intensified. I screamed with delight. The screams shifted to wild laughter as he rounded the first turn. The first lap was over before I realized it. He maneuvered the track with the ease and grace of a ballerina. As we exited each turn, my side of the car floated closer to the wall. I blinked away the mental images of cars crashing into the wall. We didn't stay tucked there long; as he took each corner, he slowed and then accelerated through the apex, bringing the car to the bottom of the track.

Before we finished the second lap, I knew I wanted to do all five. I told Luke, and he hooted in response. I decided I could sit in this car and zoom around the track all day. It was as if we were flying or dancing in circles. It was intoxicating and invigorating. My body buzzed with energy. I wished there was a way to bottle up this sensation.

Then, it was over. Luke pulled the car back onto pit road and parked. My ears still rang from the roaring engine even after he shut it off. A set of hands reached into the car and loosened the harness, freeing me. I unstrapped the helmet and passed it out the window. Getting out was going to be the tricky part. With my dominant hand out of commission, I used it to push my body sideways gently. I'd barely cleared the window when I felt Tripp's strong grip under my arms. He lifted me the rest of the way out of the car. Once my feet were back on solid ground, I turned to hug him. Wrapping my arms around his neck, I pulled him closer.

"You've definitely got this," he whispered into my ear. "Was it as fun as it sounded?"

I released him and beamed up at him. "Holy crap, that was amazing. I'm never driving the speed limit again!"

"Hallelujah!" Ava shouted, pumping her fist into the air. "We won't have to leave an hour early for everything!"

The fingers on my right hand tingled. I flexed them and

tried to stretch away the sensation. It was probably from the constant shaking of the car and would go away quickly. I caught Tripp staring at my wrist. "It's fine, okay? Just stretching my fingers."

He frowned and shook his head. "Keep an eye on it."

Liam rushed toward us and lifted me into a hug. I struggled away from him and gave him a quizzical look.

"This is footage is going to be so easy to edit! Thank you for not freaking out!" Genuine joy filled his voice.

"It's all for you, Liam."

twenty-eight

ON MONDAY, we invited Seth over to brainstorm the upcoming fundraiser and the app relaunch. We needed this to be a successful phase two.

Ava passed the takeout Chinese container to me. With a mouthful of rice, she said, "One more to go, and then it's skydiving."

I nodded. "Tripp wants to wait a few weeks before we do the fifth adventure."

"You did just get your splint off. It's probably not a bad idea."

"Yeah, listen to your boyfriend on this one, sis," Seth said. Rice spilled out of his mouth.

"Gross," Ava said, laughing as she handed him a napkin. "But, thanks, Seth."

"He's not my boyfriend ... at least not officially. And I don't know if you guys know this, but I am capable of thinking for myself." I hated when they ganged up on me like this. Not that they did it often, but that made it so much worse when they did. It was like two tiny devils on both my shoulders.

"We know you are, sweetie." Ava patted my head. "We just worry about you."

"I am drawing the fifth one today, with or without you. But first, let's get this app phase two launch worked out. It goes live right along with the NASCAR video next week. Will your team be ready?" Seth nodded. His mouth was still full of food, but this time, he gave us the courtesy of keeping it closed. "It needs to be completely bug free before the final challenge. The skydive is less than a month away. We can't afford any missteps with the campaign ending."

"We're ready. Are you?" he asked.

To dive? No. To be done with these adventures ... yes and no. When they were over, I'd be out of excuses to spend extra time with Tripp, but I'd be free to explore the challenge I hadn't signed up for. Dating. A small part of me was also starting to look forward to the challenges. "I will be." That answer would have to be enough for now.

We spent the next four hours going through every detail of the app updates and improvements with Seth. We'd already worked through the new, less thrilling adventures. I'd taken the quiz dozens of times since the first beta test, and I got a new answer each time. It matched me with bungee jumping when I took it earlier this week. I'd made my brother go back and recheck the results to ensure there wasn't a bug. But there wasn't. My answers had changed from the first time I took the quiz four months ago. I had changed. I should've expected that outcome. I hadn't, though. Even my therapist was impressed.

During my last session, I'd told her how much fun I'd had kayaking and riding in the race car. She jokingly checked her appointment book to make sure she hadn't brought in the wrong patient. Nope. I was still me.

Despite the subtle shift in my comfort zone, I still had the ability to turn even the smallest of situations into a complete catastrophe. Just this morning, Ava burned toast, and as soon as I smelled the smoke, I ran into the kitchen with my backup fire extinguisher in hand. Yes, I have a backup fire extinguisher. Four, in fact, one in my office, one in my bedroom, and one in each bathroom. You just never know when a spontaneous fire will break out. What can I say? I like to be prepared.

If I let myself dwell on the butterflies that took flight in my stomach every time Tripp sent a text to check in or called me, I'd fall down the rabbit hole of despair. I knew all the ways I could ruin things between us. I'd imagined our breakup almost as many times as I imagined our first kiss. Every scenario ended in disaster. We'd break up. He'd fire Savie. We'd be homeless. At least Ava had Heath. I'd be left with the pullout couch in Seth's living room. Sometimes, I entertained the thought of Brett and Mel taking me in, but that was the nightmare situation. I wouldn't let it come to that. Not only would I have to leave Nashville and move back to Missouri, but I'd also probably start calling him Dad or worse, start to like him. There was always the option of learning to play an instrument and becoming a street artist downtown. Or, maybe I had a promising career as an influencer who shares every panic attack as a way to relate to people or make them feel better about their own lives. Maybe a pharmaceutical company would sponsor me, and I'd get my anxiety medications free. Of course, retail and restaurant work were also on the table. The possibilities there were endless.

"Okay, so we have everything ready for the phase two launch. What about the content?" I asked, bringing us right back to the question of the day. Challenge five.

"What about it? I told you we would figure that out. Don't stress about it." The tediousness of the last few hours was getting to Ava, and her patience was running thin.

"It's like you don't even know me." I caught her rolling her eyes and rolled mine back.

"What about the camping thing?" She asked, an idea sparking. "Won't we be getting content then? It is one of the new adventures listed on the app."

"Camping thing?" Seth asked.

"Oh, you're right! I completely forgot about that." That was a lie I hadn't forgotten. I'd shoved it into my mental box and filed it away to worry about tomorrow as I packed my backpack. It was Tripp's idea. He'd always loved camping and had always wanted it to be one of Take the Leap's adventures, but he didn't think it would fit with their business model. Until we'd encouraged them to explore the less thrilling options. I'd been camping once. I was five and on a Girl Scout field trip—my last Girl Scout outing. After I freaked out when the sun started to set, the leader called Gran to come get me and politely asked that I not return. I hadn't argued.

"Can someone please fill me in," Seth said, irritated. "Did you forget I was here?"

"Calm down, drama king. It's one of the new opportunities they'll be offering with the launch, remember? We're going out to Percy Priest Lake and camping on one of those little islands." Ava said.

"Wait, what?" I asked. "I thought we were going to a campground?" No one had mentioned anything about an island to me. Camping on an island meant I had no way to sneak back to my car in the middle of the night. I doubted there were restrooms or showers or access to power. Islands might not even have cell service.

"All the campsites were booked. Liam said the islands are usually pretty open." Ava shrugged as if this weren't a big deal. "Sadie?"

"I'm fine." Another lie. My dear old friend, panic, seized

control of my body. A high-pitched ringing took hold of my ears. The massive lump in my throat made it hard to breathe. An island could also have more wild animals or snakes to worry about. What if a massive storm rolled through and flooded the island? Or a serial killer stalked the islands looking for unsuspecting campers. This was bad. Old Sadie was back. I was tempted to take the quiz again to see how dramatic the change in my results would be.

"Breathe," Ava whispered into my ear. She'd moved closer to me and wrapped her arm around my shoulder. "The islands are perfectly safe to camp on. I looked them up and read reviews from other campers. The weather this weekend is going to be perfect. No storms or rain."

I didn't have to list every detail, causing me to spiral out of control. She just knew. She kept reminding me to breathe. Her words fell into a steady cadence. Eventually, the blood thumping in my ears calmed enough to let her voice in. I focused on her and slowed my breathing to match hers. When the panic receded, I drew in one big, calming breath. For a moment, I remembered what life had been like before Tripp and Take the Leap. I remembered all the experiences I'd noped out on or didn't even consider. I'd missed so much. I didn't want to go back to being scared of everything and everyone.

"Thank you."

"Good to know everything hasn't changed," my brother said. "Our chief catastrophizer is still present and accounted for."

"Whatever." I shot him what I hoped was a mean stare. "It's getting better with every challenge, which is why I don't want to stop or take a break. I need to keep pushing forward, okay?"

"Got it. I won't argue with you," Ava said, "but I am going

to make sure whatever we do next is completely safe for your wrist and recovery. Can you work with that?"

"Deal. And I think I know what I want to do for the last challenge." The idea came to me in a flash. It was one of the few challenges that didn't immediately scare me when I'd read the list, but it would still be a challenge and out of my old comfort zone. I knew everyone wanted to wait until my wrist had more time to heal, but I was ready. I'd let them think I was taking it easy, but I'd be working with Seth on a surprise. "Seth, would you be up to help me with this one?"

"Mind telling me what it is?" Ava asked, glaring at me. Tripp wasn't the only one overly worried about my healing.

"I do mind, actually. I'll text you the details, okay?"

Seth gave me a quizzical look but nodded. He loved a good mystery.

twenty-nine

TRIPP FLUNG my backpack over his shoulder and shut the Jeep door. I glanced at the lake and smiled as the breeze tickled my cheek. Despite my mini panic attack at the thought of camping on an island, I was glad the camping trip was finally happening. I was looking forward to roasting marshmallows and staring at the stars.

"Is Liam meeting us at the campsite?" I asked.

Tripp shook his head. "He said something about food poisoning and not wanting to be far from a toilet. I didn't ask for details."

"So, they're both sick?" I asked Tripp, my voice tinged with disbelief. Ava woke up this morning with a stomach bug. She'd refused to let me in her room to check on her. Now Liam? This was starting to feel like a setup, a twist in our plans that I hadn't anticipated.

"It will just be us?" My attempt to sound cool failed. My voice trembled, giving away my nerves. I'd already been worried about camping on the island, and now it would just be the two of us. Alone. In a tent.

"If that's okay? We don't have to do this." His hopeful tone made it clear that while we didn't *have* to camp alone together, he very much wanted to. "We can leave now if you want."

"No, we do need to capture more footage, right?" I asked. After all, this whole outing was for the sake of the campaign and content. Tripp nodded, and I followed him down the dock to the small pontoon boat he kept docked at the lake.

He helped me into the boat, bracing my arm in his. His touch sent a warm shiver down my spine.

"I don't love boats," I said.

"You did list that as one of your fears. This one doesn't go fast, and I promise to drive responsibly. There are life jackets in that chest back there." He pointed to the back of the boat. "We'll only be on the boat for about forty-five minutes."

"Then we set up camp and try not to get eaten by bears or tracked by serial killers."

Laughing, he shook his head and said, "Then we set up camp, start a nice little fire, cook dinner, and roast marshmallows while we watch the sunset over the lake."

"And tell ghost stories?"

"I have a feeling that would be a terrible idea, given your propensity to catastrophize."

"Oh, I'm not scared of ghosts."

"No?"

"I don't believe in them."

"So, you're not afraid of the dark?"

"I'm terrified of the dark, but mostly because of the animal and human threats. Reality is far scarier than any ghost story."

"I can't argue with that logic." He sat behind the steering wheel and patted the seat next to him. I clicked the lifejacket on and sat beside him. Holding my breath as he backed out of the dock, I debated changing my mind. It wasn't just the boat that scared me; it was the prospect of almost twenty-four hours alone with him.

We'd all planned to share a four-person tent, which was scary enough. Now, it would just be Tripp and me alone in that tent. No Ava or Liam to distract or get between us. We'd be sleeping next to each other, but this time, I had full use of both my hands and no pain medication to knock me out. Maybe, just maybe, I'd finally know what his kiss tasted like. My fear melted into desire at the thought.

We reached the island and secured the pontoon into place. There was another boat a bit down the shoreline but no sign of its occupants. Maybe we wouldn't be completely alone, I thought with a mixture of relief and disappointment. The campsite was a short hike from the beach. Tripp carried the tent, cooler, and backpack. I'd offered to carry something, but he shrugged off the suggestion and helped me into my backpack. When we reached the campsite, it was empty. He got to work setting up the tent. I tried to be helpful, but I knew nothing about tents or campfires. We made small talk while he took care of turning the little piece of land into a home for the night. We gathered wood and sticks to build our fire.

"Seriously, what can I do to help?" I asked. "Not that I don't enjoy watching you do all the work, but there has to be some way for me to contribute."

He flexed his arm, demonstrating the cooler's weight. "Thanks for noticing."

"Kind of hard not to when you're out here sweating and lifting all that heavy wood." He smirked and raised his eyebrows. Heat rushed over my face. "I didn't mean it ...not like that."

"I'm just messing with you, Sadie. If you really want to do something more than admire my efforts, you can get the sleeping bags and everything set up inside the tent. I have a portable heater just in case the temperature drops tonight."

I hurried into the tent, avoiding further eye contact or

embarrassment. Inside, the tent felt both spacious and cramped. I unrolled his sleeping bag and placed it to the far right. I set mine up next to his. I'd also packed a small pillow and an extra blanket. I laid those out on top of the sleeping bag. I glanced around the spacious tent and smiled at how little space our things took up. Then, I scooted my stuff closer to his. I nodded with satisfaction and joined him by the pile of sticks that would become the fire.

Tripp pulled a lighter from his pocket and held a piece of paper to it. "Whoa! Cheater," I said, tsking.

"It's not cheating—it's knowing the game."

"And here I thought you were this outdoorsy manly man who made fire with his bare hands."

He nestled the burning paper beneath the pyramid of wood and sticks. "I can do that for you if you'd like another show of me and my wood skills."

Once again, a flush of pink danced over my cheeks. I decided to change the subject. "So, what's for dinner? Wieners?" What was *wrong* with me? "Hot dogs? I meant hot dogs."

Tripp laughed. He took a tentative step toward me. "You seem a little nervous."

"I am," I admitted. "I've never roasted marshmallows or slept outside."

"Are you sure it's the camping that has your cheeks turning that delightful shade of pink?"

"Yes, definitely the camping," I said, averting my gaze away from him. His boots crunched over the ground as he inched closer. When he was close enough to touch, I instinctively reached for him. "No, it's not the camping."

"Do you want to talk?" He placed his fingers under my chin and tilted my head back. I let my gaze drift back to his face. When our eyes met, a fire burned between us. No, I didn't want to talk. I'd wasted enough time on words and worrying. I shook my head. "What do you want?"

"You." The answer fell from my lips before I could stop them. My heart raced wildly in my chest. "I want to stop over-thinking this and us. I want you to kiss me. I want to kiss you. I want this to be about more than content. I want me to shut up and stop making excuses."

His face inched closer to mine. I closed my eyes and tilted my head further back, inviting him in. The warmth of his breath tickled my forehead. I sucked in a deep breath and held it, waiting. His lips brushed over the tender skin of my cheek. I turned to meet him, eager and ready for more. A soft sigh escaped my lips as his arms slid around my waist and pulled me closer to him. I melted against him. His lips hovered over mine. My lips parted slightly in anticipation. He leaned in, closing the distance between us.

"Excuse me," a voice barked over the crackle of the fire. I jumped back, pulling away from Tripp. His hand wrapped around my arm, pulling me behind him. He stood between me and the burly man in front of us. A group of four men stood behind him. How long had they been standing there? And why did they have to show up *now*? "Sorry to interrupt, but we seem to be out of gas. You don't have any extra, do you?"

"Boat gas? Yeah, I've got a few extra gallons on the boat. How much do you need?" Tripp asked, his voice thick. I slipped my hand into his and squeezed.

"A gallon or so should get us back to the dock. Thanks, man."

It took us about twenty minutes to walk back to the boat and retrieve the gas. Tripp helped them fill up their boat. We stood and watched as they drove back toward the dock. By the time we made it back to the campsite, the sun was already starting to dip back into the horizon.

"Well, that was unfortunate timing," he said, laughing. He raked his hand through his hair. "Ready for dinner?"

"Great." Whatever moment we'd been having before the interruption was gone. We settled into the chairs he'd placed by the fire and worked on roasting the hot dogs. Dinner wasn't fancy, but it hit the spot. Hot dogs, chips, and s'mores for dessert.

I held my marshmallow over the flames and waited for it to catch fire. Marshmallows tasted best when they're burnt to a crisp. Despite the fire, there was enough of a chill in the air to make my teeth chatter. I blew out the flame on the marshmallow and placed it between the chocolate and graham crackers.

"Want to take those inside the tent?" Tripp asked, noticing the chill.

"Is it warmer in there?"

"It should be; I turned on the heater when you went to find the bathroom." He laughed.

"You mean the tree to pee behind? That was a first for me."

"It's a rite of passage, really."

"One I could've done without." I shivered again.

Tripp stood and held out his hand. I took it and followed him into the tent. I took a small bite of the s'more before tossing it into the small trash bag he'd tied to the side of the tent. Marshmallow stuck to my lips. I started to wipe it away, but his hand caught mine before I could.

"I'd like a taste," he said. His voice was husky and thick with desire. He wrapped his fingers around my wrist and pulled me toward him. I fell into his chest, letting him wrap his arms around my waist. I leaned my head back and offered my lips to him.

This time, he didn't tease or hesitate. His mouth closed over mine. The first kiss was gentle and tender. His full lips lingered for a moment, and then he pulled back, grinning down at me. I raised to my tiptoes to close to distance between us. I needed more. I pressed into him, and he stumbled back. Without a sturdy wall to break our fall, he sank to the ground, pulling me down with him. I settled onto his lap, straddling my legs around his waist. His hands fell to my hips, pulling me to him. We were eye to eye. I leaned forward and rested my forehead against his.

"Is this okay?" he asked. I didn't answer. Instead, I took his face in my hands. Tilting my head, I reeled him in and brushed my lips over his, parting them and inviting him in. His tongue danced over my lips. I slipped my fingers through his hair. A soft moan escaped his lips. Heat flooded my senses, intoxicating me. This was more than okay. This was everything. He was everything.

"Tripp," I whispered his name and pulled back.

"Sadie?" His eyes were still closed. He leaned forward in an attempt to reclaim my lips. I gave in. Whatever I had to say could wait. I couldn't even remember what had been so important.

I turned my attention back to his lips and leaned into him. His arms brought me closer and I fell into him, giving him every ounce of myself I had to give.

thirty

I'D INTENDED to take things slowly, but I was ensnared the instant I tasted his kiss. There was no way I was going to be able to resist him.

Rain pelted the canvas tent, filling the silence with its gentle song. I shivered against the chill that had settled in the dark. The forecast hadn't included rain, but the spring weather didn't care what the weatherman had to say. I peered over Tripp's bare shoulder and stared at the radar on his phone. No red or yellow spots mixed with the green. It was just a spring rain shower.

"I should've packed more blankets," I said. He pulled me closer to him, and his warm skin soothed the chill. "Or I could just steal all of your heat."

"I'll gladly give it to you. No need to turn to a life of crime." I gratefully accepted his offer and nestled deeper into the cocoon of his embrace. We were a tangle of arms and legs. Moments before, it had been impossible to tell where I ended, and he began.

We spent the rest of the night curled together as the rain

continued to fall. I knew reality would be waiting for us on the other side of tomorrow's sunrise, but as I drifted off to sleep in his arms, I didn't let those fears or worries blossom in my mind. Instead, I focused on memorizing every inch of his body. From the freckles on his chest down to his strong calves that draped protectively over my legs, I didn't want to forget a single detail. His fingers trailed lazily up and down my arms as he held me. Even as his breathing slowed and his heart rate settled into a sleepy rhythm, I felt him draw me into him. By the time sleep took over, every image in my mind was a picture of him, a replay of the kiss and everything after.

I slept deeply despite the lack of a proper bed or walls around me. Morning came, and we both snoozed right through our intended departure time. I awoke to his lips painting a path down my forehead, over my cheeks, and onto my lips. My eyes reluctantly tugged open. The most beautiful sight greeted me. Tripp's grey-blue eyes were locked on mine.

"Good morning," I whispered.

"You're the most beautiful woman."

"You're only saying that because I let you in my sleeping bag." I laughed and turned away from him. I hadn't brushed my teeth or hair before we'd fallen asleep. His smile didn't waver. He gently brushed a strand of hair out of my eyes. Then his fingers flowed down the curve of my cheek, tilting me to face him.

"Don't hide from me, please. I want to see all of you."

"I'm a mess, and my mouth tastes like last night's dinner."

"I'll be the judge of that." His lips were on mine before I could protest. When his teeth nipped my bottom lip, I completely forgot what I had to protest. "Delicious."

. . .

A few short hours later, we were packing up the campsite. I would've stayed all day and spent another night in the tent if we'd brought more food. I never wanted to leave the island or the bubble we'd managed to create here. But staying wasn't an option. The little content we'd managed to capture needed to get to Liam. He had lunch plans with his sisters, and Ava had already called and sent a few texts. We may have spent the entire night and half the morning ignoring the real world, but it hadn't forgotten about us.

"I've figured out the last adventure," I said, breaking the silence that had been building between us ever since we'd boarded the boat back to the dock.

He took my now-healed wrist into his hand and drew it to his lips. "We don't have to rush to finish the challenges," he said.

"I know, but I'm ready to get back to it. Besides, the skydive is fast approaching, and we'll need to shift our focus to training for that."

He cleared his throat and smiled weakly. "I've been thinking about this whole challenge thing and the contract."

"What do you mean?" I asked. Fear coiled in the pit of my stomach.

"I never should've had them add that clause. You and Ava have done a phenomenal job on the campaign. I know we are still running up short on the app downloads, but the comments and reception to the videos have been improving. We also have the fundraiser launching this week. So, we've got plenty of content. I don't see why we need to keep forcing you into these situations. Especially after the broken wrist."

"It was a hairline fracture, and it's better," I said defensively. "Your sister and the orthopedic doctor she referred me to cleared me for normal activity. It was just a minor injury. Nothing else has gone wrong. It worked just fine last night."

My attempt at a joke fell flat. He let go of my wrist and turned away from me. I tried to pull his attention away from the lake, but he kept his focus forward. His knuckles turned white as his grip on the wheel tightened. A lump rose in my throat.

"It's not just the wrist," he admitted after a long pause. "I can't do that again."

"Do what?" I asked. If this wasn't about my wrist, was it about last night? Was it about us? Every second of last night replayed in my mind, and my imagination ran wild. "What are you saying?"

He slowed the boat to an idle. Every minute he took to answer felt like an hour. Tears pricked my eyes as I watched a wave of anguish wash over his face. I braced myself for the inevitable heartbreak,

"Sadie," he said, turning his body toward me, "I've spent my entire life pretending nothing scared me. I chased adrenaline rush after adrenaline rush. I built my entire life and career on my total lack of fear. I've broken bones and had more stitches than I can count, but none of that hurt me. Nothing could ever hurt as much as losing Noah. Or so I thought."

"Tripp, I—"

He help up his hand to stop me. "I need to say this before I lose my nerve. I didn't think I'd ever feel anything like the pain of losing him ever again. I focused so hard on the joy and fun that I'd forgotten what it meant to care about and need someone else," he said, running his hand over his chin. "Then you showed up in my office and were my complete opposite. I didn't understand how someone like you, this beautiful, smart, and talented woman, could be afraid of her own shadow. I saw you as a challenge, and you surprised me. I knew from the moment I held your hand at that stupid trampoline park that I'd do anything to keep you safe."

"You did. You've shown me a whole new side of myself."

"It's been amazing to watch your confidence grow to match the person you are. It really has, and if I've played any part in that, I'm honored. But you did the work, Sadie."

"I still don't understand what this is about?" I became more confused as he spoke. He seemed sad and distant, but his words didn't match. "What can't you do again?"

"I can't watch you get hurt. I can't feel helpless again. I can't stand back and watch you climb into another race car and drive off at 170 miles per hour. And I sure as hell can't watch as you jump out of an airplane."

"I'll be strapped to you, remember?" He rewarded my question with a sad smile. "You've got me."

He shook his head. "I don't know if I can do that. I've never been this scared of anything before."

"Scared of what?"

"Losing someone." He shook his head and closed his eyes. "I know I do this stuff all the time, and skydive with my sisters, but I never thought about the dangers before. It's just something we do."

"Okay, but I'm not going anywhere, Tripp." I meant it. I'd never been so sure of anything.

"That's not what I mean."

"Then what? Please tell me." I hated how desperate I felt and sounded. "Are you breaking up with me before we even decide things are official?"

"No, God, no. I'm letting you out of the contract, Sadie. I'm keeping you safe."

"You're what?" For some reason, that stung more than I could've imagined. He was giving up on me.

"You don't have to do another challenge or go skydiving. We'll get content for the campaign another way. A way that doesn't involve putting you at risk."

"What if that isn't what I want?" It wasn't. I wanted to continue what we'd started, even if that meant skydiving. "I meant what I said earlier. You and this whole thing have given me so much more than I expected. I'm starting to have fun."

"If you want to keep pushing forward, you can, but I don't know if I can be there to watch. I watched my brother slip away from me and was unable to save him. I won't do that again."

I sat back in my seat and folded my arms in front of me. I understood his fear. Probably better than anyone. But I wasn't ready to quit. "Then, I guess I'm doing this without you."

"As long as you're doing this for you and not to prove anything to anyone. I already know you're more than capable."

"I am."

"I respect your decision, and I'll do my best to support you. I am proud of you and how far you've come. This isn't easy for me to say."

I wish I could say the same. This was the same man who'd built an entire company around helping people chase an adrenaline rush. I wanted to understand and respect his reasoning, but I couldn't. "Can you promise me one thing?" I asked.

"Anything."

"Don't you want to know what I'm asking before you agree?"

"No, I trust you."

His answered soothed some of the fear that remained coiled in the pit of my stomach. "Promise me that none of this changes what is happening between us. Last night," I said, swallowing back the lump in my throat, "was probably the best night of my life. I want to see this through, but I don't want to lose what we might have."

He held out his hand. I took it and locked my gaze on his. "Sadie, I'm not going anywhere. I'm in this with you. I'll be there for you during the challenges as much as I can, but when I can't be there, please don't ever assume it's because I don't care."

thirty-one

BY MONDAY, I'd replayed my conversation with Tripp no less than a million and one times. With each retelling, I tried to read more and more between the lines to fish out the words he hadn't said. I was spiraling out of control. But I was more determined than ever to follow through on the contract. I would do the last challenge, and I was going to jump out of a plane. I just had to figure out how to get Tripp back on board because if I was skydiving, I didn't want to do it alone or with anyone else.

I'd also spent plenty of time remembering every detail of our night together. But every time, I landed right back at the part where he told me he was letting me off the hook. I hated dwelling on that part because everything until then had been perfect. For the first time in my life, I'd let my walls down and invited someone in. I didn't regret it. Even if it ended badly, I knew he was worth the risk. I was worth the risk. I'd never felt so sure or confident of myself or anything before. That single realization shifted everything for me. When it hit, I sent a text to my therapist and scheduled a midweek check-in. I needed to imprint that feeling into my brain and never forget it. I'd spent my entire life waiting and hoping to one day finally feel like I was worthy of something. Turns out, I'd just been waiting for him.

Maybe it was because he saw the real me and didn't run. He never tried to change me. Instead, he showed me what I could do, and I'd done it. Sure, he'd helped and held my hand, but I'd pushed past the fear and allowed myself to try. I wasn't ready to walk away from that. I had so much more to learn and experience. So much that I'd spent decades missing out on because I was afraid. I didn't want to miss anything else. But doing any of this without him seemed impossible. Those three simple words he'd said over and over had pushed me through. *I've got you.* I believed him every time he said it. So much so that I believed me when I said it to myself. I'd learned to trust myself and others.

Before the workday started Monday morning, I made plans with my brother to start the final adventure training. He wasn't an expert at rock climbing, but he did it often enough that he could teach me the basics. Seth was overly enthusiastic when he agreed to be my coach. He's already filled my calendar with training sessions. At least one person was as excited as I was to continue the adventures.

After I accepted all of Seth's meeting invitations, I pulled out my phone to text Tripp.

Hey! Are you sure you're not up for joining me on the training for the next challenge? I typed out the message, reread it, and then deleted it. I tried again, *Good morning. Still thinking about the tent.*

Me too, he replied quickly.
Good morning 😊

I've got everything set up for training with Seth.

That's amazing. I am proud of you!

There's still time to join us, if you can fit it into your calendar.
The dots indicating he was typing popped up and then disappeared. I watched them appear and disappear for several minutes before his message finally came through.

I like the idea of being surprised. Besides, the fundraiser kicks off tomorrow, and I need to review the content one last time. Want to join us? Meeting is at 3.

We'll be there!
I reread the messages again and then dropped my phone on the desk. I should've left it alone; I knew where he stood on the issue. He didn't want to be there.

Ava sensed my mood and gave me plenty of room as we worked on various projects. She then dragged me out of my office for lunch, promising me carbs and sugar.

"You're moping," Ava said, handing me a stack of Oreo creme. "Sugar rush?"

"I don't think extra creme filling is going to solve this problem," I said, "but I am willing to give it a shot."

"You know what might help?"

"A time machine so I can go back and not get injured?"

"No. Talk to me. Tell me what happened."

I groaned. I'd given her the highlights of the camping trip, but I'd yet to tell her what led to him deciding to let me off the hook. "Honestly, I don't know."

"But what did he say?"

"He said he cares too much about me to watch me get hurt again as if it's inevitable. I couldn't help but feel a pang of self-doubt. Sure, I'd had my moments but hadn't I proven that I could do this? Well, except for the whole wrist incident.

"Sadie, sweetie." Whenever she said my name like that, like it was coated in caramel and chocolate, I knew I wasn't going to like what she had to say. "It sounds like a good thing. He cares about you. He likes you."

"So? He still thinks I'm incapable of doing what he does daily. He gave up on me."

Ava shook her head in disbelief. "No, he didn't. He cares about you and wants to be with you. So, let him! I know you feel the same way about him. Even now, your face lights up when you talk about him. You're happier than I've ever seen you before, and no, I don't think that is all him. You're letting go of fear and allowing yourself to have fun."

"But he doesn't want the *fun* version of me. He wants the boring, safe version." I dropped my gaze and avoided her inquisitive stare.

"That is not what he said."

"You weren't there, Ava."

"I didn't have to be."

"Then how do you know what he meant?"

"Because I'm feeling it, too." Now, I was thoroughly confused. I told her as much. "Look, I love this free and happy version of you, but it also scares me a little. I'm not used to having to worry about your physical well-being. Your mental health? Sure, all the time, but I've never had to give a second thought to whether or not you were safe. Now, I'm standing on the sidelines and watching as you do adventurous or dangerous things."

I leaned against the counter in disbelief. "Do you want me to quit too?"

"No! Sadie, you're missing the point. The point is, people care about you. We love you and want you to be safe. This thing about me being scared is about me, not you."

"It is?"

"Yes!" Exasperation filled her voice. "And I think that scares you more than anything else."

"You being scared?"

"I swear you can be so hard-headed! No, Sadie, you're terrified of being loved and loving people back, which I get. You have plenty of reasons not to trust the feeling of being loved."

"This is way too deep for a Monday morning conversation," I joked. She playfully slapped my arm. "I hear what you're saying, okay? This is all so new to me."

"I know. It's new to me, too. But be patient with yourself and with him. It sounds like he supports your decision to keep going, but he needs to figure out how to balance his needs with yours."

"When did you get so wise?"

"Raising you hasn't been easy," Ava said. I laughed and shoved her off the chair. "But my baby is all grown up."

"Whatever." I rolled my eyes and headed back toward my office. "But thank you for loving me even though I'm a pain in the butt."

I spent the rest of the day mulling over her words. She was right. I was more scared of relationships than anything else. I'd always known that. It was why I'd spent so much energy trying to resist my attraction to Tripp. It was why Seth and Ava were the only people in my life I'd ever truly let in. It was why I continued to reject Brett's attempts at being a part of my life. I'd missed out on so many things in life because of fear.

I was done being afraid. Starting now. I grabbed my phone off my desk and walked upstairs. As I climbed, an idea formed. It seemed crazy and so out of character it surprised me that I'd even thought of it. But, if I was on a path to healing and moving forward, I needed to do this, and I needed to do it with them—him, specifically. Shutting my bedroom door behind me, I tapped his name and held the phone to my ear.

"Sadie? Is everything okay?" Confusion filled the voice on the other end of the line.

"Dad?" As soon as I said it, tears welled in my eyes. My throat closed, making it impossible to breathe or speak. I closed my eyes and pulled in a steadying breath. "Are you busy?"

"No, what's going on?"

"I've been thinking a lot lately. Overthinking and overanalyzing. It's what I do. And now I'm yammering. Sorry." *I can do this. I can do this.* "I called to tell you I'm sorry for slamming the door or every attempt you've made to make things right. Your leaving broke me in a way that I don't know if it can ever be healed, but I want to try. I'm so tired of fighting and being afraid of letting people in. I know you're not a fan of this whole adventure thing, but I'm planning something with Seth for our birthday next week. Will you come down and watch us?"

"I'd be honored to." His voice cracked. "Thank you."

I gave him the details and hung up, promising to be in touch soon. Placing my hand over my chest, I waited for my heart to quit the rapid pounding it had been doing since I picked up the phone. Then, I sent the same information to Tripp. There was no going back now.

thirty-two

WHEN WE ARRIVED at Take the Leap later that afternoon, we met Tripp and Liam in the main conference room. I'd expected to see more of Liam's team with them, but it was just the two of them. The mood in the room was far more somber than I'd been expecting. Ava glanced at me, and I shrugged. I wasn't sure what was going on.

"Come in," Tripp said and gestured toward the empty chairs.

"Is everything going alright today?" Ava asked, cautiously. She took the seat beside Liam, and I sat to her right.

"The app relaunched an hour or so ago," Liam said.

"Right, along with the ride-along video. I checked in with Seth earlier, and he said the launch was pretty smooth. Was it not?" I chewed my lip and tried to read Tripp's face. "The comments on the new video also seemed pretty positive."

"They were almost all positive," Ava said.

Liam and Tripp looked at each other, and they both broke out into wide grins. Liam said, "Surprisingly, they were. Even some of the most critical followers seemed charmed by Sadie's enthusiasm in the video."

"I'm confused. Why did you both look like you were ready to fire us?" I asked and leaned forward. There was something odd going on, and I wasn't sure I liked it.

"App downloads are up 150% since the relaunch and we've already seen an increase in experience bookings. The next race car ride along is already sold out." Tripp said.

"Are you serious?" I let their nods reassure me. I needed this bit of good news today. "And the other new adventures?"

We'd added group camping, kayak lessons with Olivia, and a few other new excursions to both the app and their website with the hopes of finally drawing in the new audience we'd been targeting with the videos.

"We're getting a great response on those as well," Liam said. "Turns out, we just needed a video where you didn't look like you'd rather be dead than doing the activities."

He turned on the screen behind me and shared the real time web and app traffic. The spikes were incredible to see. These were the numbers I'd been hoping to see with the first videos, but I guess it was better late than never. And at least now we had a stronger app and more options for people to explore. As he explained each metric and compared them to the stats from just a week ago, my optimism teased a come-back. This was good.

"So, does this set us up for a good kick off to the fundraiser and the Behind Take the Leap story?" Ava asked as she studied the data in front of her. "I know you've had reservations on sharing that."

Liam nodded. "Yes, we have the final video ready, if you're ready for it, but before we get started, I need to prep you for a few things."

Both Ava and I knew all about Noah and Tripp's motivation for starting his company. I'd also been there for most of the filming. What could Liam possibly have to share that we didn't know?

Tripp cleared his throat and stood to take over the screen while Liam pulled down the stats and loaded the video. "One of the reasons I've been hesitant to share all of this is because it's not just my story to tell."

My eyes wrinkled with confusion as the video started. A silent montage of images of a young boy who looked like a miniature Tripp filled the screen. His smile was infectious, and his round cheeks were painted the same shade of red that Tripp's turns when he's embarrassed. I knew in an instant that it was Noah. A lump rose in my throat as I studied his innocent face.

As the photos flashed on the screen, Noah transformed from an infant to a toddler to a kid. Then, the pictures took a sad turn. His diagnosis. No amount of preparation could've readied me for the way my heart hurt as I watched the progression. Tripp paused the video on an image of Noah and another boy in the hospital.

Liam sniffled. "That's me."

My mouth fell open, and I quickly snapped it shut. Liam had known Noah? Suddenly, a lot of things clicked into place. I understood why Tripp was so patient with Liam and why they seemed to have a dynamic that most CEOs and their employees don't have. When I'd first met Liam, he'd been abrasive and disrespectful to Tripp. I'd often wondered how he'd kept his job all these years with his negative attitude.

"Noah's room was next to mine," Liam said, swiping at his eyes. "I was the one who introduced him to the X Games and skydiving videos he loved. We used to watch them together."

"You were sick?" Ava asked in a gentle voice. Liam nodded. "And you were friends?"

"Best friends," Liam said with a smile. "Unlike him, I was

an only child and my parents both worked to cover the medical bills. I was alone most days, but Noah and his family kept me company whenever they visited, which was all the time."

Tripp smiled at the memory. "Liam and Noah were inseparable. If it was possible for me to be jealous of a nine-year-old, I would've been."

I glanced back up at the screen and took in little Liam. I could see hints of the man sitting across from me in the dimples of the boy in the picture. "You didn't want people to know?"

He shook his head. "My entire life I was told I couldn't do the crazy, fun things I wanted to do. I was too sick or too weak. So, I stopped telling people about my cancer and just pretended it never happened. I think that's why I was so frustrated with you when you first came on board. You have everyone cheering you on and telling you that you could do all those things."

"I had to run this whole idea by him when you suggested it, Sadie, and we both agreed it was time. We owed it to Noah. Are you ready to watch the rest of the video? Then we can discuss the fundraiser and what we'd like to do."

Ava and I nodded. Tripp pressed play and the video faded into a clip of Liam in his office. I blinked away the tears that blurred my eyes. Liam shared the same story he'd just shared with us. He talked about meeting Noah's family, and the video transitioned to some of the footage I'd captured of Tripp and his sisters. It had been edited beautifully. Between the images of Noah and Liam and the voiceover, their story came to life.

"That's incredible," Ava said, swiping an errant tear from her cheek. "I knew the basics of the story, but wow. I'm speechless."

I nodded. "Thank you for trusting us with this. Liam," I said, turning to him, "are you sure you're ready to share this?"

"I am. We'll show the team later today and then announce the revamped fundraiser. The plan is to do a renewed drive for Quest members. Starting next month, forty percent of every new membership will be donated to the Leukemia and Lymphoma Society for the first year."

"I'll match the first $10,000," Tripp said, "and we've got a few sponsors lined up to do the same."

"Incredible!" We hadn't spent much time brainstorming or planning the fundraiser. After I'd given the idea to Tripp, he and Liam had run with it. "This is the perfect way to lean into the new Take the Leap."

Tripp smiled at me. "We couldn't have done it without you guys."

I started to protest and insist it was a team effort, but Ava stopped me. "We're grateful to be here and be a part of the transformation."

"I know I doubted you guys at the beginning, and sometimes I still think this whole idea is a little crazy, but we're finally starting to see results. We just need to keep things moving." Liam stood and leaned over the table, offering up a fist bump. I returned the gesture.

"Two more challenges to go!"

thirty-three

THE NEXT WEEK, I found myself at an indoor rock climbing park with Seth. After two adventures that didn't involve wedgie-inducing harnesses, I'd forgotten just how torturous they were. Why did so many thrilling things require such uncomfortable clothing? There had to be a better way. I tried to align the harness in a way that didn't make me want to rip it off. I resigned myself to discomfort after one too many failed attempts. If the fear didn't deter me, the harness just might.

"Seth, can we just get this over with? I'm going to get rope burn in places that have no business getting rope burn."

"TMI, sis. And it's a belt, not a rope. Didn't I tell you explicitly not to wear shorts?"

I tugged at my shorts, trying to make them longer. "Your text of instructions was wordier than a YA romantasy trilogy."

He stared at me. "I understood none of that."

"I'm just saying, if you wanted me to read every detail, you should've sent it in a bullet point format."

"Sadie Genevieve Barnes, are you telling me that you didn't read the rules and directions?"

I shrugged. "What can I tell you? I'm a rebel."

"It's like I don't even know you anymore."

"Wait until you hear what I want to do for our birthday next week."

"Do I want to ask?" he asked as he expertly tied the rope into a figure eight knot. He quickly explained that the first thing I'd be learning was how to belay—or, in simpler terms, keep him from dying if he fell. Seeing that we were inside and the mat beneath my feet was pretty soft, I didn't see how that would be necessary. But, given what I had planned, the skills would come in handy.

"Have you heard of Foster Falls?" I asked. He gave a very tentative yes. "They have this rock climb called Sibling Rivalry. I've already registered us for next weekend. It's rated a 5.7, which means it is good for beginner climbers. I watched a lot of videos and think I can do it. Oh, and Brett and Mel will meet us there." I said the last bit under my breath.

He blinked at me as if I'd spoken a foreign language. "You what?"

"We're going to do an actual rock climb."

"We are? Are you sure?"

"Yup. I've already bought all the gear and made campsite reservations, too. We'll drive down on Friday afternoon, hike to the camping spot, do the whole camping thing, and then we'll do the climb on Saturday and head back." The skeptical look on his face deepened. "And, yes, I did my research to understand what the rating meant. I intentionally looked for one rated a 5.7. So, don't try to talk me out of this. I know what to expect."

"I wouldn't dream of it. But I have to ask. Are Tripp and Ava okay with this?"

I bit my lip. "I didn't tell them what we'd be doing. I just said I found a fun new camping site and wanted to go for my birthday. I suggested we could get some content while hiking."

"So, you lied?"

"No, I left out one small detail."

"Attempting a challenging rock climb two weeks after getting your splint off is not a small detail." He shook his head. A look of realization and shock passed over his face. "Wait, did you also say you invited Dad and Mel?"

Grinning, I said, "Surprised?"

"I honestly don't know which part surprises me more— that this was your idea, or that you called our dad and invited him to our birthday."

"What can I say? It's a whole new world. Now, pick your jaw off the ground and teach me how to belay or whatever. You have four days to prepare me to climb an actual rock in the middle of the forest, and I don't feel like breaking any more bones. So, let's get to it."

"Aye, aye, captain." He offered a mock salute and launched into a monologue on how crucial my role as the belayer was.

I spent the next four nights with Seth at the indoor climbing park, picking up a new vocabulary and learning how to climb a fake rock wall. I started casually throwing in words like cordelette, crimps, and jugs into random conversations. My arms and legs were sore in ways I never knew were possible, but I slept like the dead each night when I fell into bed. I don't think I'd ever slept as well as I did those nights. By the third night, I was climbing the wall almost as fast as my brother. We moved to the more challenging walls, and my confidence grew as I mastered those. My wrist occasionally reminded me that it was still healing, but I worked through the pain and did every stretch and exercise I'd learned from the physical therapist Seth insisted I visit. It grew stronger with every session.

Seth and I fell into a comfortable rhythm the more time we spent training together. After the last few months, we'd seen far less of each other than we normally did. Sure, I'd been spending more and more time with Tripp. But I also blamed him for continually trying to push me into a relationship with our dad, and I resented his ability to forgive him and move forward. But I was beginning to see that as a strength of his. I'd always been the glass-is-half-full and what-if-its-poisoned twin, where he was happy to have a drink to satiate him. He never wondered if the water was drying to drown him. He was always looking for the bright side. Even with me, he took the good with the bad. He never saw my fears as a negative thing, nor did he push me to change. Like Ava and Tripp, he'd always been patient and understanding. Even when he teased me, I knew it wasn't malicious.

Since I wanted this to be a surprise to Tripp and Ava, neither of them knew what we were up to. Seth had been sworn to secrecy. Ava tried to get me to spill daily, but I was enjoying keeping a secret—at least, this was a fun secret. I teased her with random, unhinged hints, but she never guessed what we were really up to. For his part, Tripp hadn't asked for details. When I told him we'd be camping for my birthday, he offered to drive us all to the campsite. He hadn't been too disappointed when I told him we wouldn't be alone again until I told him he'd be sharing a tent with my brother, Liam, and Kyle while I bunked with Ava. We hadn't had any quality alone time since our camping trip. I promised him I'd make it up to him once things with the campaign finally slowed down.

Friday came quickly. All day at the office, nervous energy flowed through me with increasing intensity. I couldn't sit still through our one meeting and ended up pacing behind Ava while we met with another new client. The clock moved at a glacial pace, and I was beginning to wonder if time might actually stop. For the first time since starting this campaign, the nerves were from excited energy. My fingers itched to dig into the side of a real rock. I was more than ready for this challenge.

"If you don't stop pacing, I am going to duct tape you to your chair," Ava said.

I glanced at her and rolled my eyes. Flexing my newly defined biceps, I said, "I'd like to see you try. I've got some new guns I'm dying to try out."

"One week of working out with your brother, and you're already talking like him. One Seth Barnes is more than enough."

"Are you packed?" I asked, changing the subject. I was usually bad at keeping secrets, and the closer we got to leaving time, the more I wanted to spill the beans. "You've got everything you need?"

"For the fifteenth time, yes, I am all packed for this mysterious camping trip." I pressed my lips together to keep from blurting out anything. "What time is Tripp picking us up?"

"In an hour or so."

"How long will it take us to get there?"

"Two-ish hours."

"Is Seth meeting us there?"

"He's picking up Mel and Brett at the airport now and will meet us at the campsite with them."

"I still can't believe you invited them."

"The closer we get to it being real, the more I regret it." I think I was more worried about seeing Brett and Mel than I was about the actual climb.

"Well, there's no going back now."

"I know. But, yes, we'll meet everyone else there."

"And then we camp."

"And roast marshmallows and do all the fun camping stuff."

"What's the plan for tomorrow?"

"We'll hike up to the—" I stopped and cocked my head to the side. The rapid-fire questions almost got me. "Nice try."

"Damn! So close!" She snapped her fingers in disappointment. "Well, whatever it is, I want you to know how proud I am of you for the way you've handled all of this."

"Yeah, yeah, your baby is growing up."

Laughing, Ava said, "I'm serious, Sadie. I've always loved who you are but seeing you this confident and happy is just amazing. You deserve it."

"Thank you." I resisted my long-internalized desire to push back on the compliment and tell her that she was wrong. I wasn't confident or happy. I didn't deserve any of this. But the doubt monster was wrong. I was gaining confidence and finally allowing myself to lean into the happiness around me— not just with Tripp but with everyone and everything else. I hadn't realized just how lonely and broken I'd been until the black hole started to heal.

I loved this new version of me, too. I just hoped I could hold onto her when the bottom drops out—if the bottom drops out, I corrected myself. Nothing was inevitable.

thirty-four

TRIPP FIGURED out my plan as soon as he put the destination into his GPS, and to say he wasn't thrilled would be a massive understatement. His jaw clenched as tight as his fists on the steering wheel. But to his credit, he didn't say anything or try to talk me out of it. Ava, on the other hand, was indignant. She's tried no less than five times to talk me out of the rock climb. When I refused, she called Seth and berated him for being stupid enough to go along with this plan. My brother informed her that I was more than ready and capable of doing the climb. Even though I missed Tripp during our practice, I was glad I'd had the time with Seth.

When we reached the campsite, the sun was already inching its way down. We were the last to arrive. Seth and Liam built a fire while Brett and Mel worked on their tent. I'd be sharing a tent with them and Ava, while the boys shared the tent Tripp and I had camped in last time.

"Do we have anything other than hotdogs and baked beans?" Liam asked, digging through the cooler. "I swear we talked about burgers or something."

"The burgers are under the condiments," Tripp said. He

stood to go help him and Seth get our dinner started. As he walked away from me, he turned back and offered a conciliatory smile. He knew I was nervous about inviting my dad and stepmom along, but I think he was also still upset with me for choosing this particular adventure. He hadn't said anything, but he kept looking at my wrist as if he expected it to shatter at any moment.

I settled onto a log, choosing a spot next to Brett. "How was your flight in?"

"Good," he said, smiling. "On time for a change."

"Thank you again for inviting us," Mel said. She leaned into Brett and rested her head on his shoulder. "We haven't been camping in years."

An awkward silence fell between us. I didn't really know what to say to either of them. I couldn't remember ever having a normal conversation with them. Every time I was around either of them, I was combative.

Ava was still ignoring me, so I forced myself to make small talk with Brett and Mel. It made for a long night of camping, but Ava and Tripp were in better spirits by Saturday morning. Tripp even agreed to belay for me on the climb, which meant he'd have the responsibility of keeping my rope secure if I fell.

"Thank you," I said, squeezing Tripp's hand, "I know you're not too keen on the idea, but I appreciate you being here."

"I'm learning you're impossible to say no to." He glanced over his shoulder before planting a kiss on my cheek. "Your dad keeps looking at me like he wants to punch me."

"Weird, right? He never got to play the if-you're-going-to-date-my-daughter dad role, so I think he's a little too excited to make up those lost memories."

"What about you?"

I reached down and swiped a bug off of my pants. We'd

been hiking for almost an hour and had another mile or so until we reached the climb. "I don't know. It's weird having him here, and I can't remember the last time I spent my birthday with him. He flies down every year to have dinner with us, but I fake an illness or hide out in a random hotel room for the 2 days he's here."

The truth was my stomach had been in knots ever since we'd met them at the campsite last night. Brett and Mel gave me awkward hugs and wished us a happy birthday, but I'd yet to find the courage to talk or walk with them. I let Seth take the lead like he always did. As we'd packed up the campsite this morning, I'd begun to second-guess my decision to invite them along. But it had been Brett who finally convinced Tripp to belay for me on the climb. Over campfire bacon and eggs, my dad had casually mentioned that he'd be happy to mind the rope for me. As soon as he started asking for a tutorial, Tripp jumped in and volunteered. I think Brett had played up his ignorance a bit, and I was thankful he had.

"How long have you been planning this?" Ava asked, falling into step beside me. "And how did you manage to keep it a secret."

"It wasn't easy! I wanted to tell you so many times, but I knew you'd try to talk me out of it. Both of you." I passed an accusatory glance between the two of them. "But last weekend, the idea came to me. I knew I wanted to do rock climbing for the last challenge, but the original plan was to keep it indoors. Then, I saw some photos and videos of Foster Falls. It was too gorgeous to pass up. Plus, I actually had fun camping."

"I don't think that had anything to do with the camping," Ava said, teasing me. I looked up at Tripp and smiled as his cheeks turned crimson right along with mine. "Because you sure complained about everything last night."

"Sorry," I said, shrugging, "Tripp is a better tentmate."

"I'm sure he is." She laughed as she left us to catch up with Liam. With the trip and plan being a surprise, they hadn't had much time to work out the plan for filming. I'd made sure to give him enough information on what to pack, but that was the extent. He'd been less than thrilled about being excluded from the planning, but he'd at least been on board with the idea once I shared it with everyone last night.

Tripp slipped his arm around my waist and pulled me closer to him. I rested my head against his shoulder. "I missed you last week."

"I missed you, too," I admitted.

"I was worried you were mad at me for not being there."

"I was, at first. Ava helped me understand where you were coming from, though. I'm just glad you're here now."

"Me, too."

When we reached the rock, we'd be climbing, Seth and I put on our sit harnesses, which were far more comfortable than the indoor climbing harnesses. I also made sure to wear the appropriate attire today: no shorts, nothing too loose, climbing shoes, and gloves. I also had my trusty helmet, which had gotten me through the kayak trip. The plan was for Seth to climb beside me and act as a spotter to ensure I found the right spots to grip and step.

"Ready, little sis?" Seth asked. I was a whole two minutes younger than him, but he never missed an opportunity to remind me that he was older. I stepped back and let my gaze travel the full height of the rock.

Tripp hooked the rope to my harness. "You look ready."

"Definitely not like the last time you were harnessed to a rope," Liam said, laughing. "Sometimes, when I'm having a crap day, I rewatch the video of you at the trampoline park. Cheers me right up."

"Glad to be of service," I said with a grin.

Brett and Mel approached from my right just as I was about to reach for the firsthand ledge. I jumped back, startled, forgetting they were there.

"Happy birthday, Sadie," he said and pulled me into a side hug. "Your mom would be so proud of you."

I shook my head. "Don't make me cry before I start." I blinked away an errant tear and returned his embrace. "But thank you for being here." When Brett released me, Mel stepped in for her own hug. She told me she was proud of me, which almost brought on another round of tears.

Tripp and I checked the rope tension one last time. I held his hand and closed my eyes. When I opened them, his smiling face greeted me. "You've got this, Sadie."

And I knew without a single doubt that I did. "And you've got me."

After taking a few deep, slow breaths, I gave Seth a quick nod to indicate that I was ready. Then, we were off. I followed Seth's lead as he took the first few feet without me. When I caught up to him, we climbed side by side. My fingers were used to the rubber of the holds inside the gym, and it took a bit longer than I'd anticipated to get used to the unforgiving texture of the rock. I'd cut my nails short for this and was glad I did. Otherwise, they'd all be breaking off. I was desperate to turn back and look at Tripp on the ground but knew better. We weren't nearly as high as the hot air balloon had been, but it wasn't worth the risk. As long as I kept my eyes focused on the top, I'd be okay.

One hand at a time, I reminded myself over and over again. *Don't rush.* According to my research, it should only take us twenty minutes or so to get to the top if we maintain a steady pace. At the halfway point, Seth turned to check on me, but I was already a few paces ahead of him.

"What are you waiting for, slowpoke? Are you going to let your baby sister beat you?"

"Ha! As if that's even possible."

Challenge accepted. I reached for the next notch in the rock and pulled myself up. When I moved to set my foot into place, it slipped. I curled my fingers and dug deeper into the rock. My right wrist tingled from the pressure, but I couldn't ease it until I regained my footing. My rope tensed as Tripp held it in the brake position. My knee slammed into the rock, but I didn't fall. "Ooof!"

I glanced down to see if I could find a better spot for my foot. In doing so, my gaze drifted to the ground. Tripp stared up at me. He'd tried to mask the fear on his face but failed. I smiled down reassuringly and slid my foot to the left until it found the notch I'd been looking for.

"I'm good," I shouted down to the group. With my foot securely in place, I let my weight rest on my legs while I stretched my wrist. I kept it in front of me and, I hoped, out of sight, I didn't need any *I told you so's* right now.

Despite my slip, I made it to the top a solid five seconds before Seth, but I think he let me win. I'd take it.

At the top, I hugged my brother and threw my hands in the air in victory. "We did it!"

"Hell yeah, you did!" Liam yelled at me, pumping his fist in the air as if he'd been the one to make the climb.

Tripp's wide smile beamed up at me. From up here, his lips looked as kissable as ever. An overwhelming desire to do just that took hold of me. I no longer cared about the view or the audience. I just wanted to get down to him.

"Okay, bye," I said to Seth and moved to the edge of the rock. "I'm coming down!"

The repel down felt like an eternity, even though it would only be a few minutes. I couldn't get to him fast enough. I still made sure to follow the proper steps to ensure my safety, but I moved quickly. When I neared the bottom, I turned back to ensure that Tripp was still waiting for me. I locked my eyes on him and returned his smile. He eased the rope up and guided me down the last few feet.

I fell into his arms and pressed my lips against his. I didn't care who was watching or what the cameras caught. He was the only person I needed. When I finally released him, he leaned in and whispered, "I'm sorry I ever doubted you. You were absolutely amazing."

thirty-five

IF I'D KNOWN the prep for skydiving involved another bungee jump, I might not have been so eager to get started. This time, though, I'd have to jump solo. Tripp said it was to ensure I'd be up for the diving part of skydiving.

"Won't you be the one jumping, though?"

"Yes, but I need to know you're really up for it."

"I am." At least, I think I was. I'd been hyping myself up through every single training session. I'd watched dozens of skydiving videos and read the training manuals. I knew how parachutes worked. My heart no longer threatened to jump out of my chest every time I thought about the actual jump. But when I imagined it, it was also in the safety of Tripp's embrace. "I will be."

"Great, then this should be the easy part. You've already jumped off this bridge before. And think of all you've accomplished since that first time."

I slipped on the harness and walked toward the edge of the bridge where we'd kicked this whole thing off. "Can we just go back to the trampoline park? I know I can handle that now." I was mostly joking, but it didn't sound like a terrible idea. He shook his head and leaned in to kiss my cheek before going to talk with the bungee jump crew. In the two weeks since the rock climb, we'd stopped trying to pretend everything between us was strictly professional. Neither of us could keep our hands to ourselves, but we had to when the cameras rolled. It was one thing for those around us to know, but I wasn't ready to break the hearts of all two million Take the Leap followers.

Liam and Ava stood near the edge of the bridge like they had the night we'd filmed the first adventure. We planned to film four videos for the skydiving challenge. We filmed the first two during the initial training, which involved me learning how to put on a parachute, watching a dozen safety videos, and then walking through the plane we'd be flying for the final jump. This was the third and final before the dive. Two more sleeps until I'd be jumping out of an airplane. I still couldn't believe any of this was real.

"Are you sure you don't want the boat down there this time?" Ava asked. "You know they have to pull you all the way back up, right?"

"Honestly, I'm not sure of anything right now," I admitted. "But I think it will be okay. I watched some videos of how the whole process works, and it seems like good practice." At least, that's what Tripp and Liam had told me.

"Last question," Liam asked, directing me toward the platform where Tripp waited. "How are you jumping?"

"Headfirst." Though, I'd never done anything head-first in my life. I'd always been a dip a toe in to test the waters first. "Then I'll spread my arms wide and tuck my chin." I held my arms out to my side and pulled my chin into my chest to show him. We'd gone over all of this the last time, but since I hadn't jumped solo, I didn't have to use any of the techniques.

"Perfect," Liam said, smiling. "Go get 'em."

I slipped the helmet on and adjusted the chin strap. This

time, there wouldn't be multiple cameras. It was completely up to me to gather everything we needed for content. If anything went wrong with the camera on my head, I'd have to do it all again. No pressure.

Tripp stepped aside to let them hook the bungee cord to my chest harness. I tilted my head back as he leaned down for one last kiss. I was sure the camera was already rolling, but I needed one last taste of his lips before jumping. He started to pull away, but I placed my hands on his face and held him in place. His warm lips crushed back against mine. I wasn't ready to let go yet. Finally, I let out a soft sigh and released him.

"I think I preferred the palpable sexual tension to the actual kissing," Liam said, mock gagging. "You do realize I'm going to have to watch this footage again and again while editing."

"Sorry," I said. Grinning mischievously, Tripp pulled me in for another kiss. This one was deeper and even more intense. I lifted on my tiptoes to get closer to him. I was acutely aware of Liam's continued overreaction, but I tuned him out. I never thought I'd be one for public displays of affection, but it was impossible to resist the magnetic pull of Tripp's lips.

"I'm not sorry," Tripp said when he released me.

"I am." Liam groaned and rolled his eyes. "Are you done making out now? Some of us would like to get back to work."

"Yes," I said at the same time Tripp said, "No." We laughed but pulled ourselves apart. I gently pushed him back and nodded for him to leave.

"I've got this, okay? You just watch."

"Always."

"I'm going to throw up if you two don't stop this mushy crap."

"Whatever, Liam. You're such a grump," Ava said, "But let's get a move on things. I've got a date to get to."

I gave Tripp one last smile before walking toward the platform's edge. I didn't allow myself to look down. I kept my eyes locked on the horizon and the tree line. I didn't need to look down to know the lake was waiting for me. I felt a tug on the bungee cord and heard the crew member give me the go-ahead. Closing my eyes, I took a deep breath. The wind brushed my hair away from my face, tickling my skin. The weather was perfect and clear. I opened my eyes and smiled up at the serene blue sky. All I had to do was jump. I scanned my body from head to toe, checking in on every sensation. Anticipation tingled in my toes. I was ready for this. There wasn't an ounce of hesitation or tangible fear. I tipped my head back and held my arms out wide. I took one step forward and then another. Then, I jumped off of the platform.

The blood rushed in my ears, leaving me unable to hear for a moment as I fell through the air. This time, I didn't squeeze my eyes shut as I jumped. I kept them open and focused on the surface of the lake. It called my name, inviting me in. As I drew closer, I held my hands out. My fingers grazed the water's surface. The cold sent a shiver up my arm. A flash of the first jump passed through my mind. I remembered how I'd trembled with fear and how Tripp's arms held me tight. A bubble of laughter rose from my throat and exploded from my mouth as the cord pulled me back up. I was yanked away from the water and then dropped back toward it. Each time, my hand dipped deeper and deeper into the water.

My racing pulse slowed to a steady pace as I caught my breath. Suddenly, I understood the appeal of chasing an adrenaline rush. The moment I'd jumped, everything else faded into the background. I wasn't worried about life, bills, my family, or anything. The only thing on my mind was how my body fell through the air. It was so much more than a rush. It was freedom. Nothing I'd ever done in my life had ever given me that feeling. It was as if I could fly. If I spread my arms wider and tilted my head back, I just might soar into the sun. The exhilaration was intoxicating. If I could gather all of these sensations into a pill, I'd take it every day for the rest of my life.

Somewhere between the platform and the lake, the cracks inside of me healed. Every piece of my broken heart stitched itself back together. I knew without a doubt that I'd never go back to the controlling fear I'd once embraced, as if my life depended on it. It had all been a lie. I wasn't protecting myself from anything. I was hiding and running away from my actual life.

When the bouncing stopped, I was left dangling a few feet above the water. For a moment, the world seemed to stop. Silence and calm enveloped me like a mist of peace. I'd done it. I hadn't panicked or given in to the fear like I had the first time.

"You did it!" Tripp said as he wrapped his arms around me.

I startled. One of the random crew members was supposed to pull me back up. I'd resigned myself to not feeling Tripp's touch until I was safely back on the platform but seeing him beside me now sent a rush of heat through me.

"What are you doing?" I asked.

"Taking you back to solid ground."

"Can we just hang here for a minute?" As much as I'd loved the feeling of solitude I'd felt in the moments before he joined me, having him here with me now was even sweeter. I didn't wait for him to answer. I adjusted my body so I could face him and wrap my arms around his neck. I pressed my lips against his and sighed. I'd never get tired of kissing him.

I was acutely aware of being pulled back to the bridge, but I leaned deeper and deeper into him. I didn't care who saw it or what Liam would have to edit out later. Everything I needed and wanted was right here.

I released him when we reached the top as the crew pulled us back on the platform. Ava pushed them aside and pulled me into a hug.

"Sadie! Did you enjoy that?"

The answer came to me in a rush. "Yes." I'd loved every second of the jump and the ride back up. "Can I go again?"

A chorus of laughter surrounded me.

thirty-six

"I CAN'T BELIEVE we're almost done with the campaign," Tripp said, pulling his office door closed. Ava and I were meeting with him to discuss the next steps of our contract now that we were one skydive away from completing the terms of our initial agreement. We also needed to map out phase two of the campaign. I couldn't believe we'd already made it as far as we had.

"Did Seth's team get the bugs worked out on the app?" I asked. The app had had a rough week since the rock-climbing video series. It would crash before sharing the quiz results, but we'd also managed to exceed downloads by nearly triple during the last few weeks.

"It was up and running this morning," Ava said. "Seth's team is confident the bug is fixed."

"And the fundraiser? That still moving ahead smoothly?"

"All ready to go."

With those updates sorted out, we got right into the least fun portion of the meeting. Liam joined us halfway through our deep dive into the metrics of the campaign. We spent the next four hours going over the different paths forward. It was hard to focus on anything related to work with Tripp smiling conspiratorially at me every few minutes. We had dinner plans as soon as this meeting was over. I was counting down the seconds.

"So, how do we top the Take the Leap Challenge?" Liam was asking.

I tore my gaze away from Tripp's face and turned my attention back to the meeting. "I like the idea of a contest. We have Quest members submit videos and apply to be the next face of Take the Leap. They get to pick a friend and complete their own challenges. Maybe we can break more people out of their shells."

"Is that what you did? Break out of your shell?" Tripp asked, leaning forward on his desk. A smirk danced on his lips.

"I think so, but I definitely had some help." I returned his smile.

Liam made a gagging sound. "I'm requesting the lawyers add a no flirting clause to the new contract. Y'all are disgusting."

"You're just jealous," Ava said, laughing, "I think we can wrap things up for now. Tomorrow, Sadie and I will get to work on phase two. Then, we'll all jump out of an airplane. Should be fun!"

I didn't want to rush through the work but didn't protest. I was eager to finally have Tripp to myself for a few hours. With all the skydiving prep work, we'd spent so much time together, but every second had been filmed and recorded. I was desperate for even five minutes alone with him.

I sat quietly while Ava and Liam packed up their computers and made small talk. I was far from patient and fidgeted my hands in my lap. When they finally left, Tripp sat back in his chair and stared at me. I shifted to try and find a more comfortable position but failed. I didn't want to spend another second in this office. I stood and glanced over my shoulder; his office had massive windows that gave every employee of Take the Leap a clear view into everything that happened in his office.

"Can we get out of here?"

"What's the rush, Ms. Barnes?" he asked.

"I need to kiss you. Now. But not with an audience. Think you can take the rest of the day off, boss?" I bit my lower lip and pouted at him. He shook his head, laughing. But he grabbed his keys and shoved his phone in his pocket. "You still owe me that hiking trip."

"You want to go hiking?"

"No, I just want you all to myself and the longer we stand in the office, the longer I have to wait."

"Well, then, let's get out of here." I followed him out of the office and to the elevator. He pressed the down button. I bounced from one foot to the other as we waited. I don't think I'd ever been so eager for an elevator to arrive. When the doors slid open, he held his hand out and gestured for me to go first.

His breath was hot on my neck as he stepped in behind me. He reached over and pressed the button to take us down to the parking garage. He locked his eyes on me as the doors slid shut.

"Nervous? I know you don't exactly love these things."

I shook my head. I reached over and hit the stop button. I'd always been too terrified to ever press any button other than the necessary floor button. I avoided the open or close door buttons like the plague. It always gave me intense anxiety when someone pressed them to try and make the elevator move faster. I'd always been a big fan of just letting the elevator do its job and not trying to mess with the status quo.

The elevator stalled, holding us captive between the 40th and 39th floors. I drew in a slow, steady breath.

"What are you doing?" Tripp asked, confused.

I took one step forward and raised onto my tip toes as I fell into him. He caught me in his arms. I tilted my head back and reached higher, bringing my face closer to him. "Kissing you," I whispered.

He slipped his arms around my waist and pulled me in closer, "What are you waiting for."

"My heart to stop racing," I admitted.

His lips inched closer to mine, but he stopped before they brushed against mine. Then, he pulled back. He released me and placed his hand over my chest. "What if I don't want your heart to stop racing?"

"Then you should probably go ahead and kiss me."

His hands trail down the curves of my body and land on my hips. "Or you could kiss me." I pouted and stared up at him. A look of innocence danced in his eyes. His lips twitched into a small smile, but he didn't move any closer. Was he trying to kill me?

I wasn't about to wait around and find out. This elevator was eventually going to start moving again. I didn't hesitate. I placed my hands around his neck and pulled him down to me. I grazed my lips over his as he slid his arms back around my waist. One hand dipped lower, grabbing my butt and lifting me to him. When my mouth finally crushed against his, he sighed as if he'd been waiting an eternity to taste me. His breath tickled my lips. I pressed against him, knocking us back into the wall. The elevator rocked with the movement. Tripp's grip on me tightened as he braced against the wall. He lifted me higher, and I wrapped my legs around his waist. I parted my lips and pulled him in deeper. This was exactly what I'd needed.

But then, the elevator shifted back to life and the doors opened. Tripp quickly released me. I buried my head into his chest to stifle a giggle as a group of people joined us. Their conversation quickly silenced when they noticed us in the corner.

"What floor?" Tripp asked. He reached around me and pressed the button for the first floor.

"Thanks," a female voice said. She sounded young and there was a hint of curiosity in her voice. "I'm sorry, this is weird, but are you Tripp James?"

"I am." With my head burrowed in his chest, his voice was deep and inviting.

"And, ma'am, you're Sadie, right? The one doing all the challenges with Take the Leap?"

I wrinkled my face in frustration but pulled away from Tripp. I turned and offered a shy smile. "Yup, that's me."

"I told you they were dating." Another girl said with a smug smile. "We've been following along with the challenges. We actually just signed up for one of the new camping trips. The one in Chattanooga in September."

"Awesome. That should be a good event."

"We're excited," she said and glared at her friend, the one who'd recognized us. "Well, I am. Lauren here is terrified of camping. But I think you've inspired her, Sadie. So, thanks!"

"Well, I won't be bungee jumping or kayaking anytime soon," Lauren said as her face turned red, "but I think what you did was pretty cool. I've never really been the adventurous type, but you guys have shown me it's okay to be scared and still try things."

"Really?" I asked, surprised. "I inspired you?"

The elevator stopped at the first floor and the doors opened. Lauren smiled at me and nodded. "You're pretty badass, Sadie."

Her comment left me speechless, but Tripp said, "Yes, she is."

thirty-seven

WHILE THE BUNGEE jump had given me the confidence for the dive, it hadn't prepared me for the rush of standing at the open door of an airplane at 16,000 feet. Even knowing Tripp was behind me didn't calm the intense fear that gripped my entire body. Looking down wasn't even the problem. All I could see was a blue sky and clouds. The ground didn't even look real all the way up here. It was just a brown and grey quilt of unrecognizable landmarks.

At least I wasn't alone. I glanced to my right and gave Ava a reassuring smile. At the last minute, she decided to jump with us. She was currently strapped to Seth, and despite her earlier protests, she didn't seem to be hating it. Seth was definitely enjoying teasing her. Finding the ticklish spot on her side had only taken him a few seconds, and he was sporadically torturing her. It did seem to be doing the trick, though. The color that had drained away from her face when they'd stepped up to the door was slowly returning.

Liam and Kyle were jumping, too, but they were jumping solo and would be following us. Each of us had a camera strapped to our helmets. We weren't going to miss a second of footage. This was the one challenge I was certain I wouldn't be running to repeat. I looked over my shoulder and studied their faces. Both of them had jumped dozens of times before, so this was nothing new to them. Everyone except Ava and me were calm as could be. You'd never have guessed they were on the verge of free falling from an airplane.

"I don't know if I can do this," Ava said. She pushed back, nudging Seth away from the door. "I don't have to, right?"

Ava and I had spent the last two days training with Tripp. I still don't know what possessed her to decide to join me, but I was glad she had. I loved every second I spent with Tripp, but doing this with her made it all the more special.

"You don't have to, no," I said. "But if we keep stalling, we're going to miss the jump spot." My mind flashed back to that first day in the Take the Leap offices when I'd almost missed out on meeting Tripp and doing the challenge because I'd been too scared to get in the elevator. But now the roles were reversed.

"We can circle one more time, if we need to," Tripp said. I bit back a groan. We'd already circled the jump spot two times. The longer we waited to complete the dive, the stronger my anxiety grew. I had more time to think about everything that could go wrong. The parachute could stick or we didn't clear the plane and got sucked into the engine. Neither of which were likely, not impossible, but definitely improbable.

We stepped back from the door. While I didn't hate being attached to Tripp, it did make maneuvering around the plane awkward. To be fair, we were only supposed to be strapped together for the jump, but after the first aborted attempt we hadn't disconnected. We worked our way toward Ava. Seth was already working on calming her down.

"Ava, sweetie, what's going on?"

"I get it now." Her voice shook.

"You get what?" I asked.

"What it's like to be you. I don't like it. Every worst-case scenario is running through my mind at warp speed, and all I can think about it how this is going to kill me."

"Like what?"

"Aside from the parachute malfunctioning? What if we get sucked into the engine or propellers? Or, we collide midair and all get knocked unconscious. I mean, you're right, Sadie, the possibilities are endless."

I took her hands in mine and squeezed. "Breathe, Ava." I counted her through a few sets of square breathing. "This is scary—probably the scariest thing either of us have ever done."

"Remind me why I suggested going with you?"

Grinning, I said, "I believe it was to make sure I was comfortable and didn't panic at the last second."

"Which is clearly working," Seth said with a laugh, "you're freaking out and Sadie is completely fine."

"Shut up, Seth." Ava slapped his arm. "I'm not freaking out, I'm just coming to terms with my impending death."

"You're not going to die," I said, "I promise. You're in good hands with Seth, okay?"

She nodded. I squeezed her hand one last time. We were nearing the jump point again. If we didn't go this time, we'd have to try again tomorrow, and I wasn't sure If I'd be able to do all of this all over again. I counted her through a few more deep breaths. She finally braced herself and announced that she was ready. We edged toward the door.

"On three, okay?" Tripp yelled over the roar of the wind and the plane. I nodded, hoping he could feel the movement. I didn't trust my voice. Fear had settled like a rock in my throat. I stared ahead of us and braced myself as Tripp started counting.

"One!"

"Two!"

"Three!"

He leaned forward and jumped. My heart leaped into my throat, silencing the scream that tried to escape my lips. I forced my eyes to remain open, but I held my breath. I was done jumping feet first with my eyes closed. I held my arms out and my fingers brushed against Tripp's. My head rested against his chest. The air rushed past us. It was impossible to focus my gaze on anyone spot. We were moving far too fast. He'd warned me that it would feel like forever before I felt the tug of the parachute, but everything happened quickly. The forty seconds of free falling ended before my heart stopped racing.

But it hadn't even felt like falling. For that brief moment, it was as if I'd taken flight and was soaring through the air like a superhero. I suddenly understood the appeal of skydiving. It wasn't even the adrenaline rush. It was the freedom of it all. Nothing else existed. It was just Tripp and me free-falling together. The rest of the world faded from my mind. It was like that first kiss we'd shared by the campfire. Warm and overwhelming in the best way.

The parachute jerked us up. I let out the breath I'd been holding as I felt Tripp wrap his fingers around my hand. We didn't speak. We just existed as one being floating back down to earth. The slow float down took several minutes, but the ground was beneath our feet before I was ready. We collapsed to the ground together, the parachute falling around his. I quickly released the clip holding me to him and rolled to face him. I took his hand in my face and pressed my lips against his. I could kiss him for the rest of my life and still need more.

epilogue
ONE YEAR LATER(ISH)

THE BURNER for the hot air balloon roared to life. I braced myself against the edge of the basket and tried not to tip into Tripp as we lifted off of the ground. He slipped his arm around my shoulder and pulled me closer to him.

"How are you doing?" he asked, whispering in my ear.

I sucked in a deep breath and closed my eyes. "I'm okay." I slowly opened my eyes and turned to face away from the center of the balloon. I was determined to enjoy the view this time. But, unlike our first ride last year, we weren't tethered to the ground. So much had changed since those early challenges. I'd changed. My fear still lingered just below the surface but it didn't control me anymore. I'd learned how to listen to and respect my fear without empowering it to rule my life. I'd found a deep love for rock climbing, camping, and kayaking. I'd done it all with him right by my side.

"No," I said, "I'm better than okay. This is perfect."

"Yeah?"

"Yeah."

As we rose higher and higher into the air, my heartbeat slowed to a steady rhythm. Tripp moved behind me and wrapped his arms around my waist. I rested my head back against his chest and melted into him. The sun dipped below the horizon, painting pink and orange streaks across the sky. When we reached 1,200 feet, the balloon stopped rising and we floated over Nashville. The city buzzed with life below us, but it felt as though we were a million miles away from reality.

Tripp placed his hands on my hips and gently turned me to face him. I smiled up at him, drinking in his blue eyes. As I leaned up to kiss him, he lowered, dropping to one knee, and pulled a ring from his pocket. His lips parted to speak, but I didn't let him get the words out.

"Yes," I said and fell to me knees in front him. I threw my arms around his neck and pressed my lips against his. "Yes, a thousand times. Yes."

THE END.

acknowledgments

Y'all. It's been a wild four years since my last book, *Out of Anywhere*, was released. Honestly, it feels like several lifetimes ago. I am nowhere near the same person I was then, and in many ways I am grateful for the woman, mother, and author I've grown into. It takes a village to raise a family, and it takes a village to bring a book to life.

To my family. Phew, where do I even start. Jeff, you are the epitome of a patient and loving husband. I'm grateful to have you along for this ride called life. Thank you for being amazing and designing my book covers ... even when I'm annoying.

Jackson, my sweet, anxious boy. You're growing into a little man right before my eyes, and I am so proud of you ... even if you are already WAY better at math than I am. I cannot wait to see where all your big dreams take you.

JJ (Annabeth) you have taught me more in your seven years of life than I could've ever learned on my own. I just pray you find the patience as I learn and grow with you.

Mom, I know you probably won't read this book since there isn't any magic or dragons or fantastical elements, but thank you for always being honest and teaching me to do the same.

To one of my dearest and closest friends, Leah, I honestly cannot even fathom writing a book or going through life without having you to harass with a thousand daily text messages. I'll forever be grateful to Bookstagram for bringing us together.

To my Tommy Nelson family, I never knew it was possible to have a work family that I truly couldn't live without. Sarah, thank you for teaching this elder Swiftie all the things I need to know and understand. Shannon, your wisdom and guidance in all things publishing have had a profound impact on my life and my writing. More importantly, thank you for reminding me that there are good humans in the world. Bri, you read this book before anyone else and you championed it as if it were your own. I adore you. Jen, even though you left us 😢, I will forever value the three years you worked alongside us. Ashley, the ee to my uh, I've only known you for a few months, but GIRL where have you been my entire life?????? Karissa, thank you for always being a positive light on even the hardest days —you are a true joy.

To anyone who has ever picked up, read, loved, or hated one of my books, thank you. I cherish every message you send and appreciate you more than words can say. It's been eleven years since I published my first book, and I have met so many beautiful humans because of the words I wrote. Thank you a thousand million times over for being here.

Should you stumble upon any egregious errors or typos, please feel free to email me at andreanourseauthor@gmail.com.

also by andrea nourse

CONTEMPORARY FICTION

Life is But a Dream

Happily Every Never

Lie Baby Lie

Out of Anywhere

ROMANCE

After Everything

Take the Leap

www.andreanourse.com